The Shepherds of Earth

Jack Randall

PublishAmerica
Baltimore

First printing

At the specific preference of the author, PublishAmerica allowed this work to remain exactly as the author intended, verbatim, without editorial input.

ISBN: 1-4241-2190-6
PUBLISHED BY PUBLISHAMERICA, LLLP
www.publishamerica.com
Baltimore

Printed in the United States of America

This book is dedicated to my wife, Patricia, without whose support I would never have had the time or inspiration to be able to write it. I also am indebted to my son, Randy, for his critiques, comments, and insights into the story as it was being developed; and my daughter, Sarah, for her interest and support.

As always, my blue-point Siamese cat, Vincent, occasionally accompanied by his seal-point brother, Theo, kept me company during the evening hours in my loft when the book was being written.

As I felt greatly obligated to Dr. Isaac Asimov as noted in the preface of "The Synthetic Race," (my first novel in the trilogy), I feel this way again in this second novel, for the contributions of Lester R. Brown to my thoughts about Earth and her problems. Although I haven't had the personal relationship to this man that I did with Dr. Asimov, I have been exposed to his extremely important literary work as an environmental analyst. You will find his critical comments about overpopulation, necessary climate control, global warming, and increase in water productivity all through the pages of this second novel. As a physician, I believe my novels are slanted towards the healing of society; just as my activity with patients has been towards healing them. Brown's very important work has struck a chord in my understanding of the dire straits the Earth could find itself in without recognizing the potential problems he describes so well and finding ways to correct them now. My novel finds interesting ways to deal with some of these problems, but the most important value of the book is to help people who read it recognize that these problems exist and solutions must be found to solve them if we are to progress as a viable society.

Prologue

It was the year 2105 and Ellen James had taken the Gnorman Prime Mover's words very seriously when he had left the Gnor-human colonists on Mars in 2100 to reclaim his home planet, Mekan. He had said, "My good friends, I leave Professor Ellen James in charge and I wish you great success in the *shepherding of your planet, Earth.*"[1]

The Gnormen had originally come to Earth in the time of the dinosaurs to insert their DNA into creatures that would hopefully evolve highly enough to be able to help them continue their research into the development of a totally synthetic higher-functioning brain. This would have enabled them to regulate their already synthetic bodies with a brain much less vulnerable than the composite living brain they had possessed for many centuries. The massive pollution of their planet in its distant past had led to the development of synthetic bodies by the Gnormen which were governed by living brains within the heads of these bodies; for protection from the pollution. Then later they had been forced off their planet by lesser

[1] See "The Synthetic Race," by Jack Randall, PublishAmerica, May, 2004

synthetic beings that they had created along the way towards trying to develop a higher-functioning synthetic brain. Because these lesser beings desired to retain the control they had attained, they had assiduously been secretly eliminating the living brain composites like the Prime Mover so that they wouldn't be replaced by the research the composites were doing. They feared that a much higher quality synthetic brain than the one they possessed would make them obsolete and depose them from their present position of authority and power. There had once been a colony of living Gnormen imprisoned on a satellite of their planet who had been forcibly kept there to replace the living brain of any composite Gnorman who died by death or traumatic injury. Unfortunately, these people were completely annihilated by these totally synthetic lesser beings, and Dr. Dik Ran, a Gnorman physician, had been the only living Gnorman left on the planet. He had been off the satellite when the rest of the living people were killed there by a plague introduced by the lesser beings. Without any living creatures to continue their brain research, the surviving composite Gnormen decided to seek out a planet in its early stages of development, to set up the possible evolution of brains capable of being used to create more composites. They located the planet Earth, arriving in the time of Earth's dinosaur age, and instilled their DNA and other substances into early arboreal tree mammals they found there. Then they distributed them across the planet into three sites where they hoped they would evolve into beings similar to themselves. This would enable them to have a new source of living brains for new composites; and thus allow them to continue their research when the remaining composites died off from different natural causes. When these space-traveling Gnormen returned to their home planet, they were just in time to rescue the Prime Mover and the remaining composites that were under siege by the lesser beings. They had to escape; and after destroying their last mountain stronghold, rapidly returned to Earth, arriving there in the year 2003 by using their time warp mechanism. They found that the hoped for evolutionary development of the tree creatures had been successful beyond their wildest dreams. Ellen James, a human female history professor, had been rescued by them from a flaming plane crash and she became the first Gnor-human composite successfully created; combining her living brain with a synthetic Gnor body. With

Ellen's historical research help, and using their time warp mechanism which allowed them to move forwards and backwards in time, they embarked upon rescuing numbers of humans that had perished in the past. In every case they only took people whose bodies were never recovered and who completely agreed to become Gnor-humans. Many rescues had been, and were still continuing to be, carried out; so that a thriving number of Gnor-human colonists were being built up on the planet Mars and a base on the dark side of Earth's Moon, out of detection from Earth. With the help of Ellen's organizational skills and historical knowledge, the Gnormen were able to obtain enough human brains to continue their research and finally to develop the higher-functioning synthetic brain they sought. This made it possible for the Prime Mover and most of the remaining Gnormen to become totally synthetic and return to reclaim their home planet, Mekan.

And so Ellen had been left in charge of the Martian and Earth Moon Gnor-human colonists, not really knowing what would be required to *shepherd their home planet, Earth*, but wanting to help with Earth's problems as best she could. In the meantime, the planet had fallen into unhappy times from many poor choices by mankind.

The Shepherds of Earth

Ellen, as President of the new Council of the Gnor-human colonists on Mars and the Earth's Moon, had convened a meeting in First City, which was located on Mars in a place that the Earth astronomers called the Candor Chiasma in the Valles Marineris. She was anxious to present her ideas about where they should proceed in their Earth-shepherding endeavors. The new Council was made up of the mayors of the six other Gnor-human cities on Mars, one member for the colony on the dark side of Earth's Moon, and Ellen, who was mayor of First City as well as being the President of the Council.

Representing the second city, called "Hyannisport," was Mayor Joseph P. Kennedy, Jr., previously rescued from his exploding aircraft in Earth's WWII and converted to a Gnor-human.

"Time City," the third city, was represented by Co-Mayors, chief pilot Zeltor and his navigator Rol; two of the original Gnormen who had stayed behind to assist Ellen after the rest of the Gnormen had left with their Prime Mover to return to their home planet, Mekan.

The fourth city was named "Harvard Square" by their Mayor,

anthropologist Dr. John Scott, Ellen's husband, who had been rescued from his flaming, sinking ship in the Pacific Ocean in 1932 and had also been converted to Gnor-human status as was his wife, Ellen.

The fifth city was named "Electra" by its Mayor, Amelia Earhart. Amelia and her navigator, Fred Noonan, had been rescued from their aircraft, the Electra, as it ditched in the South Pacific Ocean in 1938 and had also been converted to Gnor-humans.

The sixth city, was affectionately named "Space Band," by its Mayor, Major Glenn Miller. Glenn had been rescued from his plane just before it was destroyed by an errant German "buzz-bomb" on his last flight to Paris during the Earth's WW II, and he was also converted to a Gnor-human.

The seventh, and final city on Mars, was named "Mekan II" and its two Co-Mayors were also two remaining Gnormen, Dort and Zandor. They had been instrumental in the evolutionary development of the current race of human beings by their experimental work with Gnorman DNA and early Earth mammals at their arrival on the planet in the time of the dinosaurs.

The last Council member from the Moon colony was Atlas, the first successfully created totally synthetic Gnorman, who had also stayed behind to help Ellen with the shepherding of Earth.

Most of the Gnor-humans on the Martian colonies and on the base on the dark side of Earth's Moon had opted for utilizing the totally synthetic brain that the great Gnorman designer, Jol, had fashioned in Atlas, his first such creation. At this point in time almost all had functioning synthetic brains in synchrony with their already present synthetic bodies. The fear about losing some of the memories that had been present in their living brains when they had been composites had not been realized in the operative transfer from living to synthetic brain. The technology had been developed to be able to read and transfer the contents of the frontal lobes of their living brain into the new synthetic brain with almost complete accuracy. The other lower sections of their brains were easily transferred with no loss of functionality at all. Thus, without any serious losses experienced, all were quite happy with the transferring results. This, of course, gave them additional years that they would live; and, in fact, their ongoing cerebral functioning and memory was actually superior to what it had been in their living brain. Since their new synthetic brain's working was no longer dependent on the specifics of their former living brain, this seemed to vastly improve the new brain's speed of functioning and memory capacity. The technicians that the great Gnorman designer, Jol, had trained before he left for Mekan had blossomed into brilliant scientists themselves; and they were responsible for the continuing improvements in all aspects of the synthetic beings they created. The synthetic brain they created was able to transfer information and commands through any area of the substance of the brain as it was composed of a continuous matrix without neurons. No distinct neuron structure was necessary as each message traveled through the matrix of this brain automatically insulating that message from any other one near it. What determined which message went through was which message was first initiated. The matrix was so responsive, however, that there was no refractive period necessary for a new message to start as in the living neuron. Thus, the next message to start was only nanoseconds after the first one went through. Practically speaking, on average the speed of reaction time turned out to be quite a bit quicker than the living brain's neuronal setup. The rest of the wiring of the synthetic body was neuronal in character so this functioning was not changed. Ares, however, the son of Dr. Dik and Sarah Ran, was convinced that they might some day be able to create extremities filled with a continuous matrix like the synthetic brain had, rather than the individual neuronal structure they now had, that would allow much faster transmission of messages from the brain to the entire body.

So with these improvements, at this juncture in 2105, the mental and physical functioning of the current Gnor-human Martian and Earth Moon colonists was infinitely superior to that of the human beings on Earth. Dort and Zandor had felt somewhat saddened by this fact because back in 2003, when they had first returned from Mekan, they had recognized at that time that a human brain was actually potentially superior to a Gnorman brain. The pollution, continued political misuse of the Earth's resources, and other poor choices had led to a diminishing of the quality of the newborn members of the human race, and these changes between humans and Gnor-humans. The Earth at this time had become a far cry from the pristine planet she had been in the past. Over 1500 species had become extinct as they tried unsuccessfully to survive by moving their habitats away from the equator and the heat of global warming. It was obvious to Ellen and the other Gnor-human Martian and Earth Moon colonists that Earth was slipping into the same situation that had necessitated the synthetic solution on Mekan by the Gnormen in their past.

The Gnor-human colonists had continued to rescue dying humans to bolster their infrastructure on Mars and Earth's Moon as they had done when their Gnorman friends from Mekan had been here with them. The policy was continued that all rescued human brains could only be utilized for composite and later synthetic transfer if the involved person completely understood the situation and gave permission to do so. The fear by the Gnormen of time line future interference problems, voiced often by Rol, also had instituted the policy that was also continued that only people who died and their bodies not ever recovered could be utilized. The recovery and addition of these Gnor-humans continued to add greatly to the formation of a stable infrastructure in the Martian cities and their base on Earth's Moon. This policy of the rescue of famous people continued indefinitely as it became evident later that such increasing numbers might be needed.

Ellen James, however, was not convinced about the Gnorman policy of maintaining only very minimal changes to the time line. The current state, which the Earth and its people were slipping into, was not something that she felt would be so harmful if it were changed. She had continued to discuss this at some length with her husband John and daughter Molly, and had decided that something must be done to help the deteriorating situation on the Earth.

***

Ellen rapped her gavel on the podium for silence in the room and began her address to the Council.

"I have asked you all here," she began, "to discuss my proposal for our future direction to help our ailing planet Earth. First of all, our rescuing of accidental death humans and converting them to Gnor-humans should be continued as it has contributed very much to improving the colonist infrastructure on Mars and the Earth Moon base. We will certainly need these people in our future endeavors on Earth. Thanks to our good Dr. Dik Ran, his wife Sarah, and the talented cohort of technicians and surgeons trained by Jol and Dik, we have been able to create our present population of Gnor-people essentially without any significant problems at all. Sarah and Dik's son, Ares, has continued the family tradition by becoming one of the leading developers of new synthetic structure and has earned the distinction of becoming the director of that department. I believe we should continue our rescuing efforts; but I would like to start thinking about trying to help our Earth solve the problems she is slipping into that caused our Gnormen friends to have to develop the synthetic race that they did. If we could head off some of these problems for the Earth's peoples, we might be able to spare them the terrible trials the Gnormen had to go through. With the time warp mechanism they left us, we can find out what conditions and processes will cause irreversible changes to the Earth and its peoples and perhaps council them on how to change them and avoid these consequences. We will need to do it in secret in the beginning because of the greed and power-seeking of that small segment of humanity sometimes found in the corporate business and political world. Hopefully, we may take certain trustworthy individual humans into our confidence that are interested in the well being of all the people of Earth equally, and in that way be able to work more effectively with them to correct the problems. I suggest that it would be prudent for us to consider developing a business company of our own and a protective security force of talented, trained individuals that could act as a deterrent to detrimental changes on Earth brought about by corporations, individuals, sects, rouge governments, terrorists, or the people themselves. We will have to be careful about this phase of our activity on two counts. One, because many of that small group of powerful, and greedy corporate business people will most certainly want to control and use us for their own personal gain once they determine who and what we are. And two, we must continue meticulous Gnorman ethics so that no unscrupulous human ones creep into our activities.

Now, as we all know, the Gnormen have been very uneasy about changing the time line. But it is important to remember that they only obtained the ability to control time after their society had been in place for many years and was quite mature and very stable. The Gnormen feel that changing the time line might be disastrous for the future since apparently several terrible things happened in the early days of their using the time warp mechanism they had developed. Personally, I don't believe the Earth's timeline should be so sacrosanct. My husband, daughter, and I have discussed this at great length. We have come to believe that changing the time line by making appropriate changes on the planet might well enable the human race to survive and advance, not stagnate and decline, as is becoming more and more evident; and not unlike what happened to the Gnormen's early society.

I want you to please consider some thoughts of mine concerning the consequences of time line changes that I hope will assuage some of the fears instilled by our Gnormen friends.

In my discussions with the Prime Mover I was able to learn many of the reasons he had for not disturbing time. As I learned more and more about time I began to realize that the time warp mechanism itself could possibly be the one apparatus that all sentient beings eventually will discover, allowing them to preserve and perpetuate their own universe out into a future. By changing deleterious conditions and tendencies, they are then able to stop a possible extinction of their race by changing the future to a more compatible one than the one they may be embarking on at the present time. As the Prime Mover caused me to understand it, Gnormen feel that the universe is definitely intimately wrapped up with time. In fact, some think that time is actually the main creator of the universe and if any thing is changed in the time line, a totally different universe, or future, will be created by that change. It has been postulated that there may be phenomena called "time loops" that enable different futures to be created, but at the same time these different futures are acting to cause the universe to continue to exist. Said another way, new universes continually being created would keep some kind of functioning universe alive and present in time and space. Thus, a universe may continue to expand and develop until something is done that causes one of these time loops to be created. The phenomenon could very easily have been the invention and use of a time warp mechanism. This would then cause the whole process within the time-created universe to reset itself at the place where this particular time loop (time warp mechanism) traveled to. It could then proceed forward on a different path because of the avoidance of the past activities now known ahead of time that are going to cause harm to the society. You have all known something about our "Big Bang" universe continuing to expand on as we know it. But does it expand on into infinity?

Let me explain it another way—-when we use the time warp mechanism, I am able to go back in time and could even kill myself there in the past. Then, on the time line from that point on, I will not exist into the future and it will be a different future. We know it must become a different future because if I never existed in this future, then I wouldn't have been able to come back in time and kill myself in the original past. Hence, the future is now changed from the spot where I went back to originally and killed myself. You see, in this example time has formed a loop on a very stable line that doesn't change the past history that occurred before the spot where the time loop from the future arrived at and stopped. The future time line can change from that spot traveled back to, but the past further back from that spot remains the same. Thus, the time warp mechanism doesn't change all of the past; only the old future on the former time line from where the mechanism travels to. We can go back to the past and forward to the future that past leads us to; but any changes we make in the past will affect the future that forms. Therefore, in our current universe, if there is a definitive existence of a time line that can be traveled on (and we know this is true by our time warp mechanism activities) it may be that if we are careful and do only minimal adjustments to the time line, no catastrophic change will occur in the future that we already know. This is what the Gnormen believe and why they are so fussy about changing too much on the time line.

My feelings are different. I am not sure that changing the time line by doing something different is always dangerous. As I see it, it probably will cause time to form a different universe than the course our current one is on, but would that be so terrible? It might make for a much more successful human evolutionary endeavor; far different from what the Earth may be headed for right now. By continually monitoring the future, why couldn't we correct problems that will happen in those futures by changing our activities appropriately in the past? I can envision this activity as one way time change may be a way to preserve a continuing vital and functioning universe for all time. And is it not possible that highly evolved time-traveling beings may already be present with us now and in the future of our current universe, monitoring the time line on purpose to keep the universe stable? Perhaps they may intervene or have instituted mechanisms that won't allow a dangerous change to occur that we might try to do. Small changes may very well be tolerated without a disastrous or grossly changed future resulting. Time travelers could certainly be present among us without our knowing it if they chose to make it so. Our Gnormen friends, when they first came to Earth in 2003 and mingled with humans, are good examples of this easy concealment. Like them, perhaps these time travelers remain concealed from us because they are concerned that we might fear them to the point that they would not be able to be around to prevent us from getting into trouble.

All I am really saying is I selfishly feel that changing the time line to help my planet Earth out of obvious trouble she might be developing by the currently-ordained future time line, is worth the risk of changing the future history of this universe we are in at present. To quote one of my daughter Molly's favorite authors, Antoine de Saint-Exupery, *As for the future, our task is not to foresee it but to enable it.* I do admit, though, that it would be comforting to think that there really are time travelers present that will help us to prevent anything greatly detrimental to the future universe we will create by changing the past.

And now, most importantly, I'd like to hear what you all have to say about my speculations and the proposal to go ahead in time with the time warp mechanism to find out the consequences of our Earth's current actions or inactions. We could then return to a time when we can improve these problems of the Earth's peoples by helping them to recognize and correct the detrimental activities that will cause great harm in the future." With that Ellen sat down to moderate the discussion that followed.

Rol was the first one who rose to speak. "Madam Chair… Ellen," he began. "We Gnormen are somewhat obsessed with the possibility of harm coming from tinkering with the time line. It certainly would be helpful, as you said, if there were time travelers among us that could monitor what we do and stop us from anything detrimental. I guess I'd agree to cautiously go ahead with your plan, but if any of these time travelers exist and suggest an action we should take, I hope we would follow their advice."

"It would certainly be my intention to do so, Rol," replied Ellen.

Dort then rose to speak. "Madam Chair," he said, "one of the biggest fears Gnormen have had is in the changing of people's destinies. Loss of one soul could lead to untold consequences for the remaining people who are left to go on. There is the selfish wish to preserve and not perhaps lose forever what has been built up by past colleagues, friends, and in Earth's case, relatives. And in truth, perhaps we are a little afraid of the possibility of all of our present life and we ourselves being disintegrated in a wink from the whims of a time mechanism that we don't really understand completely. But even if we change the future of our universe, as you have said, we really haven't done anything to what has occurred in the past. People have lived and died, been happy or sad, etc.; we won't change that one iota. The new future will unravel just as the old one did. Indeed, Ellen, you, and all my other Earth friends, have changed my attitude completely about risk. I can see how the chance of a better path for all Earth's peoples is probably worth the risks it will take to attain it. Zandor and I have an obvious great attachment to you humans from our genetic work with your ancestors. We would never have been able to accomplish it without being able to come to your planet during its early years by manipulating time with the time warp mechanism. And in reality we probably changed the future then into what we now see, following the logic you presented earlier. If we hadn't intervened, perhaps this planet would be ruled at this time by a reptilian race of beings instead of the current mammalian predominance. We both feel very committed to our evolutionary experiment, the human race, and love it and want to have it prosper in the best way possible. So Ellen, as you humans say, let's do it! We will need your and your husband's expertise again for research on what is happening on Earth today. The time warp mechanism will give us the chance to see what current activities occurring now will lead to in the future, and what our appropriate changes can do for the future as well. I hope we can help, and I say *our*, Earth people to make all the changes necessary to correct their problems."

All the other members of the Council stood to give their assent to Ellen's suggested new undertaking for the Gnor-human colonists. They also agreed to go along with continuing rescues as before to bolster the Martian and Earth Moon infrastructure and increase the number of Gnor-human colonists. Everyone felt that more Gnor-humans might be needed to create the new elite monitoring force that Ellen had mentioned in her discussion; and the meeting then closed with all in complete agreement to start what the Mekan Prime Mover had called *the shepherding of your planet, Earth*. The council planned to meet again as many times as necessary to map out the strategies they would undertake as soon as the research into the future determined what should be done now to correct any detrimental activities going on at this time.

***

After the Council meeting, Ares, the son of Dr. Ran and Sarah, a very handsome young man in Earth terms, was walking back with Ellen's daughter, Molly, towards the Life Factory where he worked. Ellen, John, Dik and Sarah trailed behind them at a little distance.

"Molly," Ares was saying, "your mother sure knows how to get a point across well. Dad and Mom are very fond of her and respect her judgment explicitly, as does everyone else it seems. I really enjoyed her teaching in my schooling at the Martian Institute and it was really difficult not to like her a lot, even though she was a tough taskmistress and really pushed us hard to learn our Gnorman ethics well."

"Yes," said the attractive young woman walking beside him with the ease and grace of a trained athlete. "Mom is a great teacher and also has always been interested in trying to save Earth people as far back as I can remember. She and Dad saved me from drowning on the Titanic when it sank. Just after that they took me in as their little girl and I have been their daughter ever since. I really do love them both very much; and that human emotion has remained unchanged, even in my now synthetic brain and body. I have been with my Mom on many occasions when she organized and took part in rescues on Earth, and I can tell you, she is really a very brave, competent woman. Dad told me once that the only time he ever saw her afraid was when I had my transplant and transfer operations. I've seen her very upset only two times; the time I was kidnapped on Earth and your mom was so badly injured, and the time Dad had his second brain transfer."

"You know, you're right about our Moms," Ares rejoined. "Dad told me that my Mom had all kinds of worries when I gave up my living body and brain for a synthetic one. I remember overhearing her talking to Dad a few days before my first operation, saying that she wondered if they should be going through with the operation, and that she was very fearful of the consequences. I never got so many hugs and kisses as I did when I had recovered after the operation. And she was really scared when Dad had his two brain procedures. Dad's work was so critical for everything done on our colonies she was deathly afraid that he wouldn't come out his intelligent, loving self—but he did; much to her relief. She was nervous about my first adult body transplant as well; and I think she was a little embarrassed telling me about my sexual apparatus. She made Dad give me the lowdown on that function. They both were worried sick that I'd be out after every woman I could find to test it out. I guess they were not sure that certain emotional feelings would have to be present for me to have the mechanism work but hoped it would be the case. For instance, I have absolutely no problems with the mechanism with you." He winked at Molly and dodged a push she made toward him.

"You're incorrigible, Ares," she said with a cross look on her face. You know we've never been like that."

"I know," answered Ares. "I was just kidding. I do consider you, however," he added more seriously, "to be my best friend at this juncture, Molly."

"Yes," replied Molly with a serious smile, "and you, mine. Actually, my parents had the same misgivings as yours did; and I told them that it was a function that I definitely would want to eventually explore, but that at present I didn't think that I had the right feelings for anyone to take part in such an intimate relationship. I'll admit I like you Ares, but mainly as a friend at this time; I'm not ready to take on that experience yet with anyone. I guess Mom's ethics classes have had a good influence on me so far; and I recognize that the human emotional factor must come into play for me as well."

'I'm just teasing you, Molly," said Ares with a smile. "Listen, I feel the same way as you do about sex, and I certainly think of you as a good friend as well. You know that I really enjoy your company and hope you like mine."

"Of course I do, Ares," answered Molly with a shy sideways smile at the handsome young Gnor-human. "And our parents have certainly encouraged our friendship enough, haven't they."

"Yeah, Molly," said Ares. "You're right about that. Classic matchmakers! No doubt about it."

A few paces behind the two younger Gnor-humans, Ellen and her husband, John were observing the attractive couple in front of them.

"Well, Sarah and Dik," Ellen was saying, "you two certainly have a remarkable son. Molly tells me he is doing extremely well at the Life Factory in First City and has been able to improve several of the body-functioning designs."

"Yes," answered Dr. Ran, "he seems to have a flare for that area and is doing very well at it I'm pleased to say. He has been awarded the directorship of that division at the First City's Life Factory."

"A wonderful and well-deserved appointment I'm sure," said John. "Molly seems to be quite proud of him, Sarah; if you can go by what she says when we talk."

"It would seem that Ares thinks quite a lot about Molly as well, John," said Sarah. "It would please me immensely if those two eventually get together."

"I'm with you, Sarah," spoke up Ellen. "Those two kids seem just made for each other. Just look at them walking along there; they sure make a handsome couple."

"Well," rejoined Dik, "time will tell what may happen. Right now it seems they are just very good friends. They are two very intelligent, thoughtful, and kind individuals and are not predisposed to any irrational thoughts, feelings or acts. I'm very proud of both of them and would certainly welcome them eventually getting together if it happens."

"I'll say amen to that, Dik," said Ellen. "But to change the subject, I'm so happy that the Council has gone along with my suggestions about helping our planet, Earth. John and I will start right away to do the research necessary to see where we should go in the future and for how long to get the information we will need to plan any changes necessary to correct any deleterious changes we find in the future."

"Yes," said Sarah, "Mother Earth is in trouble, and although I now have an alien synthetic brain and body, I am ready to do all I can to protect and help her as a true Earth daughter."

"I know we all feel that way, Sarah," said John. "And Ellen and I will get right on the research needed to start the process going."

"And we'll continue with our rescues," said Dik. "Our infrastructure can still be improved with more colonists, especially if we form that elite special corrective and regulating force you suggested, Ellen, to use in our shepherding endeavors. Molly and Ares have been after me to rescue that French author-pilot, Antoine de Saint Exupery. It seems they both have enjoyed a work of his, 'The Little Prince'. They keep insisting he will be able to help us as another pilot."

"Yes, Dik," rejoined Ellen, "they have been after us similarly. I know they'll be very happy if we are able to rescue him. He may indeed be helpful to us as a pilot."

The group continued on to their respective lodgings and said their farewells at the entrance to the apartment complex. Ares gave Molly a big smile and said he hoped to see her again soon. Molly gave him a shy smile, and replied that she would enjoy that. The two sets of parents smiled broadly to one another at the little encounter between their two children, and the Rans entered the apartment complex while Ellen, John and Molly proceeded to the boarding area to return to their apartment in Harvard Square.

***

Ellen and John had decided to check into the problems of toxic and nuclear waste as their first attempt at righting the seemingly downward spiral of the living status of Earth's peoples. The problem in the U.S. had started back at the end of the twentieth century when there was a proliferation of nuclear power plants and the U.S. Congress had mandated that all nuclear waste was to be containerized and buried beneath Yucca Mountain in Nevada. There had been some misgivings about doing this as several knowledgeable geologists had been concerned about eventual leakage and spread of deadly radiation through the deep aquifer under the mountain. At that time there was no definitive knowledge of the extent of the Ogallala deep fossil aquifer. If this aquifer extended under most of the southwestern United States, and if the buried Yucca Mountain containers leaked, deadly radiation would spread to most of that part of the U.S. making the area uninhabitable; or at the least dangerously habitable without sophisticated protective technology not yet invented. And this section of the U.S. supplied about eighty per cent of the world's grain.

Ellen and John were discussing their plans for future travel with the time warp mechanism to be able to define what dangerous trends were now happening on the Earth.

"You know, John," Ellen had said, "There was a person who suggested a good solution for the nuclear and toxic waste problem back in the 1980's."

"There was a good solution in the 1980's, Ellen?" John replied to her statement incredulously. "Who offered it and what was it? Maybe we could use it to help with the problem if it's feasible."

"Well," Ellen replied, "back in the 1980's there was a congressman named Silvio Conte, who was chairman of the very powerful Ways and Means Committee of the House of Representatives of the U.S. Congress. Every year he would hold a symposium about current problems going on at that time; and because of his very influential position on appropriations, he was able to get most of the then current administration's Cabinet officers to come and speak at his symposium. Conte's constituents from his district in western Massachusetts were invited to these symposiums, and they were very popular because of the president's Cabinet members who spoke at them. What transpired at these meetings was available to me in the Congressional Records, and I was able to uncover a very interesting one that occurred on May 9, 1984.

During that symposium in 1984 William D. Ruckelshaus had been invited to speak concerning the increasing problems with waste disposition, especially nuclear waste. Ruckelshaus was serving his second term as EPA (Environmental Protective Agency) chief. He had started the agency during his first term in 1973-75, and had brought about several changes to protect the environment. After he completed his speech in which he had stated nuclear power was one of the clean sources of energy that should be further developed, he asked for questions from the audience. Dr. David Jackson, a surgeon from Northampton, Massachusetts who was attending the symposium, asked Mr. Ruckelshaus if there were any place on the planet that he thought nuclear waste could be stored safely? Ruckelshaus answered that unfortunately there was no known place on Earth that he knew of where nuclear waste could be safely stored at this time; which was one of the main problems of utilizing nuclear power for energy. Jackson then offered that there might be one place where the waste could be safely stored, and even utilized for fuel by the storage facility. He suggested to Ruckelshaus that the nuclear waste, along with other toxic wastes could be gathered by a crack newly-formed company that would safely transport the waste to an island segregated from other inhabited areas and then to an orbiting space platform or the Moon. From there it could be propelled in a safe trajectory into the sun. He added humorously that it might give the Earth a few more milliseconds of longevity thanks to the added fuel; and it certainly would spawn a very lucrative new business for whatever company was able to take it on. Mr. Ruckelshaus laughed at this science fiction solution and it obviously was never considered seriously. And yet this method might very well be successful in ridding the planet of these polluting wastes that are choking off the Earth peoples' lives. Back in the early twenty-first century there was no vehicle that could raise the collected wastes safely to an orbiting space platform or the Moon; the rockets utilized then had a failure (and sometimes disaster) rate of one in two thousand launches. But since our scout vehicles climb the magnetic lines of force in the Earth's magnetosphere allowing them to hover or move slowly (or rapidly) up, down, backwards or forwards, waste could be transported to a space platform or the Moon fairly easily and safely; and then it would require very little energy expenditure to fire them off into the sun. Astronomic calculations of the trajectory could easily be done so that no other heavenly body would receive any of the waste and the sun, of course, would burn it up as fuel. If we were to start such a company ourselves we could use our scout vehicles for transporting and with our Gnor-human bodies, there would not be the risk that humans would have in piloting the waste-loaded ships. What do you think about it, John?"

"It is a very interesting proposition, my dear," answered John.

"It's too bad that Ruckelshaus didn't listen to that Massachusetts surgeon and at least undertake study of the possibility of doing what he had suggested. We know even now how much damage toxic wastes are causing to the human condition. Our scans now show that a few of the radioactive waste containers buried in other sites have already started to leak. Jackson's idea might work well with our ships and Gnor-human bodies ferrying the wastes as you have stated. I think this idea is well worth exploring. We will need to go far enough into the future to determine what is going to happen with the Ogallala deep aquifer and any possible radiation problems if the containers under Yucca Mountain begin to leak. I agree we should consider taking on this endeavor as our first step in our 'Earth shepherding', as it is a fairly straightforward proposition."

"I'm sure all of the pilots will want to fly this future exploration expedition," said Ellen, "but I think Zeltor and Rol should be the ones to go with us. Since we can't be sure how far we have to travel into the future to obtain the needed information, I would like those two skillful space travelers to be our pilot and navigator when we take off. We may have to go some distance into the future to see what the wastes will cause, or we may be fortunate and get the information we need in only a few years' travel. I'll speak to our Gnorman friends in the morning about preparing for the space expedition. John, you know that Molly will want to come along with us. I think it'll be good for her and will continue to teach her how important you and I feel it is for us to try to help Earth's peoples."

"I agree, Ellen," said John, "Molly would be very disappointed if we didn't let her come along. We can tell her tonight at home; I know she'll be very excited about going. You know, Ellen, the nicest thing that has ever happened to me, after meeting you, was my rescuing Molly from the Titanic's sinking and taking her on as our daughter. She's developed into a wonderfully kind, thoughtful, intelligent person, and I love her very much and am very proud to be her Dad."

"I feel the same way, John dear," answered Ellen. "She makes our lives complete. It remains obvious to both of us that our human emotions, in spite of our now totally synthetic brain and body, are very much in play and will probably always be so. Let's get back to our apartment and tell her. She will be so excited!"

***

Indeed, Molly was very excited when her father and mother informed her about the upcoming sojourn into the future to determine what should be done about the Earth's toxic and nuclear waste problems. She had listened and learned from her mother the reasonable ethics and morals of the Gnorman society and was firmly committed to them. It made it easy for her, like her mother, to want to help the people of Earth with their obvious impending problems.

"Mother," Molly asked, "how far into the future do you think we will have to go to find out what changes must be necessary and when we must make them?"

"That's hard to tell, dear," Ellen answered. "But we have Zeltor and Rol to fly and navigate for us so I'm sure it will be as quick as possible.

Thinking about the future and the company we will have to form, Molly, we will need a crew of Gnor-humans that will be able to man the ships and transport the wastes safely and efficiently. I think we will have to start a special school to train these individuals to be able to do this work properly. We will probably have to form units of Gnor-human Special Forces similar to the US Navy Seals. I was thinking that in your school of young athletes where you've been training we might be able to find the ideal candidates. We would train them to undertake this mission and later missions where trained disciplined operatives might be necessary for success of what we undertake. How do you think your friends and fellow athletes would feel about this?"

"Oh, Mom!" Molly replied enthusiastically, "I think that's a great idea! I know most of my friends in the school would jump at the chance to be part of this, including me!"

"Now, just a minute young lady," interjected her father. "I'm not so sure I'd be happy seeing you on a toxic and nuclear waste ship just yet. What does your mother think about you doing this?"

"Well," rejoined Ellen, "I know how Molly feels but I would think we should see what type of training is necessary and then we will decide exactly who should be chosen for the task later on. I don't think we should make any binding decisions just yet; but it makes me proud that you are as interested and willing as you are Molly, dear."

"I guess I should have known how *your* daughter would react to such a challenge," said John. "I am certainly fortunate to love two of the most fantastic women on two planets and a satellite."

"And we love you too, Dad," answered Molly. She ran and threw her arms around him and gave him a huge hug. Ellen gave the two of them a loving glance and smiled. John looked over at Ellen and returned her smile.

***

The next day the three of them with Zeltor and Rol met in a briefing room and began planning what they would need for the expedition into the future to determine exactly what was going to happen to the nuclear wastes to be buried under Yucca Mountain in Nevada.

"Our newer scanning devices should enable us to find out what we need to know fairly easily," Rol began the discussion. We can do most of our scout work at night and use jamming to prevent anyone from picking up our scout vehicle on their monitoring screens. It is prudent that we do this since there is a military presence near the mountain that was put up to deter any possible terrorist attacks on the facility there."

"A very good idea," rejoined Zeltor. "We certainly don't want Molly to be shot down on her first mission. He looked over at Ellen's wide-eyed daughter and winked. I should be able to get us close enough with electronic jamming in place so that we will be undetected, and our sensors should be able to tell if the buried containers have started to leak or not."

"I'm fairly certain," said Ellen, "that there is a good chance we will get confirmation of significant leaking and radiation pollution because of it, since we already have some evidence that leaks are beginning to happen at other sites where containers have been buried. What will be the most compelling reason for us to return and act is how much of the western United States will be affected by the pollution. I believe the Ogallala deep fossil aquifer's extent will be the key to this whole problem; and our preliminary scans show that it extends much further than most of the United States Congress has realized. There may be a chance that radiation pollution could extend across the entire western part of the United States."

"I hope we don't find this to be true, Ellen," said John. "But if it does turn out to be the case, we definitely will have to consider Dr. Jackson's suggestion of shooting these wastes into the sun. It will be important to go back further in time before anything was buried under Yucca Mountain and start the nuclear waste removal program then. I think we may have to utilize the base on the dark side of Earth's Moon to fire off the wastes at present since it would be difficult to establish a space station for this activity without the whole world knowing what we are doing."

"On the other hand," Ellen countered, "if we can establish ourselves as an Earth company that is doing the waste removal plan, we can build the space station ourselves and be able to transport the wastes there much more openly and easily than having to do it surreptitiously on the Moon to avoid detection. At this time in Earth's history I would not want certain corporate business people or governments in power to know about us as yet. Their self-serving nature is too prevalent and dangerous to let them know about us now. We will need to find someone with enough power and authority in the U.S. government that we can trust to keep our true nature confidential. That person will have to be able to arrange for us to intercept and collect the nuclear and toxic wastes without any interference or discovery by any corporate businesses or the government. At the same time he or she must make it possible for us to transport the wastes to a collection facility on Earth that we will construct undetected, where we can then transport these wastes from there to the space station in our scout vehicles. I am hopeful that we will find someone who may have that ability and power within the United States Environmental Protection Agency that will be genuinely interested in protecting all people primarily and carrying very little political baggage. Such a person would be extremely valuable in helping us complete the mission of a successful facilitation of Earth's nuclear and toxic waste removal."

"As usual, Ellen," said John, "you again make great sense. But it may be hard to find such a person in the EPA; although that area of service to the public is certainly the most logical place to begin looking."

"Well, all these things will need discussion and determination later," broke in Zeltor. "Right now Rol and I will get the ship prepared for flight within the next couple of days. We pretty much have a ship in mind that has everything necessary for the mission, and we'll secure a functioning time warp mechanism and install it for our use."

"That's great!" said Ellen. "The three of us will be ready to go when you send for us. We're very happy and greatly appreciate that it will be you two taking us on this mission. See you in a couple of days!" With that the five exchanged smiles and left the room.

***

The mission flight had extended to the year 2255 and by this time severe radiation leakage had occurred under Yucca Mountain. The Ogallala deep fossil aquifer definitely did extend under the entire western part of the United States and it had already become seriously contaminated with radiation, even as far as northern Mexico. The first casualties of that radiation were the farmers who pumped that aquifer for irrigation of their crops. Farm family after farm family came down with outbreaks of devastating cancers and gastrointestinal disorders; leading to drastic weight loss, diarrhea, painful mouth ulcers, hair loss, and finally, premature death. It was finally realized that radiation-polluted water was the cause of the problem, but it was too late to do much about it. The water had to be pumped or else the crops would die and famine would break out over many parts of the United States and the world. Since this area produced a commanding percentage of grain and other food products for much of the United States and the rest of the world, these farmers did what they could to lessen the radiation effects and sacrificed themselves and their families by continuing to farm the polluted ground. They received very little help from the alternative medicine of the day, and scientific medical progress was unable to invent any effective new techniques and drugs for the conditions the farmers developed. The average life span of these farmers dropped to 45 years and many of their infants either died in childbirth or soon thereafter. Many were born with disabling defects that caused them to have stunted growth and very short, miserable lives. Sterility became commonplace in the men and women, and most were happy that this was true since they found it too difficult to face the birth defects and short lives of their offspring. Soon the disastrous secondary effect happened with corporate businesses continuing to supply other more distant people with the radiation-contaminated food and they became ill in similar fashion. Between the effects of this radiation pollution, toxic wastes per se, water loss with desertification, and the effects of global warming, mother Earth was facing the possibility of a slow extinction of her human population.

It was at this juncture that Ellen and the rest of the crew on the mission came to the obvious conclusion that it would definitely be necessary for them to return in time to make changes to get rid of the nuclear and toxic wastes in the fashion they had discussed earlier.

"We've seen enough, Zeltor," said Ellen. "Let's get back home to Mars in the proper time and plan our toxic and nuclear waste Sun-Shoot project. It's obvious that it must be done. It also looks like we will need to concern ourselves with solutions for water losses, desertification and global warming as well in the future. But for now we can start with the toxic and nuclear waste problem. At least we should have a definitive chance to correct it. It is also obvious that we will need to continue to rescue and convert accidental death humans and train them to run the needed company we must create as it will most likely require continued support by the more resilient Gnor-humans."

"I don't see any great problems with the time line per se at this juncture," said Rol. "But there definitely will be changes in the human populations in the newly-forming future different than what we saw in the current future. Another future problem could continue to be overpopulation with its obvious pollution problems. Each new human presents another source of pollution that must be reckoned with if the Earth is to remain pristine. As you said Ellen, let's hope we can keep a close eye on what our new future creates and also hope that we are being monitored by time travelers that will keep us out of trouble!"

Zeltor set the time warp mechanism to return them to 2105. As soon as they arrived in that time over the southwestern United States, Zeltor rushed the scout vehicle to the Starship and then back towards the Mars colony and docked smoothly into the First City's spaceport.

On arriving back at their quarters Ellen immediately called for a Council meeting the following day where they would discuss their findings and what they felt should now be undertaken to help the inevitable disastrous plight of the people of Mother Earth.

***

The Council met early the next morning and Ellen explained to the leaders what they had found in the future and what they thought might be the best way to transport these menacing wastes from the Earth. She also made it clear to them that the more resilient Gnor-humans probably would be needed to safely collect and transport the toxic and nuclear wastes to a holding site that they would also have to construct, prior to the wastes being shot into the sun. She stated that it would be reasonable for Gnor-humans to form a clandestine company to take on these tasks as humans per se might not be able to tolerate this work safely. It was made very obvious to everyone that the attempt at removing the wastes from the planet would be a reasonable first priority. One of the Council members asked if consideration to burning at least the toxic wastes with fusion generators might be an easier solution than shooting both types into the sun. Ellen and Rol both counseled against this because of the air pollution it would add to an already deteriorating situation that itself might have to be looked at as a future corrective undertaking. In addition, burning the wastes on the moon or Mars would most likely leave residual that would make the area less habitable or useable in the future. Another Councilman suggested that perhaps they could drill to the Earth's molten core at a remote hidden spot and deposit the wastes there. Dort stated that it would not be certain what would come forth from that opening and more importantly, what it would do to the spinning liquid core that caused the Earth's magnetosphere. He added that the magnetosphere is what protects the Earth from the disastrous effects of the solar wind with its radiation produced by the sun. The planet's life could not survive without this protection. Also, if something happened to the magnetosphere there would be no way to recharge the batteries that powered both the Gnor-humans and Gnormen. After lengthy discussion the Council unanimously agreed to undertake the waste disposition in the manner Ellen and her colleagues had proposed.

"Thank you, my friends," said Ellen. "We will now get started to prepare our first "shepherding" maneuver for Earth. We will need the help of an Earth person preferably high up in the US government that we can trust to be able to collect the wastes for transportation safely, and without our true nature being discovered. My suggestion would be that we get this Earth person to help us pose as an Earth company with entrepreneurial expertise in this problem. The danger of the wastes and the threat of terrorist compromise should allow that person to help us to keep the project safe from prying eyes. We can build the space waste-holding site as a private company similarly to the way the International Space Station was constructed. John, Molly, and I will search for such a person immediately. We plan to look at the Environmental Protection Agency and hope to find someone there who has no political baggage and is genuinely interested in protecting all of the people from environmental harm. I would like to thank the Members for their consideration and input into our concept for ridding the Earth of its damning waste pollution. We will report back to the Council periodically as we develop the definitive infrastructure and train the Gnor-humans that will run the company. We will hope to start soon in getting rid of these wastes in the manner we have proposed."

Back in their apartment Ellen, John, and Molly sat down with Zeltor, Rol, Dort, and Zandor to discuss how they should infiltrate the EPA's staff to find the person who could be trusted not to reveal their presence and be genuinely interested in the health of all the people and not in his or her own advancement by use of Gnor technology.

"This may be a difficult kind of person to find at this time," said John. "As regards many of the corporate businesses, they have become so cunning and cutthroat in their attempt to outdo and steal from each other that it may be next to impossible to find anyone in business that would be trustworthy."

"That is why I suggested the EPA," said Ellen. "I think there would be a better chance of finding such an ethical person in that governmental department than one from the current business environment. Also, we don't need a corporate business to finance this since we will build and maintain it ourselves. If we don't find that person in the EPA, we will have to find one in another area; perhaps the scientific or medical community, or maybe even the clergy."

"At any rate," broke in Dort, "Zandor and I have had extensive previous training in infiltrating human institutions and organizations. We can and will be glad to show you how to accomplish this activity without the people becoming suspicious."

"Thanks, Dort," answered Ellen. "I knew you two, from your prior experience, would be invaluable in helping us get started on this quest. My plan would be for John, Molly, and I to approach the EPA headquarters in Washington, D.C. as a family having problems on our farm in Nevada near Yucca Mountain. We will arrive there a year or so before the Congress passes the legislation mandating the burial of nuclear wastes under the mountain. This will give the company we form a chance to start collecting the wastes before they are buried there. Saying that we are from that area in Nevada may hopefully get us to see someone who might be having second thoughts about burying nuclear wastes there. There were, after all, several geologists at that time that were dead set against this idea. If the person we see shows genuine concern about our little family living there, it would be indicative that he or she was sincere about protecting the people from this problem. Since we know the administration and Congress are in favor of this Yucca Mountain disposal site, an EPA person being against it would make it more likely that he or she has no political baggage that could hurt us. We can then study that person and find out if he or she qualifies as someone we can trust to help us and not reveal our presence on Earth. I expect we will find that this person will not be too high up in the organization, but hopefully high enough to be able to do for us what will need to be done regarding protecting our anonymity. We'll start our infiltration in Washington next week after Dort and Zandor have taught us the proper technique to accomplish this during the next few days."

"Mom," said Molly, "I apologize for changing the subject, but when are we going to be able to rescue the poet-pilot, Antoine-Marie-Roger de Saint-Exupery? You know how much Ares and I have always loved his story 'The Little Prince'. And when you told us that the author had been shot down and killed by German planes in WWII over the Mediterranean Sea on July 31, 1944 you had said that you and Dad probably would be able to rescue him from that crash. Is it possible that we could do that rescue before we start the waste project since it will be taking up all of our efforts for a long time once we start? Ares and I were so looking forward to going with you on that rescue; and I was thinking that Saint Exupery was a pilot who loved adventure and by his writings seemed to espouse very high ethics and morals. Wouldn't he perhaps be valuable as another Gnor-human able to fly scout vehicles?"

"Well, Molly," said Ellen, "we did promise you we'd do that, didn't we; and we have put it off a couple of times already, it's true. Let us identify and secure our Earth friend who is to help us first. Then, while we're preparing the plans for the collection, transportation, and space station infrastructure and training the personnel for the project, we can go about rescuing your poet-pilot. I suspect that he will be quite happy to join our Gnor-human society and might indeed be valuable to fly for us. Will that be satisfactory?"

"OK, Mom," answered Molly, "you're a peach, and I love you." Molly gave her mother a hug, took leave of the others and rushed from the room to find Ares and tell him the news about the upcoming rescue of their favorite author. In the meantime Ellen and John made plans to work with Dort and Zandor to help train them for their infiltration into the EPA in Washington, DC. They hoped to be able to find the person they would be able to trust to help them with their waste disposal project and keep their presence on Earth secret.

"We can brief Molly later," said Ellen. "Right now she's very happy about the upcoming rescue of her poet we promised her and wants to let Ares know the good news as well. Zeltor, I hope you and Rol will be able to take us. There may be a problem with security around the United States' capitol area, and I know you two will be the best able to keep our flights hidden from discovery."

"Of course," smiled Zeltor. "We wouldn't let you go without us, Ellen. After all, we certainly must protect our first Gnor-human family."

"Thanks Zeltor," Ellen smiled back at the Gnorman. "I knew you'd be there for us. I found out that the congressional debate about placement of the nuclear wastes under Yucca Mountain in Nevada took place in 1997-98. We should plan to be in Washington during 1997 if we are to stop the Yucca Mountain project before anything gets buried there."

With that they all smiled and took leave of one another, setting up the training program to start in the morning.

***

About two months had gone by and Ellen, John, and Molly were now well prepared for their plan to infiltrate the EPA as a concerned family from Nevada with a farm that was located close to Yucca Mountain. They would say that they were worried about possible pollution of their farm from the nuclear waste to be buried there. At this time there were a lot of protesters from that state that were actively seeking to halt the Congress from passing legislation to put the wastes under the mountain, so their doing likewise in Washington would not be looked upon with any suspicion. And since they were a 'nice, grassroots family', they might very well end up being shunted to a person known in the department to be sympathetic to such local people's fears. Fortunately for them this is exactly what happened when they applied to be seen by someone in the EPA about their fears.

They were given an appointment to see Jack Nelson, a 54 year old African American former physics professor from Johns Hopkins University whose wife, Cecile, had also been appointed to the EPA by the President as one of the under secretaries of the agency. Both she and Jack were from Nevada originally and had met at Johns Hopkins during their undergraduate years. He had gone on into physics and become an assistant professor in that department; and she had gone into the EPA, to pursue environmental protection activity. She had always been interested in preserving the natural environment and rose in respect and expertise in that department steadily over the years until she was close to the top of the organization. Her husband, Jack, had always been proud of her dedication to the environment and his feelings gradually became almost as strong as his wife's concerning protecting it and the people affected by it. Jack and his wife had two children; a son, Joshua, now 23, and a daughter, Jeanne, who was 19. Tragedy had struck this loving family two years earlier when Jack's wife Cecile was discovered to have widely metastatic breast cancer and was now expected to die within the present year. To make matters worse, his daughter Jeanne was discovered to have some sort of rare, as yet undiagnosed, metabolic disease and was literally wasting away in front of her frightened family's eyes. To lose the two female members of this very close-knit family was almost too much for the two men left to bear; but they were trying to endure it and both did as much as they could to make the two women's remaining time as pleasant as possible for them.

During Jack's wife's illness the EPA Secretary, acutely cognizant of how dedicated Jack had become to the environment through his wife's tutelage, had asked him if it would be possible for him to help Cecile with the job that she loved so much since she had continued to struggle with it and wouldn't give it up. When she could no longer carry it on, she and the Secretary both encouraged Jack to take it over and abandon his physics professorship. They both knew that he had never been happy with his teaching job, and so it was easy for him to acquiesce to their requests. Later on Jack was officially appointed by the Secretary to his wife's job in the Agency; and he had vowed to her that he would pursue it in the same dedicated fashion that she had always done. Because he soon developed a reputation as a "bleeding heart" environmental person, it was natural that Ellen and her family would have been referred to him for discussion and disposition.

***

Ellen, John, and Molly entered Jack Nelson's office and were greeted in a warm, friendly fashion by the still quite fit and handsome African American man. He rose quickly from his chair behind a magnificent walnut desk bathed in the sunlight from a large window behind it and invited them into the room.

"Come in, come in," said Jack to the three. "Please take chairs there and tell me how I can help you. I'm Jack Nelson, one of the many under secretaries of the EPA; and incidentally, both my wife and I also were from Nevada originally. Now, tell me exactly who you are and what it is that you want me to do for you and I'll try to do whatever I can to help you."

"Thank you, Mr. Secretary," said Ellen in reply. "My name is Ellen James and this is my husband, Dr. John Scott. And this young woman is our daughter, Molly, who is also interested in this problem as well. We were hoping you could help us with the concern we have about the proposed burying of nuclear wastes under Yucca Mountain in Nevada. That site is close to our farm and we are very worried about it. Will the wastes definitely have to be buried there now, or is there a chance that another method and place could be utilized instead?"

"This does seem to be of concern to a great deal of Nevada citizens at the moment, Ellen," answered Jack. "I really don't know how to answer you at this time. The law has already been passed in Congress and it is just waiting to be enacted. It has been held up because of legitimate fears by geologists about the aquifer under the area; how deep it is and how far it extends. It does look like, however, that nuclear wastes will eventually be buried under Yucca Mountain. We are awaiting more information about the site, so I'd like to have a rain check on any answers to you until we get that information. Because I was originally from Nevada, they have put me in charge of overseeing how the waste gets buried, who transports it, and how it is brought to the site, so I'd like to give you an appointment for next week to give you some answers then. Would that be OK?"

"Indeed, Mr. Secretary," answered Ellen, "that would be quite acceptable to us."

"Please, Ellen," smiled Jack. "Don't bother to call me 'Mr. Secretary'. It'll get confused with the big boss of this agency. I'm just a little cog in this EPA machine, not the big wheel. So Mr. Nelson, or better still, Jack, would be appropriate from three fellow Nevadians."

"That's good of you, Jack," answered Ellen. "Then we'll plan to see you a week from today, and thank you." With that the three left the office and returned to the scout vehicle where Zeltor and Rol were waiting to pick them up.

When they entered the ship Ellen could hardly contain herself. "Zeltor, Rol, I believe this man we just met will be perfect for our needs," she exclaimed to the two Gnormen. "He has told us that he has a wife with end-stage breast cancer and a daughter who has some sort of rare metabolic disease that is slowly killing her also. His wife had an impeccable reputation for preserving the environment and protecting the people; and her husband has followed her lead since he took over for her. We have a wonderful chance to get him on our side since we will be able to save both his wife and his daughter. If they agree to his wife's brain transfer, her husband can cover up the surgery by saying that she was treated successfully at a private medical clinic where they had found her disease wasn't as far spread as originally thought. At the appropriate time his daughter could have the operation as well with the same subterfuge about successful medical care. If I am correct, I believe Jack and his son probably will also opt for Gnor-human change eventually since they are such a close-knit family. Even more fortuitous for us, they have no other living relatives, so that problem won't be a factor either. In addition, Jack Nelson seems to me to be a man who would accept the Gnorman ethical and moral values easily. I can hardly wait to come back next week. I think we have found our liaison on the first try!"

***

The following week the trio returned to Jack Nelson's office, but on this occasion he was rather somber and didn't seem to have much to say during their interview.

"I apologize to you people," he finally said soberly, "I'm afraid my heart is not in my work today. My wife is at home with a terminal illness and took a turn for the worse last night. I fear we may lose her very soon." With that a tear formed in the corner of his right eye and started to run down his cheek. "I'm sorry," he continued, dabbing his face with a handkerchief. "Perhaps we should continue our talk in a day or two when I'm a little more composed."

"We're sorry to hear that, Jack," replied Ellen. "It must be a very difficult time for you and your family."

"It is indeed," answered Jack. "And to add to our family's woes, my daughter also has a serious problem as well and I'm afraid she will have a great deal of trouble handling what is happening to her mother." He wiped his eyes with the handkerchief and rose to escort them to the door.

Ellen glanced anxiously at her companions and then said to the secretary, "Jack, we understand your sorrow about your wife and daughter. Won't you please sit down? We have something to offer you that will solve the problems with the women you love if you, your son, and they are willing to accept it."

Jack clumsily slumped back into his chair, a quizzical expression on his face. "What do you mean, you can solve my wife's and daughter's problems," he asked. They are both dying (his voice cracked), my wife sooner than my daughter. What could you possibly do to stop that when all the doctors say there is nothing more that can be done?"

"We may be taking a chance telling you what I am about to say," Ellen rejoined, "but my heart goes out to you in such a terrible situation. We have researched you and found that you appear to be a very decent, loving, and intelligent man who is motivated to help the people and the environment, rather than himself. We are not from Nevada. We come from colonies on the planet Mars and are former human beings that have been transformed into a different living being called a Gnor-human. My husband John was about to drown in a packet boat off San Francisco in 1932; I was about to die in a burning plane crash in 2003; and we rescued my daughter Molly from the Titanic disaster in 1912. I know this will be hard to believe, but we can show you and prove it to you. It will then not be hard for you to see why we must remain hidden from the people of Earth at present, but we are hopeful that later on we can drop our clandestine ways. Most important to you now is that we have the technology to save your wife and daughter if they, and you and your son, agree to it. Our story is much more complex that this hurried explanation, and it will be told to you in full measure later on. We are here actually to try to get the help and trust of someone in the United States government that can help us to set up a clandestine system to get rid of toxic and nuclear wastes. We have the ability to travel forwards and backwards in time and have seen widespread devastation to the Earth in the future from these wastes. Again, I am sure it will become obvious to you why we need to remain hidden from the people of Earth at this time, but we are hopeful this will not be true in the future. We are dedicated to being Shepherds of the Earth to protect her from wrong paths that could lead to her peoples' destruction. Will you come with us and let us prove what I say is the truth? It would seem that time is of the essence as far as your wife is concerned. After her recovery we can talk about your daughter's recovery as well. Will you come?"

Jack had slumped back against his high-back chair and was staring at Ellen. "This is fantastic!" he murmured. "How could you ever prove such a preposterous tale to me?"

'We will take you to our ship and fly you to Mars and explain in detail how and why we are here," said Ellen. It is a relatively short trip with the type of propulsion in our scout vehicle; and we can manipulate the time so that we will be back the same day to go with you to talk to your wife and family about saving her. Remember this; we can only do what you wish us to do. Our ethics and morals, although we came from humans, are far more advanced now than they ever were as humans. We are not able to harm you in any way; we only want to help Mother Earth escape from that same destruction that occurred to the race that came here and created us, as they had to similarly create themselves in order to survive on their self-blighted planet. Will you come? The time may be growing short for your wife and daughter."

Jack looked Ellen straight in the eye and said, "I read only kindness and concern in your eyes, Ellen; certainly not madness. If you can save the loves of my life, I will be eternally grateful to you. If all this is true, I could never be anything but your staunchest ally, and you can believe me implicitly that no one in my family would ever disclose your presence here on Earth. Please take me to your ship!" With that he quickly arranged with his secretary to be off that day, presumably because of his wife's worsening, and then left his office with his three visitors.

***

When Ellen entered the bridge of the scout vehicle with John and Molly, Zeltor and Rol greeted them warmly, but then were completely taken aback when a fourth person followed them in.

"Zeltor, Rol," Ellen began, "I'd like you to meet Jack Nelson of the U.S. EPA, who needs our help as desperately as we need his. Jack, these are two true Gnormen, the race from the planet Mekan that created us and trained us to be able to save your wife and daughter as they did us. Zeltor is our pilot, and Rol is the navigator of our ship."

Jack looked incredulously at the two Gnormen and the surrounding instrumentation of the ship's bridge.

"Good day, gentlemen," he said haltingly. "I'm very pleased to meet you but it's hard to believe that I'm not in some fantastic dream with what I've been told already by Ellen and John, and with what I'm now seeing in your ship. Please don't take this as any disrespect, but you don't look very much different than most humans. I must confess that I am quite a bit apprehensive about all this; but if it can save my Cecile and Jeanne, my wife and daughter, I will be grateful beyond belief."

The two Gnormen smiled at the remark about their similarity to humans.

"Hello, Mr. Nelson," said Zeltor. "We're pleased to meet you as well if Ellen vouches for you. Ellen will have to tell you about two other Gnormen you will probably meet soon whose manipulation of your ancestor's DNA during the time of your dinosaurs has caused us to look very similar." He then looked at Ellen and John, suspecting that something had probably escalated with Jack's wife's illness necessitating this unplanned encounter and asked them what the problem was.

"Jack's wife Cecile's illness has taken a turn for the worse," explained Ellen to the two Gnormen, "and isn't expected to live very much longer. We will need to work fast to save her so it has necessitated us to explain everything to Jack now so that we can set in motion the steps necessary to do so."

"So brain transference is being considered is what you mean," said Rol.

"Yes," rejoined Ellen. "But we haven't yet explained to Jack fully what will have to be done to effect Cecile's cure. I am sure if this path is not chosen by Jack, his wife and the family, we will return him to a few days before meeting us and thus maintain our incognito position here on Earth. Otherwise, I would not have brought him here to the ship. I felt we needed the presence of the ship and the ride to Mars to convince him of our truthfulness and what we will be able to do to save his wife and daughter. Since we don't have the Prime Mover's eloquence with us anymore, on the way back to our Mars colony I will try to describe Gnormen history and the reason why the Gnormen came to Earth in the past. I will try to explain how they actually helped create the current human race to help them finish the research necessary to develop the totally synthetic brain they needed to go back to their planet and reclaim it.

Ellen then turned to Jack.

"I hope I will be able to show you, Jack, how similar Earth's burgeoning pollution is to what happened to the Gnormen's planet Mekan that necessitated them having to create synthetic bodies able to survive on their polluted planet. We have gone ahead in time with the time warp mechanism I told you about and seen the devastation caused on Earth by nuclear and toxic waste pollution. We know how to rid the Earth of this pollution, but the greed of a few power-minded people in the business community at this time necessitates us doing it in secret. We need someone like you to help us set up a company that will be able to collect the waste and transport it without discovery. If you can help us form a company that won't be discovered for who and what we are, we will then be able to set up a satellite waste holding space station from where we can propel the wastes into the sun where they will do no harm. Our Gnor-human crews will fly the collecting ships as we can tolerate wastes both nuclear and toxic far better than humans. Our ships climb the magnetic lines of force in the Earth's magnetosphere at any rate of speed we choose so accidental spill is very unlikely. So Jack, if you and everyone else here is agreeable we can start now; and with the time warp mechanism, we can get you back to Earth again before your family starts to wonder where you are."

"My head is spinning," said Jack, "but let us proceed at once and I will listen with all the concentration that I or anyone else could muster while flying in an alien space ship to a colony on Mars!"

With that, everyone smiled and Zeltor started the ship on its flight back to Mars; first directing the ship off the planet by utilizing magnetic drive with slow miniscule jumps up each of the Earth's magnetic lines of force. When they were high enough he shut off the detection-jamming sensors and the magnetic drive and began a more rapid flight towards Mars using fusion power.

"You see, Jack," Zeltor directed to the awestruck passenger, "that slow climb up the Earth's magnetic lines of force enables us to ascend slowly and safely; something that can't be said about your rocket launches. At least one in two thousand such launches end up in disaster as I'm sure you already know. With our ships collecting and transporting the wastes, there would be little problem with inadvertent spills as we could ascend slowly and carefully using our magnetic drive."

"Yes, I can see that," answered Jack. "That technology would be extremely valuable for Earth's air and land travel as well. I believe I read somewhere that the Germans were developing a magnetic technology for rapid train travel."

"Now perhaps you can understand, Jack," interrupted Ellen, "why we must remain hidden from corporate businesses for a time yet. Until they develop the ethics and morals of the Gnormen that we have now, it would not be safe to give them this knowledge. At the right time we will do so, perhaps in incremental fashion."

"I'm beginning to understand you, Ellen," Jack replied. "I know all about corporate business lobbying and its extremely detrimental effect sometimes to the environment. My wife Cecile often gets quite vehement about the topic! I must say, though, this conversation is making me more and more excited about my wife and daughter. I'm also fascinated with your idea of propelling the wastes into the sun. I remember some time ago, in the early years of the EPA, my wife Cecile came home one night and told me that someone in a congressional seminar had suggested doing that to Secretary Ruckelshaus. She said they all laughed about it at the time, but Cecile thought that maybe it might be a reasonable thing to try to do."

"That's interesting, Jack," said Ellen, "because we obtained the idea ourselves from that symposium of Silvio Conte in 1984 when a Northampton, MA surgeon suggested it to Secretary Ruckelshaus. Isn't it a small solar system?" Jack smiled at Ellen's use of 'solar system' instead of 'world'.

On the way back to the Martian colony Ellen and John related to Jack the story of the Gnormen's coming to Earth and how living human brains were transferred into synthetic Gnor bodies with spontaneous hookup and completely normal functioning of these bodies. They also conveyed to him how the transplanted living brain's functionality could then be transferred into a totally synthetic brain with only minimal inconsequential losses of any of the living brain's past memories and emotions. They told him how several hundred more years of life were bestowed on the people and how much better off they were physically and mentally in their synthetic state. Their mental processes were improved and chemicals placed into these synthetic brains helped to induce a higher plane of ethical and moral values that were necessary in these now long-lived and powerful people. In this way a living person's abilities, awareness, memories, and emotions, could be preserved for a very long period of time. They said that it could be seen to be a way of preserving a race of living beings caught in a deadly environment of diseases and pollution, as what happened to the Gnormen. Ellen also explained how the bellows apparatus in their chest cavity allowed them to speak through an almost identical anatomy to the human one. She also discussed how power to run their synthetic body was obtained by very long-lived batteries that were constantly recharged by the electric current obtained from an electromagnetic device within their bodies that utilized movement through the magnetosphere of Earth and other planets as the source of power. It was also possible to recharge at night while sleeping by plugging into another outside source in planetary systems where the magnetosphere was not as well developed as it was on Earth and Mekan. Although he didn't request it, John explained to Jack how the male and female sexual apparatus worked, and that it had much better function and sensation than the old human one had, and without the mess of secretions. Ellen somewhat embarrassedly remarked that it was very much better in the female body also, and that all sensations were heightened as well.

By the time they had reached the Martian colony, Jack was limp with processing everything that had been told him. After they arrived on the landing pad, he was helped into a life support suit and he and the others left the ship to transfer to the hospital Oxygen Quarters. On the way to that destination Jack marveled at the Martian landscape and a roaring dust storm swirling over the top of the force-field-protected dome of First City. The reduced gravity effect he noted at once; and he was acutely aware that only he required a support suit to survive in the Martian atmosphere. He knew from his physics' professorship that it contained ninety-five per cent CO2 and only 0.13 per cent oxygen. He took in the beauty of the reddish to black sky and stood wide-eyed at the bustling colonists moving about the city without any life support suits of any kind.

When they entered the hospital Oxygen Quarters John helped Jack remove his life support suit; and the visitor remarked that he felt a little giddy but that it was probably more from emotion than anything else. Ellen introduced him to Dr. Ran, his wife, Sarah, and their son, Ares. She told Jack that Ares was the first mating of a living Gnorman, Dr. Ran, with a human female, Sarah. This had bolstered the belief that humans and Gnormen did indeed have similar genetic makeup. Of course, by this time all three had already transferred to totally synthetic bodies and brains; although later Jack related that he could not tell the difference between humans and Gnor-humans.

"I'm happy to meet you, Jack," said Dr. Ran. "Ellen has told you most of the story of our arrival here on Earth and Mars. This is the hospital where all the transference surgery and rehabilitation is done. An Earth atmosphere is kept in this building for support until you no longer need it. I will be glad to explain the details of the surgery and recovery to you. I'm sure you realize by now that your wife will lose her human body with its human brain and exchange it for a synthetic one that, I must say, is much stronger, smarter, and longer-lived than her human one. A very important thing that Ellen and John may not have mentioned to you is that human thoughts and emotions are not lost with this transfer. You still feel both physically and mentally that you are "you" and are still human. Also, sexual feelings and the apparatus to express them are not lost either, and actually are enhanced."

"John did mention that part, doctor," Jack spoke up with a smile. "But what will my wife have to go through, doctor? Will it be painful, and will she suffer much after the surgery?"

"There will be almost no pain or suffering," answered Dr. Ran, "and the body she receives first will feel just like her old one did, only better. It will take six to eight weeks for her living brain to connect up with the synthetic body's brain stem, but she will have no awareness actually until it has joined and she is functioning normally. At that time everything will function better than it ever has; and believe me, she will be very happy with her new body as all the other Gnor-human women have been. One thing is critical, as I'm sure Ellen and John have already told you, Cecile and the entire family must concur with doing this as our ethics and morals do not allow us to go ahead otherwise. It will mean a family conference must take place to have a full discussion of this, and we will have to arrange it with the time warp mechanism so that if you decide not to do anything we must be allowed to place you back in a time a few days ago so that you will have no recollection of this or us. If you are agreeable to the procedure, and you think your wife may be, we will go back immediately and arrange the family conference."

"Doctor Ran," said Jack, with a slight throb in his voice, "what you are proposing to me looks like it may be able to return to me the love of my life, which I thought I was about to lose forever. Of course I want to proceed at once. Also, from what you've explained to me about your mission here and what you've been doing with the accidental death humans that I have seen all over this colony, I am one hundred per cent in favor of your project to spare Mother Earth's peoples from harm and devastation. I would be very proud and honored to be a part of it."

Across from Dr. Ran and Jack, seated in a chair, Ellen beamed and said enthusiastically, "I knew we could count on you, Jack. Even without the chemicals in your brain that we have, you have ethics and morals very similar to ours. I could sense this in you all along, and it gives me extreme pleasure to know that we can restore your wife and daughter to you. We have been looking for someone exactly like you to help us start our project to get rid of the Earth's toxic and nuclear wastes before irretrievable damage is done. I have a suspicion that your wife will want to be on board with this project as well when she is better."

"There is no question about that, Ellen," replied Jack. "I'm ready to start back as soon as you people are. Who will come back with us to help explain all this to Cecile and my family?"

"We will take the same pilot and navigator," said Ellen. "Dr. Ran, John and I will also accompany you to give the explanations necessary. At a later time, Jack, we will have you come back and introduce you to several human heroes that we have rescued and that are now working with us. It will be fascinating for you to converse with them as it has been for us. Rol, let's set the time warp mechanism to have us get back to Jack's home just a couple of hours after we left his office."

"Amazing!" remarked Jack All this way and back in two hours!"

***

When they arrived at Jack's home, they were greeted by his son, Joshua at the front door of a comfortable two-story Tudor house.

Joshua was a twenty three year old, tall, athletic-appearing, handsome young man, who had spent his undergraduate years at MIT in physics as his dad had been, and was now a graduate student there at this time. He was looking sad as he greeted his dad with a hug. He quickly released his father and stepped back in surprise as he saw the strangers who were standing behind his father.

"How's your mother, Josh," Jack asked of his son, "is she comfortable now?"

"Yes, dad," Josh answered, "the medicine you gave her this morning seemed to ease the pain she was having and she's been sleeping peacefully most of the day."

"How's Jeannie," his father went on, "has she been taking your mother's setback badly? You know how upset she has been with your mother's illness."

"Yeah, dad." replied his son, "she has been a real trooper about it, what with her own problems and all. She tries to cheer me up about it, knowing full well that she may soon be in the same situation herself before long." A small drop of water welled up in the corner of his right eye and he quickly brushed it away. Jack put his arm around his son and smiled at him.

"Well, Josh," I have some wonderful news for you and your sister. These people with me have the ability to cure your mother's problem if she chooses to go along with their operation. Josh, this is Dr. Dik Ran, Dr. John Scott, and Professor Ellen James, who are here to discuss with your mother and our family a process that will restore her to perfect health. We believe that your sister Jeanne could also benefit from this process as well." The enthusiastic light in his father's eyes was very infectious and Josh found that the pall that his mother's moribund condition had caused was beginning to lift.

"Is that right, dad," he said. "Cured? That's wonderful! How will this be done? Is it an operation or drug therapy? Oh, my gosh! I'm very pleased to meet you people!" Josh spoke to the three strangers enthusiastically, and shook all three hands warmly.

"It is both an operation and drug therapy, Josh," said Dr. Ran. "But first we must get your mother, sister, and you together to explain what we have already presented to your father. Jack, do you think your wife is up for this discussion now?"

"I do," replied Jack. "Although she is very weak, she is perfectly alert and knows her prognosis completely. She is a real trooper, as is her daughter, and thinks more of us than she does of herself; as she always has."

"Good," said Dr. Ran. "It seems then that we should make the decision as soon as possible to be able to affect the best transplantation results. Can we all get together in her bedroom or should we meet in another room?"

"Our bedroom is quite large," answered Jack, "and I'm sure we can bring in a couple more chairs to all meet and have the discussion there. Josh, go and get your sister and wheel her into the room. These people will need acceptance by all of us before they will be able to help your mother and sister."

Jack quietly opened his bedroom door and saw that Cecile was awake and looking much better than she had when he left that morning. He advanced to the bedside and kissed his wife gently on the cheek.

"Hello, darling," he whispered in her ear. "Are you feeling better? You look much better to me."

"Yes, dear," she said, "I do feel a lot better since you gave me the medication this morning. I actually slept most of the day and now feel quite rested and raring to go."

Tears started to form in Jack's eyes and he took his wife's hand and squeezed it gently.

"That's my brave darling," he said, "Cecile, I have some wonderful news. I have brought some people with me that feel they will be able to cure your illness and leave you normal again."

"What!" she said with hope rising in her eyes. "What do you mean, Jack."

"Darling," he replied, and waved the three up closer to the bed, "let me introduce you to Dr. Dik Ran, Dr. John Scott, and Professor Ellen James. They will explain to you in great detail what they have to offer to you if you accept their proposal. They must have your acceptance and ours as well before they will take it on. What you are about to hear will be fantastic, but it is all true; I have just been taken there and witnessed it myself... on the planet Mars!"

"Mars!" breathed Cecile, and the name was echoed by Joshua and Jeanne as well, as they had just entered the room. "What are you talking about, Jack?"

"Wait now, Cecile," replied Jack, "let our visitors explain everything to you and the kids."

"Good evening, Mrs. Nelson," began Dr. Ran. "We would like to explain to you who we are and what we can do for you to correct your devastating illness." He then went on with aid from Ellen and John to explain exactly who they were and what they would be able to do for her if she accepted the synthetic transference.

After he had finished, Cecile and her two children seemed dumfounded by what had been said. Ellen then began to speak.

"I know this is hard to believe and accept but let me tell you that two of us standing here before you are such Gnor-human transplants. I was rescued from a burning airplane and my husband, John, from a sinking ship. Jeanne; feel my arm and face. Does it not look and feel exactly like yours?" Jeanne approached slowly from out of her wheelchair and did as Ellen suggested.

"It is amazing," said Jeanne, with wide eyes. "I feel no difference whatsoever!"

Jeanne was a frail creature, very thin and pale, but had an extremely beautiful face with chiseled features and tight-curled black hair. She looked a lot like her mother as both of their eyes were a striking dark brown that sparkled similarly from out of the pale facial skin they both had. Jeanne went back to her wheel chair and sat down.

"Now Josh," Ellen went on, "Come and take my pulse, and note the temperature of my hand." Josh also approached and tried unsuccessfully to find any pulse after trying several spots on Ellen's wrists.

"I can't find any pulse!" he said incredulously. "And her hand is cold!"

"And, as Dr. Ran has said," recommenced Ellen, " human memories and emotions are not changed one iota; you are just given a new body and mind that still is completely yours but you are now stronger, smarter and much more long-lived than any human being. All of the hundreds of rescued Gnor-human colonists on Mars have enjoyed their changes immensely; and we exist there now only to save planet Earth from destruction in the similar manner that caused the Gnormen to have to develop the synthetic body to survive."

Cecile's eyes, which had become sparkling with excitement, grew misty.

"I would certainly love to be a part of that endeavor, Ellen," she said. "Then, with a sudden resolve she sat forward in the bed and looked her husband in the eye and said "Since I really have nothing to lose, Jack, I for one am ready to undertake this procedure right now if you think I will survive it."

"We haven't lost anyone yet," smiled Dr. Ran. "I don't think you will be an exception to that record."

"If everyone else will please step out for a minute," said Ellen, "I want to talk to Cecile and Jeanne woman-to-woman for a moment. After the others had left the room, Ellen removed her clothing and revealed her attractive body to the two women.

"I want you both to feel my breasts and examine my sexual apparatus. I am not trying to be a pervert, but I want you to see that my body looks and feels like a very healthy young adult woman. Sensation in my synthetic body is much more enhanced for the better, and I will remain with this shape for the hundreds of years I can now live barring any traumatic mishap. I still have the same human emotions and memories I always had, but my psyche has been improved by chemicals in my synthetic brain that have raised my ethics and morals to that of the Gnor race that created me. The funny part of it is, this race actually created we humans by what they did to our ancestors back in the age of the dinosaurs. That is why we look so similar to them. Dr. Ran was the only living Gnorman, and he successfully mated with a human female, Sarah, to have a son. They all opted for transference to the synthetic state that they now are in. But it proves how similar we are to them although certainly not in the high-minded ethics and morals they have had centuries to develop. They laugh at us accepting a salary for doing something for one another. They are rewarded enough by being able to be allowed to perform whatever tasks they do well for the benefit of all. The chemicals in their synthetic brain help to quell any feelings of violence, jealousy, anger, or envy, but non-detrimental emotions as love and admiration are unchanged and they have also had millennia to develop into their high ethical and moral state. We Gnor-humans still continue to have these emotions; but they are no longer overpowering and easily handled in a logical manner with the help of the chemicals within our brains. I don't know how you two women feel about sex, but you can see that I have the usual accoutrements necessary to perform the function. Let me tell you, however, that the sensations as a Gnor-human are very much more intense and much more satisfying than I ever had before as a human."

Ellen quickly replaced her clothes.

"I hope I didn't embarrass you too much ladies," said Ellen. "I did embarrass myself, but I can't blush anymore as I have no blood vessels so it wouldn't show. I did think that it was important to show you that you are giving up very little and gaining a lot. There is one problem that would more extend to Jeanne than to you, Cecile. That is the fact that you cannot reproduce anymore with this synthetic body, even though you feel all the yearnings and joys of sexual activity. There are no internal organs like you have now; no organs to get cancer or other diseases that can kill you, or to have periods with. We have been rescuing children and supplying them with synthetic bodies that are changed at varying intervals to simulate growing up. We do the same for adults, changing their faces at hundred year intervals to simulate aging. It apparently was to keep the same feature alive that the Gnormen had early in their living history. You would probably find it hard to believe that I have been a Gnor-human for 102 years, added on to 33 years as a living human being. Two years ago I was scheduled to have my face aged to about what you would call a forty year old. I still wanted to look my best for my husband, John; so I approached that change as any forty year old human woman would.....with great fear and trepidation!" Ellen smiled broadly after she said this.

"Adoption of the children by Gnor-humans has worked out well for all concerned. As far as human children are concerned, there are enough of them destitute in the world today to supply anyone who wants to love and bring them up."

"Ellen," said Cecile, "I want to thank you for doing this. It has answered many of the secret things I was pondering and made me more convinced to go ahead with this. Jeanne, how do you feel about all this? If your metabolic disease doesn't relent you may have to consider this also."

"Mom, I am flabbergasted about all this," replied Jeanne, "but if it works out well for you I will love these people forever, and wouldn't hesitate doing it myself at all." She went over to her mother's bed from her chair, threw her arms around her and kissed her on the cheek.

"Well then," said Ellen, "it's all settled. We will make arrangements to transport you to Mars for the operation and rehabilitation. We will let the family visit and stay as long as you like. Remember we can use the time warp mechanism to get you back here any time we want to, so there won't be any suspicion aroused. When you are well, Cecile, and back to work after a suitable period of time, you can say you were at a mountain health clinic in Switzerland where you underwent treatments successfully for your condition. Now let us bring the others back in and tell them the good news."

***

Cecile, Joshua and Jeanne were as spellbound as Jack had been when they were transported to the First City on Mars for her procedure. The two children and Jack were installed in a suite of rooms in the hospital Oxygen Quarters to await Cecile's operation. Dr. Ran was worried that there might be some metastatic breast cancer present in her brain that could slow or even have a deleterious effect upon the synaptic acceptance of her living brain by the synthetic spinal cord. Cecile, however, had decided to progress directly to the transference to the totally synthetic brain right away after her first operation, so the doctor felt that the procedure would ultimately accomplish what she wanted and she would be free of the cancerous human body as well.

The day finally came for Cecile's operation and Ellen, John, Sarah, Molly, Ares, and the three Nelsons accompanied her to the operating room door. As she was wheeled toward the OR door, her two children gave their mother a big hug and kissed her on the cheek, saying they'd see her soon, free of that horrible disease forever. The Gnor people smiled and wished her good luck; and Ellen squeezed her hand. Jack stepped forward, put his arms around his wife, smiled and kissed her on the lips.

"I'll see you later, honey, "he whispered. "Now I want you to promise that you won't wear me out with your new body after this operation."

"You are a tease, Jack, darling," and she threw him a kiss as she was wheeled through the OR door.

The operation went very well and the usual four to six week rehabilitation period went by with eventual full recovery of Cecile. Ellen was able to ease their concern during the time when the synthetic spinal cord was accepting the living brain and Cecile was totally unresponsive. She had explained how very worried she had been when her daughter Molly had had her first operation, but that everything eventually worked out very well.

On a morning when Cecile was completely well and Ellen was visiting with her she began to tell her that she wanted to stay on Mars for a little while to get used to her new body, but then she confessed to Ellen that secretly she really wanted Jack to get used to it as well.

"He has been a little hesitant with me, Ellen," she said that morning, "and I really have a great desire to become intimate with him again. You were right about the sensations. They are far more intense than they ever were before. My chest anatomy is like it was at Jeanne's age; and you say it stays like this forever? I can see why the Gnor-human women have no complaints about their bodies." She smiled after saying this.

Ellen smiled back at her. "It's perfectly natural that Jack should feel this way now, Cecile" replied Ellen. Just tell him so and help him to get over it. He will love it; and so will you, believe me. Don't worry about the fluid problem; it won't hurt your apparatus at all."

Jack was very hesitant with Cecile at first, but there had been so much love between the two of them over the years that he soon lost it. He reported to Dr. Ran, who had queried him on how he and Cecile were getting along on an intimate level, that being with his wife again was like the time they had spent on their honeymoon. It was very obvious to all how happy and grateful the two of them and their children were for this gift from the Gnor-humans.

As Cecile became stronger and stronger, she suggested to Jack that the two of them approach Ellen and suggest that they get back to Earth and start on the project. She said she felt wonderful and now that she was well again she wanted to get back to her work, especially to help Ellen and the Gnor-humans with their project.

Ellen was delighted with Cecile's request but she wanted Dr. Ran's OK that she was ready to return to Earth.

"I have examined Cecile, Ellen," Dr. Ran responded to her question, "and she is as fit as you are; even though she is actually much younger than you and not experienced with her new body."

"Thanks, Dik," said Ellen with a wry smile. "You sure know how to make a woman feel great!"

"Well," smiled Dr. Ran sheepishly, "what I meant was that despite the age difference you two look about the same. I'm sorry but I didn't mean anything disparaging by my statement."

"I know, I know," Ellen replied good-naturedly, "I was just kidding. I'm still trying to get back at you for kidding me about John and me in our courting days."

Cecile and Ellen looked at each other and laughed.

"Well then, "said Cecile, "since I'm well enough, let's get back to Earth and start the project. I'm raring to go!"

"Whoa, slow down my love," said Jack. "We'll have to let you start back slowly or the people at the office will get pretty suspicious."

"Oh, that's right, dear," Cecile replied. "I'd forgotten about that."

"Perhaps, said Ellen, "what we should do is send Jack, Jeanne and Joshua back and you stay here, Cecile. Then we can bring you back at a time that would be equivalent to your having gone to a medical clinic in Switzerland. You can see the Secretary and return to work part time with your husband at the office. In the meantime Jack can help us get started with our bogus company that will be formed to handle the wastes. I was thinking that Jack could suggest to the Secretary that you be the liaison with our company. He could be led to think that this would be a good way to let you start slowly towards getting back to work, and you would be infinitely helpful as a double seal with Jack to keep our project secret."

"Ellen," said Jack, "I can see why everyone thinks so highly of you. I would say that plan is the one we should follow. So the three of us can return to Earth now and we will see you later on, my love; although the wait to see you again will be interminable to me. We will spread stories about how we took you to a famous private Switzerland clinic where the treatment there has a chance to affect a cure of your illness. We will be vague about the clinic's name and location so it will not be able to be traced. Ellen, if other people want to get working positions in the company you form, I will say that all positions are filled as they require super specialists to do them. That way we can keep only Gnor-humans on the job within the company."

"Great!" replied Ellen. "We'll have to think of a name for the company so you can identify it to the Secretary. I thought something simple like "Waste Management" might be a reasonable name. We can tell the Secretary that our company wants to build a space platform to try a revolutionary new concept for getting rid of toxic and nuclear wastes. He will understand that we must remain secretive so that other businesses won't be able to steal our technology. This will help us to keep prying, greedy eyes from realizing what we are doing and who we are. I fear there may be trouble in the future from a few of these business people, but we will have to deal with this as it occurs. Well then, it appears to be all settled; and Jeanne, if your condition becomes intractable and you concur, we can do the same for you that we did for your mother. But that's for another time and place; let's get you three back to Earth."

***

Jack returned to work and spread the story about Cecile's treatment program overseas. He brought word from time to time how well everything was going and how optimistic everyone at the facility was about her condition. In the meantime he dropped word to the Secretary that a company had approached him about a revolutionary new technique for getting rid of nuclear and toxic wastes. He was able to convince the Secretary that this was a legitimate, exciting new company and about the necessity for complete secrecy to avoid piracy of the new technology it had invented. The Secretary had agreed to this and given him permission to investigate this company and to keep him apprised of any progress the company was making with the project. He also wanted Jack to arrange for him to meet with the company CEO as soon as he thought it appropriate. He said he would try to stall the congressional effort to bury the wastes under Yucca Mountain for a time longer, but would eventually need definite proof that this new company's method would work safely and well.

The Council in First City on Mars suggested that Ellen be installed as the CEO of the company, which she accepted with pleasure. She started work on the waste-holding facility in a desolate spot in the badlands of South Dakota that Jack had arranged for them to use. This location would be very hard for unwanted corporate business people to investigate. Jack planned that the Gnor-humans, being trained as guards, workers, and truck driver/pilots by Ellen, would be set up as U.S. Special Forces personnel engaged to protect the facility from 'terrorists'. A fleet of these specially-designed waste carriers, that would be able to be converted from truck to scout vehicle and back again, would be built on the Earth Moon base and flown to Earth to the South Dakota waste-holding facility under the cover of darkness and electronic jamming. There they would be housed in large secure garages built for that purpose until they were needed to go and pick up waste from around the nation and deliver it to the South Dakota facility. The trucks, which would be designed to be able to convert to scout vehicles without disturbing the cargo of wastes they carried, would then be able under electronic-jamming cover, to fly slowly and safely up the magnetic lines of force of the Earth to the space station. If the right circumstances allowed, and the trucks en route to the holding facility were traveling in a desolate area, they could convert to a scout vehicle and take off for the space station from that spot, saving time and the confusion of many vehicles arriving at the holding area at the same time. The electronic jamming devices would be present on all the scout vehicle/trucks, so prevention of discovery in flight could be accomplished easily. There would be the problem of inadvertent discovery by someone in the area not seen by the truckers; so this out-of-facility flight would not be undertaken unless there was a great backup of loaded waste vehicles arriving at the holding facility at the same time, and their on board sensors could be accurately employed to assure non-discovery. Eventually, with the process working well in the US, the company would expand to the rest of the world when they felt they could establish enough security to do it without discovery as to who they really were. That might require bringing the waste by ship to US ports where transport to the holding area could be accomplished if they were unable to establish other secure holding areas in other parts of the world. They would try first, however, to establish the secure holding areas worldwide.

The space station would be constructed in a high Earth orbit very far removed from the low Earth orbit site where a US administration was considering putting orbiting platforms powered by dangerous nuclear reactors for protection against terrorists and other threats.

Ellen thought she could convince the Secretary that the high orbit was necessary for protection of lower orbiting Earth satellites from the radiation effects of the nuclear wastes on board the space station. She was certain that she could also convince him that her company had the facility to place such a station into that position safely because of their invention of a different type of propulsion other than rocket launching. Of course she requested that the Secretary guarantee absolute protection by him of this new technology which her company had developed at considerable expense and would consider sharing later on. She went on to explain that she didn't want any one country to have exclusive rights to this technology to avoid international squabbles about it which might delay its construction. She intimated that the power needed on the space station would be much safer than the nuclear power that he knew had been commonly utilized by the Russians in the past Cold War. She definitely did not intend, however, to give any specifics about the fusion and solar power she would actually be utilizing there.

Thus the wheels were placed in motion for ridding the Earth of the wastes that the Gnor-humans had discovered were to cause so much devastation to Earth in the future.

***

In the meantime, enough days had gone by to be able to return Cecile to Earth for a triumphant return to the EPA office. Everyone there, and especially the Secretary, was genuinely pleased to see her looking so well and to notice how jubilant Jack was on her return. Great care was taken to divert questions about the facility she had been treated at; and the story given was that her condition was not as bad as what they originally had thought and her cure was much easier than they had expected. Cecile was so well liked that the details of her cure soon became unimportant as everyone was so happy to see her back working and looking so well. The Secretary suggested that Cecile come back part time for a while until she became stronger before she took up her job full time again. This played right into her hands and she asked if she could help her husband on the waste removal project he had told her about. This would give her a chance to work back into her duties easier than anything else she could think of. The Secretary was delighted to agree with this plan, so Cecile was set up nicely as a double seal with Jack for protecting the Gnor-human company's anonymity.

The main frame of the space station was constructed at the base on the Earth's Moon. It was to use solar as well as the fusion generators as its power source, but those large winged panels would be placed on the station later. Jack's son, Joshua, expressed great interest in the space station project as he was an ardent space and alternate energy enthusiast and had taken several courses in his undergraduate years at MIT; studying many futuristic technological papers about these two fields. He had been doing graduate work at MIT on theoretical space stations and their power sources but was currently on sabbatical because of his mother's illness. He had asked Ellen if it would be possible for him to observe any of the construction of the space station, perhaps from one of the scout vehicles. Ellen had informed him that his father and mother would be doing just that in an Earth-atmosphere-equipped scout vehicle to keep the Secretary posted as to the progress of the station and she didn't see why he couldn't come along as well. She did intimate that utmost secrecy had to be maintained about this project as certain corporate businessmen would pay large sums and do almost anything to get their hands on this technology. This project was for all the peoples of the Earth; not for a few wealthy businessmen to get even richer. Josh understood the problem and completely agreed with the confidentiality needed. He was very excited that he would be able to witness this fantastic waste removal undertaking first hand; a problem that his mother and father had been involved with for some time now with very little hope of ever seeing their endeavor succeed.

"My daughter, Molly, has also shown a great interest in becoming involved in this waste project," Ellen had said to Josh. "Perhaps she would be able to help give you a young person's approach to the proper technique of observation on one of our scout vehicles."

"Thank you, Professor James," replied Josh. "I would appreciate your daughter's help very much. I'm sure this type of travel is "old hat" for her, but to me it is exciting beyond words!"

"Believe me, Josh," smiled Ellen, "it wasn't too long ago that Molly felt as you do now. Actually, she loves traveling on the scout vehicles.

I think the only reason our chief pilot Zeltor hasn't taught her to fly one herself is that he's afraid she might go off by herself and get into trouble. She's a very independent young woman and sometimes takes on more than she should."

"I suspect I know who she gets that from, ma'am," smiled Josh in return. "I will look forward to meeting Molly again and especially observing the space platform construction."

***

Back in her apartment on Mars Ellen was talking to her husband and daughter about the coming space station construction.

"As soon as the infrastructure is built at the Earth Moon base," she was saying to John, "we will transport it to a high Earth orbit and begin fleshing it out. We should be high enough above the usual orbiting satellites to avoid much detection. We have put a priority on establishing good electronic jamming facilities on the station from the beginning to help avoid any detection from snooping eyes below. Jack and Cecile have been great at protecting us, and have already obtained permission to use the designation and uniforms of US Special Forces for our people working at the waste-holding facility and on the truck/scout vehicles. The Earth Moon base has already started on the space platform infrastructure so it won't be too much longer before we can transport it to the high orbit position and start putting it together in earnest. I told Jack and Cecile that we will let them see the construction first hand from a scout vehicle and give them appropriate non-revealing pictures which they can show to the Secretary to keep him apprised of the construction's progress."

"That's a great idea," said John. "I'm sure we can doctor the photos so they won't give away any of our technology, and they will certainly be exciting for the Secretary to see."

"Oh, another thing, Molly," said Ellen, "Jack's son, Josh, has expressed a great interest in observing the space station's construction. He has been working on theoretical space stations at MIT and might have some helpful suggestions about the construction, although he is in awe of the whole undertaking. I knew you would be observing at the site yourself so I told him you would be happy to give him some tips about travel on a scout vehicle if you're there together."

"I'd be glad to do that, Mom," answered Molly. "Only I hope he's not one of those constantly questioning humans that drive you wild after a while. He did seem to be a nice fellow when he was here with his family for his mother's operation. He certainly was a fit, nice-looking fellow."

"I'm sure he will act appropriately, Molly," rejoined her mother. "Perhaps you could get him to meet Ares. I believe the two of them would have a lot in common."

"Yes," said Molly. "I think you're right about that. And it is important that he keep our secrets so becoming friendly with him is most important to inculcate that in him."

"You know, Molly," interposed Ellen, "I was just thinking that it might be fun for you to take Josh with us on the rescuing of Antoine Saint-Exupery that we are about to do while the space station is being put together at the Moon base. He will get to know you two and will see how we are able to rescue people from certain death. This concept should help him to realize what we are all about and we could discuss with him again about Gnor history and the time warp mechanism and the dire things we have seen in the future if things go on unchanged. He will be experiencing first hand the time warp mechanism in action as we rescue your poet-pilot. You can go on a scout vehicle that is equipped with an Earth atmosphere as well, since Josh will need it. What do you two think about that suggestion?"

"I think it's fine," said John. "I'm sure Josh would love it. How about you, Molly? What do you think?"

"I agree; let's do it!" answered Molly. "Do you want me to go to Earth with Zeltor and speak to him about coming? We could bring him up here to the Oxygen Quarters where he could hang out while we prepare the rescue and in that way we could include him in the preparations. I'm sure he would enjoy that."

"That sounds like a good idea," said Ellen. "But I believe he's taking care of his sister Jeanne right now so that Cecile and Jack can continue with the clandestine setup of the waste project."

"Well," replied Molly, "why can't Jeanne come up to the Oxygen Quarters too? We would only be a few days with the rescue and I'm sure Dr. Ran and Sarah would be happy to entertain her for that short time. It would give Jeanne a chance to see how well we all do in our present state. You know, Mom, I didn't think she looked too well when she was here, and from what I've heard about her condition, she may need transplantation herself at some time in the not too distant future."

"You know, Molly," said her father with a smile, "even though you and your mother are not from the same genetic makeup you sure think alike. I guess that's why I love you both. I agree with you that if they want to come; and Jack and Cecile OK it, we should bring them both here to Mars."

"I guess it's settled then," said Ellen. "I'll contact Jack and Cecile from the special line I have to them, and if they agree, Molly, you can go with Zeltor and bring Jeanne and Josh back if they want to come. I'll also check with Dik and Sarah, although I'm sure they'll be glad to watch over Jeanne while we're on the rescue mission. Molly, make sure you talk to Ares about this; it wouldn't be fair not to get his opinion."

"OK, Mom," rejoined Molly. "I'll talk to him right away. You know, this is exciting; especially since we are rescuing one of my favorite authors!"

"And I hear he's also one of Josh's and Jeanne's favorites as well," said Ellen.

And with that Molly rushed out the door to look for Ares.

"You know, John," said Ellen. "I'm looking forward to this rescue myself. I guess it's because we're showing what we can do to help mankind in a very dramatic way to a young person that we want to convince to stay on our side and help us be successful with our Earth-shepherding project."

***

Ares concurred with the others about Jack and Cecile's son, Josh going with them on their rescue of Antoine de Saint-Exupery. He too had formed a positive opinion of the young man when he had been on Mars during his mother's operation. The two young men were quite similar in that they were representative of a fit human and a fit Gnor-human. They both had nimble brains with nimble bodies to match, and they both had a flair for technological thinking as well. It seemed inevitable that they would probably become friends if given the chance.

Ares decided to go to Earth with Molly and Zeltor to pick up the two Nelson siblings to bring them to the Oxygen Quarters on Mars. Josh could then take part in preparation for the rescue of Antoine de Saint-Exupery and be able to see how the time warp mechanism could enable them to rescue someone from a death that had already taken place. In the case of Saint-Exupery, no one knew the exact way he died for sure, and being able to possibly find this out was exciting to all involved in the rescue.

After landing on Earth, Ares and Molly were soon at the front door of the Nelson home. Zeltor had landed them close enough to the area that with their superb Gnor athletic ability they were able to traverse the distance to the Nelson's home in a short time. They were concerned about transporting Jeanne to the sight where they had left their gravity packs for the ascent to Zeltor's scout vehicle. They thought Josh would be able to make the trip but they weren't sure about Jeanne. If it became necessary, they reasoned that Zeltor could always use the Portal to transport her aboard the ship.

As they approached the front door it suddenly opened as the Nelson's had been watching for them to arrive and had seen them coming up the walk to the house. Jack and Cecile stood in the doorway with Jeanne and Josh in front of them. Jeanne was sitting in her wheel chair with her brother leaning on the handles of the chair and both were smiling and looking excited about the coming trip. Jack beckoned Molly and Ares to come in and the six of them entered the spacious living room of the Nelson's elegant tudor home.

"We're happy to see you young people again," said Cecile. "Although I guess that even though you four look about the same ages, Molly and Ares are a bit older."

Molly answered, "Even though we have passed more Earth years, Mrs. Nelson, our bodies and brains have actually been progressed very similarly to the way Josh's and Jeanne's Earth bodies have grown naturally. So we feel actually about the same age as they do, and as you say, we certainly look the same age. Of course our bodies stay the same until we change them, but that change is progressed much slower than natural human development occurs because we live so much longer."

"Yes, Molly," answered Cecile with a broad smile, "and I'm quite pleased with that fact about my own new body."

"As am I," added Jack, with a squeeze of Cecile's shoulder.

"But come in and sit down. This trip for Jeannie and Josh sounds like something that will be exciting and extremely memorable for them both! I'd offer you something to eat or drink but I know you don't do that so please come and sit down and we'll talk about the upcoming trip."

Molly and Ares smiled and entered the room and sat down together on a soft leather couch. Josh pushed Jeanne's wheelchair up closer to them and she rose to take a chair opposite the two Gnor-humans while Josh placed the wheelchair out of the way in the corner of the room. Ares rose quickly to assist Jeanne into the chair and she gave him a shy smile and murmured, "Thank you." She was very impressed with his good looks and the strength in his arm when he took hers to help her into the chair. Ares smiled back at her and answered, "You're welcome." Josh came back over and sat in a chair next to his sister, and his two parents sat together on a love seat in between the four young people.

"Tell us a little about this upcoming rescue and these rescues in general," asked Jack. "I saw some very famous people walking around when I was on Mars for Cecile's operation. Ares, your father has offered me a return tour there to converse with some of these people and I am really looking forward to it."

"Yes," Molly began, "the Gnormen who came to Earth and created us were worried about changing the time line and also exactly what humans they could trust with Gnor bodies. Until they were able to be sure about both factors, they established a policy that no humans would be rescued unless their bodies had never been recovered. They felt that this would cause minimal shifts in the time line. As regards trust; they used my mother's and father's research knowledge of the people being rescued to be sure they were ethical and reasonable people. What you probably don't know, is that there are certain chemicals developed over centuries of time by the Gnormen that are placed into our brain that helps to suppress negative feelings like greed, envy, jealousy, and violence. We still have those feelings just as you do, but we are able to control them with logic and the help of these chemicals. A hard workout in the gym helps a lot also." Molly, Josh, and Ares all smiled at her last remark.

"So all the rescues are done with these two factors in mind," resumed Molly. "During the rescue on the Titanic several people with dubious reputations were deliberately not rescued. So far we have not had any problems with any Gnor-human transplant going awry, although my mother and father were worried about it in the beginning rescues. We don't expect that our poet-pilot-philosopher, Antoine de Saint-Exupery, will be a problem either, considering his writings. His work, "The Little Prince" is a great favorite of both Ares and I."

"That's really interesting, Molly," Jeanne spoke up enthusiastically with her eyes sparkling, "Josh and I also love that work ourselves!"

"Yes," said Josh, "both of us studied Saint-Exupery in courses in college and really enjoyed his work."

"Well," said Jack, "it looks like your upcoming rescue mission will be very interesting on all counts. And Jeannie, Dr. Ran and his wife Sarah are very nice people and I'm sure you will enjoy your visit with them. However, right now I think we had better get you back to your ship. I can drive you close to the spot and that will make it easier for Jeannie."

"That will be wonderful, sir," said Ares. We were wondering how we would arrange to get Jeanne there undetected."

The six rose from their chairs and proceeded to leave by the front door, with Jack rushing out a side door to his garage to bring his car around front. Josh retrieved Jeanne's wheelchair, helped his sister into it, and pushed her out to the driveway as his father drove up with the car and invited the four to get in. As Jeanne went to get up from her wheelchair, Ares came over, took her arm and assisted her into the car. She smiled shyly up at him and thanked him. Ares smiled back and whispered, "You're welcome." Josh sat in front with his dad and the other three sat together in the back seat with Jeanne in the middle. Cecile smiled and waved to them as the car sped off down the street. On the way back to the ship's landing site a lively conversation ensued between the four young people. They were very excited about the trip and it was obvious that they felt very comfortable with one another. Ares had begun a conversation with Jeanne.

"You should have a great visit with my mom and dad," he said to her. "You'll have to forgive me if I start praising my dad, but there isn't anyone I know who can put a person at ease like he can. And my mom was a policewoman on Earth in the past and has an amazing knack of being able to recognize when people are troubled or nervous and knows how to get them to relax. I know you'll have a good time with them. It would be even nicer if you could join us on this trip, Jeanne; but perhaps you'll do so on a later one."

"I would enjoy that, Ares," returned Jeanne. She turned to him and he noticed how her eyes sparkled as she said, "Yes, perhaps later on."

In the meantime, Josh had turned around in the front seat and was conversing earnestly with Molly about the upcoming space station to be built in high Earth orbit.

"I can hardly wait to see the construction being done there, Molly," he said to her. "This type of space structure is what I've been studying in theory in grad school at MIT, but it will be spectacular to see the real thing being done before my eyes. And, incidentally, I really appreciate your being willing to keep me out of trouble when I'm on the ship with you observing that construction."

"Think nothing of it, Josh," answered Molly. "There's not much to learn and pilots like Zeltor make observing a snap. My mom says that you might be able to give us some pointers on the construction, and that space stations are one of your pet projects."

"He certainly has been sketching them at home for many years, Molly," broke in Jack from the front seat. "I know how much it means to him to have this opportunity to see and maybe even help in the construction of the station."

"Dad," said Josh, with his face blushing bright red, "you two are embarrassing me. But I do see this trip as the opportunity of my life. And to carry it further, it may be the opportunity of all our lives if we are able to help Earth avoid a catastrophe later on by what we do now."

"You are certainly speaking the truth there, son," said Jack soberly; and they drove on silently for the next couple of minutes contemplating what Josh had said.

Soon they arrived at a desolate area in the woods where Molly and Ares had stowed their gravity packs. The five emerged from the car and all bid Jack farewell. He kissed his daughter Jeanne and hugged Josh, telling them to be careful but to enjoy this experience which would be one like nothing they had ever had before. He then turned to Molly and Ares and told them to take good care of his 'babies'.

"You can count on it, sir," they both answered and smiled at the other two. Molly then said, "We look forward to our trip and the beginning friendship with your two offsprings. We'll see you again when we return, Mr. Nelson. Goodbye."

With that, Jack returned to the car and drove off, waving as he did so. The four returned his wave.

"I'll get Zeltor on the communicator," said Molly, "and Josh, Ares, and I can go to the ship with the three gravity packs we left over there in that thicket. Jeanne can be transported to the ship by the Portal after I give Zeltor the coordinates here."

Ares showed Josh how to adjust his gravity pack and the three made ready to ascend to the ship which had arrived and was hovering high above them under electronic cover. Jeanne had already been beamed aboard, and was waiting for them on the ship. She greeted the three excitedly when they arrived.

"Such an exciting experience," she said. "First I was on the ground on Earth, and the next thing I knew I was here in the ship. And Molly, your very nice pilot, Captain Zeltor, was so kind to me and explained everything, telling me to wait for you here in the cargo bay. It must have been spectacular, Josh, to fly up here to the ship as you did."

"Oh, it was spectacular all right, sis," Josh answered. "I'll tell you truthfully, though, I was a little scared at first. But thanks to Molly and Ares, who guided me up all along the way, we arrived in good shape and I was really enjoying it at the end of the flight; although it did start to get a little cold."

"He did very well, Jeanne," said Ares, who smiled at her and walked over to give her his arm to help her mount the steps to the bridge of the ship. "Josh is a natural at it."

"Yes, Josh," said Molly, smiling up at him, "you really handled yourself very well for the first time doing this kind of transportation. Congratulations!"

"Thanks, Molly," replied Josh. "I appreciate both your comments and your help very much."

With that the four ascended to the bridge where Zeltor was already making rapid progress back to Mars. The four continued their lively conversation all the way back to Mars and it certainly was obvious that they would soon be fast friends. What the relationship between Ares and Jeanne and Molly and Josh would develop into at this point was difficult to know, but they did seem to enjoy each others' company very much at this time.

***

Dr. Ran and his wife, Sarah, were at the docking port on Mars to greet the four when they landed. They helped Jeanne and Josh don their survival suits to escort them to the Oxygen Quarters. The two humans marveled once more at the stark Martian landscape with its reddish-black sky and listened to the fierce sand storm winds howling over the force field dome covering First City. Even through their survival suits they could feel the intense cold present on this forbidding planet as they stepped onto the landing platform before entering the protection and heat retention of the overhanging force field dome. Josh was very impressed with the many Gnor-humans they encountered on the way into the dome, including also their own party; because they seemed to be able to move with ease and comfort through the harsh Martian surroundings. He knew from his studies at MIT that Mars was very cold and had an atmosphere of 95 per cent CO2 and only 0.13 per cent oxygen. The Gnor systems apparently allowed easy passage through this challenging climate and obviously were constructed in an amazingly hardy manner. For a brief moment he envied Ares and Molly their wonderful Gnor bodies; and had a beginning insight as to why his mother was so happy with hers. He could see that his sister might very well be the next one to consider adopting this form if and when her own malady began to overwhelm her. He even secretly began to consider the transition for himself but dismissed it for the present time.

Once inside the Oxygen Quarters Jeanne and Josh removed their survival suits and were shown to their rooms by Dr. Ran and Sarah. A schedule for meal times in the cafeteria was given to them as well as instructions about the locality of all the other facilities in the building necessary for all the living humans that were there following their rescues and operations. Ares and Molly took their leave of the two to return to their two homes; Molly in Harvard Square and Ares there in First City with his mother and father.

"My mom has made arrangements for the preparations for the Saint-Exupery rescue to be arranged in the Oxygen Quarters," said Molly. "That way you can be a part of the expedition, even though you're not going to go with us, Jeanne."

"That would be wonderful!" answered Jeanne. "Your mother is so thoughtful. My dad said it was she who suggested this whole idea that will be so great for Josh and me."

"Yes," said Ares. "Molly's mother is known far and wide for her thoughtfulness. I guess that's part of the reason why the Prime Mover of the Gnormen left her in charge when they returned to their home planet. Molly lives in the fourth city down from here; about 15 Earth miles away. But even on foot, with the decreased Martian gravity, it's easy to traverse the distance in a relatively short time."

"That is," smiled Josh, "if you have a Gnor body."

"Of course," Ares smiled back good-naturedly, "but it doesn't matter because Molly will be coming with her mother and father in some sort of conveyance anyway. We are getting almost as addicted to easy transportation as our Earth relatives. In the meantime you two rest up and we'll see you both in the morning in your library to start the rescue preparations."

Ares and Molly then smiled goodbye with Molly starting for Harvard Square and the three Rans to their quarters in First City.

***

The next morning the preparatory group met in the Oxygen Quarters library to arrange the rescue of the poet-pilot, Antoine de Saint-Exupery. Present were Ellen, John, Molly, Ares, Zeltor, Rol, and the two Nelson siblings.

"I have found out," started Ellen, "that Saint-Exupery was a rather eccentric adventurer-pilot who would read in his plane while flying. Sometimes he would circle an airfield several times while he was finishing reading a story in the plane. He had over 6500 hours flight time in all sorts of airplanes and under all kinds of conditions, and had weathered several crashes in the past. The French army had stopped his flying for a short time but had reinstated him to fly reconnaissance missions against the Germans in WW II. At the

French air base of Bastia Borgo on the Italian island of Sardinia he had been flying an American twin-engine Lockheed P38 Lightning for about a year doing reconnaissance for the French. He had crashed a previous Lightning on a hard landing, and ended up flying his final plane, another Lightning, #2734L. Saint-Exupery was rather old for a pilot at age forty four and he knew that these reconnaissance missions were probably the last ones the French Air Force would let him fly. After checking a favorable weather report from operations officer Duriez on the morning of July 31st, 1944, he took off from the field at 7:30 am to start his photo mission over France. At 8:45 am he reported that he was descending, had entered a cloud layer, and saw nothing. After that, nothing else was ever heard from the pilot; and neither his airplane nor his body was ever recovered for about 60 years. In 1998 a bracelet bearing his name was picked up in a fisherman's net near Marseille, but most people thought it was a hoax. However, in April of 2004 the wreck of his plane was finally found in 300 feet of water on the Mediterranean Sea floor about three miles off the coast near the cliffs of Provence. The cause of the crash has still failed to be ascertained, but we should be able to find that out and it will determine when and how we will be able to rescue him.

We should join his flight over the mountains to avoid recognition near his airbase and see if we can find out what happened to him. We can then retrace with the time warp mechanism and proceed to rescue him from whatever it was that occurred. Does this seem a reasonable plan, Zeltor?"

"Yes," rejoined the Gnorman pilot, "it would seem to be the right way to approach it, Ellen. Rol and I should be able to get the ship ready for travel in two days if everyone agrees to this plan."

Everyone agreed that this was what they should do, so Zeltor and Rol left the library to prepare one of the scout vehicles and to set up a time warp mechanism in it.

"I'm very excited about going back in time to WW II and especially about the rescue of this fascinating man," Josh remarked to the others.

"I guess we all are," said Ellen. "It's interesting that some historians say that Saint-Exupery, the intrepid eccentric adventurer, seemed to have become tired by all his past escapades and plane crashes and was beginning to see the end of his flying career. Perhaps his incessant smoking had something to do with his fatigue as well. I would hazard a guess, however, that when he realizes what kind of a marvelously hardy and long-lived body he will obtain if he agrees to our transplantation, that he will rekindle his great love for adventure and flying again, and can help us as another one of our pilots."

Everyone concurred with Ellen's remarks; and Jeanne wistfully said that she wished she could go on the rescue as well, but looked forward to the others telling her all about it when they returned. Ares smiled at Jeanne and said that he would be glad to give her a play by play description of what occurred on the rescue when they returned.

"I would really appreciate that, Ares," Jeanne shyly smiled back at him. "I will look forward to it." And her face became a little flushed.

"Well," said John, "we should all review the plan and Ellen's research on Saint-Exupery this next day or two to be ready for launching the rescue mission when Zeltor and Rol notify us that the ship is ready for us." With that John, Ellen, and Molly left for their Harvard Square apartment and Ares departed for his apartment there in First City. Josh and Jeanne were left alone in the library.

"I sure wish you could come with us, sis," said Josh. "It's such an impossibly fantastic adventure!"

"I know," Jeanne replied. "But Ares said he would tell me all about it, and that's pretty exciting to me, Josh." Her brother smiled and looked over at his sister.

"Yeah, Jeanne," he said with a twinkle in his eye, "I noticed that you and Ares seem to be hitting it off pretty well."

"Well, Josh," Jeanne replied, blushing, "You and Molly seem to be developing a nice relationship also. I hear she's going to show you how to behave in the scout vehicle when you two go to observe the construction of the space station."

"Oh, well," said Josh, himself blushing a little, "that's because they don't want me to get into any trouble on the ship and Molly's an old hand at scout vehicle travel. Actually, sis, I really do like Molly a lot. She's intelligent, kind, very athletic, and not bad looking either. She probably would have little interest in a weak human like me, though. Ares is more her type I would think."

"What do you mean?" said Jeanne. "Weak! There aren't too many people as fit as you are. And you never know about things of the heart, Josh. Don't rule anything out if you find you really like her a lot.

I think she's great and really enjoy her company. With my current problems, I guess it would be futile for me to think Ares would be interested in me, either. As you said, a Gnor-human like Molly is more his type."

"I'll give back to you, sis," said Josh, "the same advice you just gave me. I also like Ares a lot; and don't forget, we always have the option of transplantation as well. To be honest with you, I'm thinking more and more about possibly doing it. What these people are trying to do with their lives is pretty great, and I wouldn't be averse to doing the same thing with mine."

"You know, Josh," said his sister, "I'm having the same thoughts and have just about made up my mind to do it if they'll let me. Mom's body is magnificent, and she's absolutely no different than she ever was with me in the past. And there's the problem that my illness could suddenly get worse, and maybe even.....kill me!" A tear formed in the corner of her eye and she quickly wiped it away. Josh walked over and put his arms around his sister.

"Don't you fret, sis," he said. "These people have brought us a chance to live a wonderfully long and productive life, and to have an extremely noble cause to spend it on. You saw how well Mom did with the procedure and Dr. Ran says they have never lost anyone yet!" At that moment Sarah Ran walked into the room.

"What haven't we lost, Josh?" she asked.

"Oh, I'm sorry, ma'am," Josh replied sheepishly. "Jeanne was worried about her metabolic condition and we were talking about the transplantation operation that your husband did on my mother."

"Jeanne, dear," said Sarah. "You can rest assured that nothing will happen to you if you undergo the operation. We always worry that something might happen because of our human emotions, but it never does. I know my husband and the technicians will do their usual marvelous job if you decide to do the transplantation. I for one would love to see you do this and be able to cheat the metabolic problem that threatens your life." At that moment her husband walked in with a serious expression on his face.

"Whose life is being threatened?" he asked Sarah. "What are you talking about?"

The three of them smiled at one another and explained to Dr. Ran what they had been talking about. All four then laughed at the situation that had been caused by the disparate entrances.

"Jeanne," said Dr. Ran, "anytime you decide that you want to do the operation we will do it for you. You must realize, however, that you probably would not be able to return to your current Earth life because of your enhanced abilities. At least, you would have to monitor them very carefully when interacting with humans while on the Earth so as not to reveal these abilities."

"I understand that very clearly, sir," answered Jeanne. "And it doesn't seem to be a factor to me right now. I will have to think more about it and let everyone know how I feel about it in the very near future."

"Of course, dear," said Sarah. "Don't worry your pretty head about it right now. I'm sure there'll be plenty of time to think about it in the future. Right now Dr. Ran and I were wondering if you would like to take a little motorized tour of some of our Martian cities."

"Oh," said Jeanne, "that would be wonderful; but won't I have to wear a survival suit?"

Sarah smiled broadly in response to her question.

"No, dear," she said. "We have a small shuttle vehicle that maintains an Earth atmosphere within it. We actually built it to be able to take people around the Martian colony before their transplant operation so they could see what they were getting into here. There is a garage-like setup on one end of the Oxygen Quarters where the vehicle is parked, and it can be entered there without having to don a survival suit to get into it as it would if it were outside. Josh, I know you want to read up on your coming rescue mission, but we're sure you'd enjoy the trip with your sister. We'll make sure you get back with enough time to do your research."

"That would be wonderful!" said Josh. "You people are so great to us. It would be wonderful if human beings could all be like you are."

"Thanks for the compliment, Josh," answered Sarah. "Although I still feel that I'm very much a human being although I'm called a Gnor-human. I do have the advantage of the Gnor chemicals in my brain that influences how I think about and relate to others. It is easy to be nice when one is not controlled by the emotions of greed, envy, jealousy, and violence. Human beings really do know what's the best way for them to relate to one another; they just have too many of these powerful emotions uncontrollably present within their minds that often stop them from doing what they know they should do."

"OK, people," said Dr. Ran, "if everyone is agreed, as humans say, let's get this show on the road! Follow me!" And he led the group to the garage described earlier by his wife with Josh pushing his sister along in her wheelchair.

The tour in the shuttle vehicle was like a science fiction movie to the two young Nelsons. The different cities were fascinating to them, and they were greatly impressed by the buildings that were partially underground in all the other cities except First City. On the trips between the cities they traveled in a force field corridor and often saw and heard the raging dust storms of Mars swirling around the corridor. The vehicle was heated so they didn't feel the stinging cold of the planet; but they did hold in awe the stark Martian landscape and the overhanging reddish-black sky.

"This landscape and sky is very impressive," said Jeanne, "but I'm afraid I prefer the vegetation and the clear blue sky of Earth, Sarah."

"As do I prefer the same blue-green sky and plants of my home planet, Mekan," said Dr. Ran with a smile. "However, I guess I love Earth's sky almost as well. Part of that love is because I know that my Sarah was born and has lived under it." His wife was sitting beside him in the front seat and he gave her hand a squeeze and smiled at her. She turned back to the Nelsons in the seat behind.

"There must have been an Ireland on Mekan, kids," Sarah said smiling broadly. "And my husband must have come from it with the blarney we're hearing from him right now." She smiled fondly at her husband and squeezed his hand back.

"It's too bad we can't visit with Ellen and her family, as well as some of the famous humans we've rescued in the past," said Dr. Ran. "We would have to have you don survival suits to do it, however, as there are no functioning Oxygen Quarters in the rest of the cities. We will get you to meet some of these great people in your Oxygen Quarters in First City, Jeanne, when Josh is out gallivanting with Molly and Ares on their rescue mission. Just kidding, Josh; we'll get you to meet some of them as well. Right now I think we'll head back to First City. There is a meteor shower expected and I always worry about the force field protection in these corridors. The cities themselves are fine; but not as much power is placed in the corridors and some of the larger rocks have been known to break through the force field over them. Because of the thin Martian atmosphere, meteors strike the planet with much more regularity and are not all burned up as they are in the Earth's thicker atmosphere."

Just as Dr. Ran finished saying this there was a loud tattooing sound heard all around them in the corridor they were in between Harvard Square and Mekan II. Just ahead of them a huge boulder smashed through the force field and was rolling toward them at a rapid clip. Dr. Ran swerved the shuttle vehicle sharply to the right and the boulder rumbled by them, just missing their left side. The shuttle bounced off the side of the corridor force field and Dr. Ran pulled it back into the center of the corridor. He then put the shuttle into high speed and almost rocketed through the remainder of the corridor to emerge suddenly into Mekan II.

"I guess we'll stay here in Mekan II for a while," he said to the others, "until I can find out what's happening ahead in the corridor to Hyannisport."

He opened a conversation through the vehicle's communicator and was told that that corridor was OK. They then traveled much more sedately through that corridor into Hyannisport and finally through the last corridor back into First City to the parking garage in the Oxygen Quarters. As they disembarked from the shuttle and were moving back from the garage to the library, Josh thanked the doctor and his wife for the wonderful tour they had just taken them on.

"To be able to experience first hand the planet Mars is mind-boggling to me," he began. "I had studied much about the planet in school, but never in my wildest dreams did I ever think I would actually experience it in person. I thank you so much for taking me on the tour. I loved it!"

"As did I, Dr. Ran and Sarah," added Jeanne from her wheelchair that Josh was pushing. "The corridor ride was exciting as well. It is certainly hard to believe that Josh and I are here on Mars experiencing this fantastic adventure. We feel so fortunate to have met you people, especially for what you have done for my mother and also for our dad because of her rescue from death. I am beginning to feel that I should definitely consider joining you. It's hard not to admire and like you people."

"Well, dear," rejoined Sarah, "believe it or not we all feel the same about your whole family as well. Oh, of course we are synthetically enhanced with strength and longevity, but we are still very much human beings with the same emotions and love for nice people that you have."

Sarah went over and helped Jeanne out of her wheelchair to take a chair as they entered the library. Jeanne again had tears in her eyes and gave Sarah a big hug which the Gnor-woman returned with a broad smile.

"You know, Jeanne," said Sarah, "I always wanted to have a nice daughter like you. I envy Cecile, she is very lucky to have you."

"Thank you, ma'am," Jeanne replied. "But you do have Ares, and he seems like a wonderful person."

"Of course, dear," Sarah returned. "He's his father's son all right. And we do love him very much. I'm very glad you all have hit it off so well. We all look forward to a great relationship between the Nelsons and the Gnor-humans."

"Actually," said Josh, "We may all end up as Gnor-humans. Something my sister and I are not too averse to at this point in time."

"That's good to hear, son," said Dr. Ran. "Our plans for shepherding Earth would be greatly enhanced if this comes to be. But for now we'll leave you two alone and you can get busy on your research, Josh. Jeanne, you get some rest and make sure you two get your meals in the cafeteria. Everything has been set up for you so that you just have to appear there and a menu will be brought out for you to choose what you want to eat. There is also a bathroom in your quarters for you to use."

"Thank you so much, Dr. Ran," said Jeanne. "I'll make sure Josh eats something. He sometimes gets lost in his studies and forgets to do so back on Earth. Will I see you tomorrow?"

"Yes, dear," answered Sarah. "I'll be around in the morning and we can have a nice gabfest about Gnor history and any questions you might have about us. My arrival here is pretty interesting; it is thanks to Molly's mother, Ellen that I am present here today. I'll tell you all about it tomorrow. And you can tell me what you have been doing on Earth and what you had wanted to do before this metabolic problem happened."

"Oh, I would enjoy that very much, Sarah," said Jeanne. "Then I'll see you in the morning."

"Right," returned Sarah, "And don't forget, if you need anything or are having any trouble you know how to contact us right away."

"Yes, we do," Jeanne replied. "Thanks again. See you in the morning!"

The four exchanged pleasantries and the Rans left the library to return to their quarters in First City.

"They are great kids," Dik remarked to his wife as they left the Oxygen Quarters."

"Yes they are," Sarah returned, "and my policewoman's intuition tells me that Jeanne may be developing an attraction to Ares. He also seems to be interested in her as well; or haven't you noticed it."

"I have noticed it, Sarah," answered her husband. "But I know of a certain person who became enamored of an Earth woman a while ago and it hasn't turned out too bad."

Sarah picked up her husband's hand and gave it a squeeze.

"Not bad at all," she whispered, and reached up and kissed him on the cheek.

"I realize, Sarah," Dik remarked "that we had always pictured Molly and Ares eventually getting together, but right now they are only friends. Molly and Josh seem to be getting along pretty well right now so it isn't certain what might come about there at this time either. One thing is certain to me about the four of them, and that is that whatever happens I suspect they will all remain good friends."

"Yes," said Sarah, "I agree with that. To be honest with you, those liaisons wouldn't be bad combinations at all. I like them all and it would certainly help our shepherding of Earth project."

"Yes it would do that, dear," returned her husband, "Well, we shall see!"

***

The preparations for the rescue of Antoine de Saint-Exupery were completed and the crew started out in the Starship to intercept the French poet-pilot. When they reached Earth they entered the specially-prepared scout vehicle and Zeltor swiftly navigated it to the island of Sardinia. Along the way he utilized electronic jamming to keep both ships from being discovered. Using the time warp mechanism to get them to the right date and time, they arrived in the early morning of July 31st, 1944, and soon came upon a Lockheed P38 Lightning flying just above a thick cloud layer just above the cliffs of Provence. They identified #2734 L on the tail of the plane and knew they had found the French pilot. The plane below suddenly dived into the clouds and Zeltor followed. There was an explosion below them and they broke out of the clouds to see the Lightning, with one engine on fire, plummeting towards one of the mountain gorges. Saint-Exupery was able to pull up the P38 before it crashed into the gorge and he turned the plane around to return to his base in Sardinia. Then, as he approached the edge of the Mediterranean Sea, a larger explosion occurred which engulfed the cockpit of the plane and pieces of the aircraft flew apart as it plunged into the sea below about three miles off the coast near the steep cliffs of Provence. The P38 sank immediately to a depth of about 300 feet.

"So this is how your poet died, Molly," said Zeltor. "No wonder no one ever found out what happened to him. The wreckage of his plane would have been very hard to find, especially since our sensors showed that he was unable to get a radio message out to tell people where he was. Rol will reset the time warp mechanism and we will go back to rescue our French pilot friend!"

Rol proceeded to do just that and they came again onto the P38 flying above the clouds below them. Rol prepared to transfer Saint-Exupery to the cargo hold of the scout vehicle with the Portal and sent Ellen, John, Molly, Ares and Josh down there to greet him.

"But I don't speak French!" said Josh, in a panic.

"Don't worry," said John. "All the rest of us do. We'll speak to the poet."

And they all rushed to the cargo hold awaiting Rol's transportation of the pilot to the ship.

The Frenchman looked around him with an incredulous expression on his face when he found himself no longer in his P38 but instead inside a much bigger craft, the kind of which he had never seen before. The five people in the cargo hold noted that the pilot had on an old stained shirt riddled with cigarette burns, and was wearing a silk heating suit and a well-worn leather pilot's cap.

"Where am I? Who are you people? How on Earth did you transport me here in this fashion?" the pilot fired at the five people standing there in the cargo hold.

"Please don't be concerned, sir," said Ellen. We have come here to rescue you from a death you were just about to encounter. If you'll accompany us upstairs to the bridge of our ship we will show you what is about to happen to your ship."

"What do you mean my death? And how do you know what is about to happen to my P38?" asked the French pilot.

"Because we have already been into the future and seen what has happened to your ship," replied Ellen. We have captured it on our sensors and will play it back for you to view when we get to the bridge of our ship."

The six of them ascended the stairs towards the bridge of the scout vehicle with the French pilot staring at his surroundings with widened eyes. When they arrived on the bridge Ellen asked Zeltor to play back on the telescreen the explosion and crash of the P38 into the sea, which he promptly did.

"Sacre Bleu!" exclaimed the Frenchman. "How did you get that film? How can you know what is to happen in the future? Who are you? But please excuse my bad manners and thank you very much for apparently saving my life!"

"You are entirely welcome," answered Ellen. "But to answer your questions, Captain Saint-Exupery; we are a race of people that has the technology to go forwards and backwards in time. We will explain all this more fully to you shortly. In the meantime, let me say that the three of these young people here before you are great admirers of your writings, and especially your fable, 'The Little Prince'. When your plane was lost and no one ever knew for sixty years what had actually occurred to cause you to crash into the sea, these three prevailed upon us to come here and discover what did happened to you and to rescue you. We followed you out after your takeoff from the airfield on Sardinia this morning on what, unknown to you, was to be your last mission on Earth. We noted the explosion of your plane and its crash into the edge of the Mediterranean Sea; which you just saw on the telescreen. Then we reversed time back to just before the crash and rescued you. If you want to stay with us as a survivor you will have to make some serious decisions after you have heard all about us, what we are doing here on Earth, and what we propose to offer you."

Ellen and the others then proceeded to relate to the French pilot the history of the Gnormen and the Gnor-humans they created and the project they had taken on to shepherd Earth away from all of her developing problems. He was informed that he could never go back to Earth again as his old self; and that if he decided not to join the Gnor-human race, they would honor his choice and return him back in time to his plane. There he would not remember what had transpired and would continue on to the crash into the sea and his death.

"What does "joining the Gnor-human race" entail, Professor James?" the French pilot asked.

Ellen and the others then described the operation he would have to undergo, and underscored the usual excellent result with greatly improved strength and longevity that he could expect to obtain. The pilot then asked in what country the operation would be done, and was dumbfounded when he was informed that it would be in a place they called First City in their colony located on the planet, Mars.

***

"On Mars, you say!" said Saint-Exupery incredulously. "You mean this ship is going to fly us to Mars?"

"No, we will change ships to fly to Mars, sir." said Zeltor. "But please don't be concerned. Our ships have an excellent supply of oxygen for you and our young friend, Josh, here; who is a living, breathing human being just like you. On Mars you will stay in Oxygen Quarters that will supply you with an Earth-type environment until you decide if and when you'll have your operation; and then if you do, you won't need that support any longer."

"Professors," the Frenchman queried, addressing Ellen and John, "would it be possible for me to think about this overnight? I must say that up to this point I have been quite depressed about my current life situation. My marriage has been very unsatisfactory to me, and I knew that the French Air Service was going to stop me from flying after this mission. In addition, my body is weak and tired from all the plane crashes and adventures I have taken part in over the years. At this juncture it would certainly be possible for me to feel that the crash of my P38 might be the kindest thing that could happen to me. But now, with what you have told me about how I will be after the operation, I suddenly am beginning to feel like I did when I first began my adventuresome quests into the sky as a young man. Your project to shepherd Earth is a noble and extremely worthwhile endeavor; and, without doubt, any human being should be honored and very happy to be a part of it. I just feel I need to have a little time to be sure I could again be of service to myself and your project."

"Of course, Captain Saint-Exupery," replied Ellen, "my husband and I understand completely. He did the same before his operation. Please take all the time you need to decide. The Oxygen Quarters on Mars are very comfortable so there is no reason to hurry along your decision; especially with our time warp mechanism enabling us to easily be able to comply with whatever you finally decide to do."

"Captain," spoke up Molly, "my two friends and I are sure that there are many more literary gems waiting to be written by you. We are selfish enough to hope that you will join us and give us the pleasure of reading them after you create them."

"You are too kind, Molly," replied the Frenchman. "You know, 'The Little Prince', that you have said you loved so much, was actually a compilation of many of my own thoughts that occurred when I was flying mail across the Sahara Desert. Many of those thoughts that were expressed by the Little Prince were some of the things that I considered during the times I was waiting to be rescued after I had crashed in my plane on that desert."

"Whatever inspired them, sir," said Ares, "we are all of us very much the better for you to have produced them for us to read. I, too, would very much appreciate your continuing on with your literary work."

"We all must remember, though," said John, "that Captain Saint-Exupery's work will have to remain within our colonies or at least be written under a pen name if it gets distributed on Earth."

"Incidentally, Captain," interjected Zeltor, "No one has told you yet, but it is most assuredly possible that I will be able to train you to fly one of these scout vehicles so that you will be able to directly contribute to our project to shepherd Earth."

"Ah, my good Captain Zeltor," replied the pilot, "making it possible for me to continue to fly would be like a gift from the gods.

And the manner in which your Professor Ellen has described you Gnor-humans, that may actually be an appropriate statement. If I decide to join you, I would look forward to that happening with great joy!"

"Well, then," replied Zeltor, "Let's get back to First City and see how the space station project we told you about is progressing."

And with that he and Rol began preparations for the flight back to the Starship and then on to Mars.

***

By the time the Starship had docked on Mars, Captain Saint-Exupery had just about decided to join the Gnor-humans in their Earth-shepherding project. He too, like all the other humans before him, was overawed by the desolate planet's landscape with its howling wind storms, and he especially marveled at the ability of the Gnor-humans to comfortably exist in these harsh Martian surroundings. It was this last realization that convinced him to join their project, and he announced this to all after they had assembled in the library of the Oxygen Quarters after disembarking from the ship. The French pilot had been introduced to Dr. Ran, Sarah, and Jeanne, who were waiting for them in the library when they entered.

"My friends," the pilot began, "and I hope I can now call you my friends; I have decided to join your project and will undergo the operation to make me a Gnor-human like yourselves. The choice between death and existence as a resilient, long-lived, thinking being engaged in a very noble project is no longer difficult for me to make. It actually has become easy for me to make it from the heart as you yourselves are also all doing with your Earth-shepherding project. Some of you may remember what the Little Prince said to the pilot in his story:

"Voici mon secret. Il est tres simple: on ne voit bien qu'avec le coeur. L'essentiel est invisible pour les yeux."

"Let me tell you my secret. It is very simple: it is only with the heart that one can see rightly. What is essential is usually invisible to the eye."

Jeanne's eyes misted over as the pilot recited the passage from his famous story.

"I remember that phrase so well," she thought to herself, casting a furtive loving glance at Ares. "And I certainly know how true it can be!"

"Well then, Captain," said Dr. Ran, "we will make arrangements for your transplantation very soon. In the meantime you can enjoy the Oxygen Quarters with Jeanne, Josh and the few other humans that are undergoing transplantation or recovering here from their operation. Perhaps after your operation you might also find it interesting to observe first hand our high orbit space station construction. This is to be utilized for our first Earth-shepherding endeavor to get rid of the wastes that in the future we have seen to become devastating to the Earth and its people. It would not be known yet by you, of course, but in the future atomic energy will be utilized in plants to produce electric power. The nuclear wastes produced by these plants will devastate Earth as time goes on as there is no completely safe place to deposit them and they stay as deadly contaminants for thousands of years. By 2004 your own country, France, will get 80% of its electric power supply from nuclear power plants."

"We have mastered the power of the atom? My good doctor," rejoined Saint-Exupery, "the more you talk and the more I hear, the more excited I become about my upcoming future! I look forward to my operation!"

The people in the library split up into two groups that became engaged in separate conversations. The four young people all were crowded around the French pilot and were asking him many questions about his writings; while Ellen, John, Dik, and Sarah were quietly conversing about the trip and the space station project. Dr. Ran brought in some drinks from the cafeteria for the three humans and all enjoyed winding down and relaxing after their strenuous recent endeavors.

"I'm afraid we don't have any cigarettes for you, Captain," Dr. Ran apologized when he handed the pilot his drink, "but after your operation you won't have that nasty craving any longer. Of course, with the bellows mechanism in your chest you would still be able to smoke, but it will give you no pleasure; although I guess it could be used to help disguise you on Earth. You know I never thought of that until just now!"

Eventually the gathering broke up and the Frenchman was shown to his room by Dr. Ran. Soon after Dik returned, Ellen, John and Molly took leave of the others and returned to their apartment in Harvard Square while Ares and his mother and father retired to their quarters in First City. This left Josh and his sister alone in the library.

"Well, sis," said Josh, "I'm really beat. The rescue was fantastic, what with going back and forth in time and all. I'll tell you all about it in the morning. Let's get back to our rooms and hit the silk. You can tell me all about what you did here while we were on the rescue mission."

"O.K.," replied Jeanne. "You know, most of what Sarah talked about was her husband and son, and especially how much she missed Ares when he was away on the extended technical trips he has to make in his position as director of his department. I kind of missed him myself, Josh; he seems like such a nice person. What do you think of him, big brother?"

They had reached their apartment door and went inside.

"Jeannie, I like Ares very much," Josh replied, "He is smart, athletic, kind, and downright thoughtful. He's great fun to talk with and knows Earth jargon pretty well. He said they had to learn it for their forays on Earth. He even knows the music and told me that Glenn Miller was rescued and has a band here on Mars that plays for the colonists here! And sis, he seems to have some interest in you from some of the things he asked me about you!"

Jeanne blushed a little at her brothers words, but was excited inwardly at the revelation by him.

"Well, I'll confess, Josh," she said, "I'm certainly attracted to him also." With that the two retired to their rooms to sleep.

***

In a very short time the French pilot underwent transplantation of his living brain into a synthetic Gnor body and then to continue further with assimilation of all of his memories and abilities from his living brain into a fully synthetic one like the other Gnor-humans had done. After his recovery Saint-Exupery could not keep himself from constantly expounding on what a marvelous body he now had with fantastic sensory and athletic abilities he had never experienced before. Zeltor kept the promise he had made to the pilot and started teaching him the fundamentals of flying a scout vehicle, and also to start him on the technique necessary to run the two massive interplanetary Starships left by the Gnormen when they returned to their home planet, Mekan. He also made arrangements for him to continue his learning process by accompanying them on their upcoming mission to fly the space station's platform to high Earth orbit from the Earth Moon base where it had been constructed. The fact that this project was to cause Earth's toxic and nuclear wastes to be disposed of by shooting them into the sun was mind-boggling to the French pilot. Nothing like this was even conceivable in his time.

"I have much more to write about now, my friends," he said smilingly to Molly, Ares, Josh, and Jeanne. "It is too bad that the Earth people followers of mine will not be able to read it."

***

Progress on the formation of the space station on Moon colony had progressed to the point where they were ready for the transport of its base platform to the high Earth orbit where it would be fleshed out with the secondary structures necessary for receiving and firing the wastes off into the sun. Very little energy would be needed to fire the material; the main difficulty would be the accurate calculation of the proper time and trajectory to fire it so that it would miss any other object in space on its way to the sun's gravitational capture of it. This could be done without very complex astronomical calculations and all were looking forward excitedly to the launching and completion of the project. Zeltor and Rol had determined that four scout vehicles would be needed to attach to and ferry the space station's base platform to its high Earth orbit and had asked three other pilots to assist them to accomplish the task. They would fly one of the front two ships and Ellen the other; Lt. Joseph Kennedy and Amelia Earhart would fly the rear two ships. Josh, Ares, Molly, and Captain Saint Exupery would be on Zeltor's ship while Ellen's husband, John, plus Jack and Cecile Nelson would be accompanying Ellen on her ship. John planned to do appropriate non-revealing filming of the platform in high Earth orbit from Ellen's ship for the Nelsons and her to show the EPA Secretary at a scheduled meeting back on Earth. The Secretary was to meet with the CEO (Ellen) of this enterprising new company, Waste Management, at this meeting and she was hoping to convince him to continue the project and the secrecy associated with it to protect her company's considerable investment. Lt. Kennedy's friend and fellow pilot, Lt. Willy, would accompany him on his ship; and Amelia Earhart was to have her navigator, Fred Noonan, to help on her ship. The front two ships had an oxygen facility installed for the humans on board while the two rear ships had none. They did always carry survival tanks, however, in case of an untoward occurrence where they might be needed. All these pilots and their crews were very experienced and skillful at flying the scout vehicles, and Zeltor was sure they could accomplish the feat of carrying the huge space platform into high Earth orbit without incident. The day finally came for the launching of the platform and all involved personnel had been transferred from Mars and Earth to the Moon to accomplish it. Ellen's and Zeltor's ships had been equipped with an oxygen atmosphere for the humans on board; and the four scout vehicles had been previously fastened securely to the four quadrants of the space station's platform.

"We must do this in synchrony," Zeltor had explained to the three other pilots in his preflight briefing. "We should be able to get off manual control once we get about five hundred meters off the ground and go to auto pilot immediately. Remember to have your electronic jamming mechanisms in place and running. You never know who may be trying to find out what we are doing up here in high orbit, and some of these business people have some very expensive sophisticated equipment to spy with. Once we reach the proper orbital site we must watch out for former Soviet Union nuclear-powered space vehicles that have been fired up to a high Earth orbit from a lower one for disposition. Apparently this was done to allow the dangerous nuclear reactors present on them to stay up longer, as they would do in this higher orbit, before eventually falling back to the Earth. It is amazing to realize that they utilized reactors on their space platforms containing plutonium 238, a radioactive substance with a thousand-year plus half life. And there was no known technology to recapture them if and when they fell back to Earth where they could contaminate everything below. I guess they were going to rely on them staying up long enough for mankind to come up in the future with a method to contain them. Of course with the frequent meteor showers that occur, an accident could nullify that reliance very quickly. Our own space station will have protection from force fields, something they don't have."

"With this mentality prevalent in the world," said Ellen dryly to Cecile and Jack Nelson, "you can see why we must remain incognito for some time yet."

"I never doubted your words, Ellen," replied Jack. "I know it's extremely important to do so with the kind of people in power at this time on our Earth. I hope it never comes to this, but you may need an elite special force of people for protection to continue your Earth shepherding in the future."

"I agree, Jack," replied Ellen, "and we are already contemplating training such a force. I have talked with my daughter Molly, and she and some of her athletic friends may become the nucleus of such a group."

The pilots and their crews moved quickly into their ships at the close of Zeltor's briefing and made final preparations for takeoff with the space station platform. Zeltor gave the signal over the inter-ship intercom and the four scout vehicles with the space station platform between them simultaneously began to rise off the Moon's surface by a slow climb up Earth's magnetic lines of force, manually controlled by each pilot. Everything went smoothly and at five hundred meters Zeltor gave the signal to change to automatic pilot and engage the fusion generators for a rapid trajectory to the platform's final high Earth orbit destination. Zeltor reminded everyone to engage their electronic jamming devices to avoid any detection from Earth.

The flight went uneventfully and they soon arrived at the proper high Earth orbital site. Just as they approached, they narrowly missed one of the Soviet platforms Zeltor had mentioned that came tumbling by just as they were about to set their own platform into position. They made sure it was significantly further ahead and in a different orbit than the Russian satellite before detaching the four scout vehicles from the platform and leaving it there in its final orbital position. Lt. Kennedy and Ms. Earhart, after detachment from the space platform, immediately took their ships back to Moon Colony to gather more structures, supplies, and engineers to begin construction of the space station. Zeltor and Rol also took off after the other two ships following a final check on the proper orbiting essentials of the platform. Ellen stayed behind to facilitate the non-revealing filming of the space platform being done by John. Then she pointed her ship back to Moon Colony where Jack and Cecile put on survival suits and with Ellen, boarded Zeltor's ship to be transported back to Earth for the meeting planned with the Secretary of the EPA. Ellen's ship would be flown by Lt. Willy with Captain Saint-Exupery to help him as they also were to deliver more structural material for the space station construction.

On Zeltor's ship there was a grand reunion of the Nelson family and their Gnor-human friends. After several hugs and animated conversations about the recently completed space maneuver among the group had finished, Josh and Molly decided to transfer to Ellen's oxygen-enabled ship, now being flown by Lt. Willy and Captain Saint-Exupery, to continue their observation of the construction of the space station. Fond farewells were said by all as Josh donned a survival suit for the change of ships by him and Molly. Ares had decided at the last minute to return to Mars and help his parents entertain Jeanne as well as attend to his duties at the Life Factory. Secretly, Ares was very excited about and looking forward to spending some time with Jeanne on Mars. The two Nelson parents, as well as Ellen and John, were all cognizant of the attraction that seemed to be developing between Ares and Jeanne.

"It seems to me that Ares definitely has some interest in my daughter," Jack said, as the four were conversing together.

"Yes," replied Ellen. "John and I have noticed changes in both Molly and Ares lately. Up to now the two of them have been just good friends, but we have always felt that they would eventually get together. Now I'm not so sure. Ares seems quite interested in Jeanne; and in addition, Molly and Josh have also hit it off very well. I don't think this is a bad thing; all four are wonderful people, and no matter what happens, both John and I feel they will all always remain good friends."

"You can't know how happy Jeanne's interest in Ares has made me feel," said Cecile. "She has not had much to look forward to, especially romantically, and her obvious happiness at present does her mother's heart very good."

"You may not know, Cecile, said Ellen, "that Josh and Jeanne have both expressed to me an interest in having a transplantation operation like yours."

"Well, listen you people," broke in Jack, "if every one else becomes a Gnor-human I certainly hope I'll be able to do so also. Besides, I'll probably have to, to keep up with Cecile here!"

Jack smiled broadly, as did his wife, who reached over from where they were sitting together and kissed him on the cheek.

"If we want to continue on this Earth-shepherding project for the time it may take, Jack dear," she said, "it might definitely be a very good idea to do so."

"Just as our kids have already come to understand, Ellen and John," said Jack with a shrug. "I have just about come to the same conclusion myself. I'm sure I would be able to perform my role on Earth much better in the Gnor-human state."

"If you really are all sure about this, Jack," said Ellen, "we can start thinking about having it done. With the use of the time warp mechanism we can easily arrange to do it without causing any suspicion at your jobs. We can return you to work on a Monday after the usual weekend off your job by utilizing the mechanism; even though you may have been recuperating for weeks on Mars after your operation. The future will restart again on the Monday that you return to work, erasing what has transpired after that while you were away."

"Yes," answered Jack, "I see that clearly. Well, after the space station construction is finished and waste disposal is progressing well, I'll take that long weekend; hopefully with my two kids as well. You know, thinking about this gets me really excited!"

"So does it me," smiled Cecile, with her eyes sparkling as she squeezed her husband's hand. "I have hoped for some time now that you would decide to do it. I don't want to be around without you, dear; just as you were not happy about losing me when I had the breast cancer."

Jack reached over, put his arms around his wife and kissed her. They separated a little sheepishly and Jack apologized for the outburst of emotion between the two.

"Please don't apologize for a poignant moment that both John and I feel privileged to have witnessed," said Ellen. "If I could cry, I'd have been drowning us all."

She smiled and walked over and squeezed Cecile's hand. John was also smiling and shook Jack's hand as well.

"The love between your family members," John observed, "has been one of the reasons that has made us confident that you were going to be the people on Earth who would be best able to help us."

At that juncture the subject returned to how they would present CEO Ellen to the EPA secretary at the upcoming meeting with him back on Earth. From their position on the bridge, Zeltor and Rol noted how much the Gnor-human and human friends were enjoying each other's company and smiled broadly at one another as the scout vehicle flashed back to the great Starship that would then transfer them to Mars.

***

Ellen, John, and the two Nelsons had been transported back to Earth by Zeltor and two days later were being ushered into the office of the EPA Secretary by his assistant for the meeting they had been worried about on Mars. The four of them had arrived there filled with a certain amount of trepidation as Jack had been called at home by the Secretary the evening before and told that a Senator Greene from the Congress would also be present at the meeting the next morning. It seemed that there was strong congressional pressure to get the enacted nuclear wastes burial legislation implemented as soon as possible. Senator Greene had apparently assigned himself to investigate this new company that purported to have a unique technology for disposing of wastes that the EPA Secretary had told him about. If it turned out that he was satisfied that this company had a legitimate claim to be able to do this in a safer manner than now proposed, then the Yucca Mountain burial site could be delayed or perhaps even abandoned.

The fear of discovery, which was ever present in the minds of the Gnor-humans, made them somewhat more apprehensive of this upcoming meeting with a stranger they had not had much time to do any research on.

"Come in Jack and Cecile," said the Secretary, rising smilingly from his desk and walking around it to shake Jack's hand and give Cecile a perfunctory hug. "Please introduce me to your guests and I will in turn introduce you all to Senator Lyle Greene, who has come from Congress to evaluate your claim to have a safer way to get rid of the nuclear and toxic wastes than burial at the Yucca Mountain site." The Secretary looked at Ellen and John in anticipation of Jack's introduction of them.

"Mr. Secretary," said Jack, "this is Ellen James, the current CEO of Waste Management, and her CFO, John Scott."

"Pleased to meet you," said the Secretary, moving forward to shake first Ellen's, and then John's hand. "We have heard a lot of marvelous things from Jack and Cecile about your company's work with waste disposal."

"Thank you, Mr. Secretary," said Ellen, "my company is extremely grateful to you for considering us and allowing us the security to protect our investment in the unique technology we have developed to get rid of toxic and nuclear wastes. We have already been able to put a space platform into place in high Earth orbit, prior to constructing the space station necessary to accomplish the task of waste disposal. We have filmed some of the platform placement and have it here to show you our progress." Ellen indicated the briefcase that John was carrying.

"Well, Ms. James," rejoined the Secretary, "that is very interesting; I look forward to seeing those films, as will my guest, the Senator."

He then approached a chair on the side of the room where Senator Greene was sitting. The senator rose as they approached him and he smiled graciously at Ellen as the Secretary introduced them.

"Senator Greene," said the Secretary, "this is Ms. Ellen James, CEO of Waste Management, and her CFO, Mr. John Scott."

The senator shook both Ellen's and John's hands, and said he was very happy to meet them.

"My committee," Senator Greene added, "is especially interested in your company's new technology for getting rid of wastes. Your mention of a space station being used to get rid of the wastes is very intriguing and I look forward to your explanation of that statement."

The Secretary then asked them all to follow him into the next room and they all sat down around a conference table while some audiovisual apparatus was brought in to enable them all to view the films Ellen and John had brought. The lighting was dimmed and John prepared to run the filming he had done at the space platform; filming that would not give away any important information about the technology being utilized there.

"Mr. Secretary, and Senator Greene," began Ellen, "my company believes that the safest way to dispose of both toxic and nuclear wastes would be to move them off the planet to a site that would be a reasonably safe place to deposit them. We feel that place is the sun."

"The sun!" exclaimed the Secretary, "you mean our sun, old sol!"

"Yes sir, Mr. Secretary," continued Ellen. "They would not have much effect on the sun and actually would most likely be burned up as additional fuel. The problem is that to transport them out of Earth's gravity today would require a very unsafe method such as the utilization of rocket launching. Since one in every two thousand rocket launches ends up with some serious problem, it would not be too wise to consider this method for toxic and nuclear waste disposal at the current time. Our company, on the other hand, has invented a technology that uses a totally different kind of transport propulsion that is very safe and has little chance of causing the catastrophic spill that rocket launching might. You may have heard of an engineer who has been considering the use of locked-on laser power to cause small ships to be safely propelled up through Earth's gravity. Our company has been able to develop a somewhat similar drive in principle that is very reliable and safe. This will allow us to transport these dangerous wastes safely to a space station from where they can then be easily fired off into the sun. We understandably want to keep our discoveries private and have been quite happy so far with the help to accomplish this that you have given us, Mr. Secretary. If you would like, John can run the film we recently took of the space platform that we elevated to high Earth orbit using this new propulsion technology. Of course this is the bare bones platform you will be seeing; the space station that will be used to fire the wastes into the sun is to be built upon this structure and will be far more sophisticated."

"Please do start the film, Mr. Scott," answered the Secretary with enthusiasm. "Senator Greene and I are looking forward to seeing it."

John ran the film and the two men were obviously impressed with it and what Ellen's company had accomplished so far. Several persons had been photographed on the platform in space suits which showed how very large the platform was and consequently how large the space station would be as well when it was finished.

"This is indeed impressive, Ellen," said the Secretary. "I'm certainly glad I went along with Jack's initial request to engage your company in this endeavor. If we are able to safely dispose of toxic and nuclear wastes in this manner, a large problem for mankind's future will have been solved."

"Yes, indeed," added the senator, "My committee will be pleased to hear about your progress to this point. I hope you will be able to keep me informed as well about your space station construction and when you figure you will be able to start with the toxic and nuclear waste disposal."

"Of course, Senator Greene," replied Ellen. "At the present time we cannot be sure of that time frame but we will get it to you as soon as it is available."

"I don't believe that cost of this project should be a limiting factor if it is a process that works well and safely," said the senator, "but have you any idea what the price of this project may be eventually? I'm sure someone on my committee will ask this question."

"My company is not interested in the gross profits that could be accrued by its administration as is often seen in some of the business ventures of today," answered Ellen. "We are satisfied with a reasonable payment for our services, overhead, and the salaries of our workers. Anything extra will be spent on new products created for the protection or improvement of our technology and for mankind in general. Our company's current mission, formulated by our founder, is to create products and services that will protect and improve the lives of mankind all over the Earth. We are not interested in allying with small groups of powerful people or individual governments for bottom line profits. What will be the price tag of our products and services? I can only say that I'm convinced their cost will be far, far less than their value."

"Well said, Ms. James," commented the Secretary with a broad smile on his face. "Your founder's philosophy fits right into the EPA's mandate. We will await the further development of your project. Please keep me informed, Jack; this is really an exciting undertaking and holds out great promise for a future solution to a developing problem for mankind."

With that the meeting broke up and all parties left the Secretary's office. Ellen and John went to the rendezvous agreed upon with Zeltor and signaled him to pick them up. Zeltor arrived promptly in a scout vehicle and transported them up to the Starship, returning with great speed to First City on Mars. Jack and Cecile returned to their home to continue their preparations for creating, organizing, and protecting the waste holding station being built in the badlands of South Dakota.

"I think in general the meeting went off well," remarked Cecile as they entered their front door. "I feel the Secretary is with us one hundred per cent; and he is giving us free rein to proceed just as we'd hoped."

"I agree, Cecile," said Jack. "But I'm worried about Senator Lyle Greene. He has had a somewhat unsavory reputation in the past and is on the committee involved in the waste removal project. I would not trust him too far. He will bear watching!"

***

Senator Greene entered his inner office, closed the door, and took out a special red telephone he kept in the top drawer of his desk. He punched in a number and listened while it rang twice at the other end of the connection. A man with a low voice answered.

"Hello! What's up, Lyle?" said the voice. "You haven't called me on this special line for some time. Have you received some important congressional information I should know about?"

"Well," replied Senator Greene to the voice, "I thought you might be very interested in what I just witnessed at a meeting in the EPA Secretary's office. It seems an obscure company has developed the ability to transport large payloads into Earth orbit with some sort of safe, new propulsion. They plan to get rid of toxic and nuclear wastes by transporting them to a space station they are building in orbit and firing them into the sun. To my untrained eye their technology seems pretty far advanced, and they appear to be well into the construction phase as well. At this meeting I saw very impressive films of the supporting platform already in place in high Earth orbit. This could put a big crimp into the plan I have encouraged in my committee to utilize your company to collect and bury the wastes under Yucca Mountain. The committee has been influenced by the EPA Secretary to slow down enactment of the Yucca Mountain legislation; I presume until he sees if this new process will be effective. Fortunately, he has not told the committee about this company as yet; and, of course, I won't inform them about it either. However, if you can't find some way to stop this company or take it over, you and I stand to lose a very large sum of money if they get the job instead of your company."

"What's the name of this company, Lyle," said the voice, "do I know them?"

"I don't know who they are," replied the senator. "I never heard of any of them. They call themselves 'Waste Management', and they have a real Boy Scout mission statement. The CEO is an attractive young woman named Ellen James, and the company's CFO is John Scott, another no name without any business history that I can find. It's funny; I had an internet name search done and came up with an Ellen James who was a college history professor and had died in a flaming plane crash. In that same search John Scott was identified as a promising young anthropologist at Harvard, but he apparently had died in a shipwreck in the 1930's. Other than those hits, I drew a blank on their background identity or that of their company. It would seem that they are chummy with two undersecretaries in the EPA, Jack and Cecile Nelson, who the Secretary has left in charge of developing this project. The Nelsons might be a source you could use to gather information about them."

"Hmm, yes," said the voice. "Well, no worries, Lyle; I'll put my staff to work to find out about them and their company. This new transportation you mentioned that they have developed would be a nice thing to acquire. It ought to be easy to relieve them of it if they are the Boy Scouts you claim they are. If we are not successful in taking over their company or obtaining their technology, then we will have to sabotage their project or discredit it in some way to prevent it from replacing the Yucca Mountain waste-burial plans we have already set up."

"I'm relieved to hear you say this," said the senator. "Please get busy on it. They seem to be progressing rather rapidly on the project. Believe me, the films showing the size of just their platform makes the

Russian space station look like a toy. Their technology seems far advanced over anything I've ever seen. Let me know your progress as soon as you find out anything. Goodbye!"

"Goodbye, Lyle," answered the voice. "No worries; I have invested too much capital in this waste project to allow some "Johnny come lately" to take it away from me. I'll talk to you soon."

***

On Mars, late in the afternoon in the landing port lounge in First City, Ellen and John were discussing their recent meeting in the EPA Secretary's office with Zeltor. He was waiting for his ship to be loaded with material to be taken to the Earth orbit platform for use in the space station construction and was obviously concerned about the possibility of inadvertent discovery.

"Ellen, how does it look concerning protection from prying eyes?" asked the veteran pilot. "Will this EPA Secretary continue to allow us a free hand to develop the space station without interference from anyone?"

"So far, Zeltor," answered Ellen, "it does appear this will be the case. He appears to be happy so far with what we have shown and said to him; and also seems to be quite satisfied with Jack's and Cecile's handling of the project and the reports sent back to him on our progress. He is continuing to delay the congressional implementation of the Yucca Mountain legislation; although we did have a senator from the involved congressional committee at the meeting to see what we were doing."

"Do you think this new person could become a problem?" queried the pilot.

"I don't know," replied Ellen, "but John and I both feel he should be observed closely and not allowed to learn too much about us and our project."

"We intend to discuss this with Jack and Cecile when you take the four of us to the construction site again next week, Zeltor," said John. "I'm sure they probably have already considered the potential problem this Senator Greene could create."

"Incidentally, Zeltor," said Ellen, "where's your navigator, Rol? He usually flies with you, doesn't he?"

"Most of the time, he does," replied Zeltor, "but every once in a while he takes off and no one sees him for a short time. Then he just as mysteriously reappears. I think he goes off reading or taking part in some other project he wants to do by himself without any interference from anyone. He never lets these sojourns ever interfere with any of his duties so no one worries about them. I'll probably see him before we have to go back to the space platform with our load of construction material."

Just then Rol strolled into the room.

"Hello," said the navigator to Ellen and John. "I hate to break up your discussion but they just told me to let Zeltor know the load is ready to fly. It's getting late and they want us to take off as soon as possible. I guess they need something in this load right away on the space platform."

Zeltor smiled at Ellen and John.

"See what I mean?" he said, and winked at them. "We'll pick you four up for your platform trip next week. See you then!"

"Goodbye, gents," replied Ellen, "see you then."

With that the pilot and navigator left the room; and Ellen and John also left to commandeer a shuttle car back to Harvard Square and their apartment.

When they were back in their quarters Ellen changed into a comfortable lounging outfit and flopped into the couch next to her husband. She reached over and kissed him on the cheek.

"It's feels good to be back in our apartment again, doesn't it John," she said with a sigh, "but I miss Molly. Don't you?"

"Of course I do, my dear," John returned, and put his arm around his wife's shoulder and drew her closer to him. "But it does give me more time and space in which to enjoy my beautiful wife's company in private."

Ellen smiled and snuggled closer to her husband.

"John," she said demurely, "you are so incorrigibly delightful. She reached out and put her arms around him and kissed him on the lips. After a brief tender moment in his arms she then sat back and a serious expression appeared on her face.

"John, dear," Ellen began, "There's something I've been thinking about that we should discuss. I'm really worried about our shepherding project on Earth being discovered and utilized for the wrong reasons by the wrong people. We Gnor-humans tend to think that our more advanced synthetic bodies and brains are more than a match for any humans that would try to force us to use our technology or even ourselves in a manner we would deplore. That fact may be true, but we should not underestimate the resourcefulness of the criminal human brain. At that meeting with the EPA Secretary there was something about Senator Lyle Greene that my intuition tells me could become a possible danger to our Earth project that we must be ready to recognize and deal with. Forces could be mustered that we are at present unable recognize and may not be able to cope with. I think we should go ahead post haste with the formation and training of the elite police force of Gnor-humans that we discussed here with Molly earlier. Practically speaking, even without any abject threats, we will need such a force to monitor and protect our waste collections and transportation to keep our technology from being discovered and stolen. I confess that I'm concerned enough to want to start the training as soon as possible. Perhaps we should retrieve Molly from her space station construction observation and get her to help us start on this at the fitness academy where she and her young friends work out."

"As always, my dear," replied John, "I have to agree with you completely; and although Molly may be a little reticent to leave the construction site and the company of Josh right now, I'm sure she will come back immediately if we ask her to. There is one logistical problem, though; who will teach the course?"

"You're quite right, John," Ellen rejoined, "I thought that we should ask Jack Nelson if he knows of a person who would be skilled in this kind of training and could be trusted to keep our identity secret while training this force. I'll broach this subject with Jack when I contact him tomorrow about our platform visit next week."

Ellen snuggled back against her husband, started to unbutton his shirt front, and whispered that it would be nicer to be in bed right now. John rose from the couch and hurriedly finished removing the rest of his clothing. He strode into the bedroom where Ellen had already entered, disrobed, and was waiting for him with the bed sheets pulled over her chest and an anticipatory smile on her face. He raised the bed sheets and climbed into bed beside his wife.

"Although I miss Molly very much, my love," said John, "being all alone with you without having to worry about sound restraints helps a great deal to assuage the loss of our daughter's presence."

"Less talk, my loving, verbose husband," whispered Ellen. She pulled him over to her and shortly the Gnorman designer Jol's marvelous sexual apparatus[2]was placed into full function by the loving couple with intimacy and definitely no sound restraints.

The next morning Ellen contacted Jack Nelson at his office through the special line they had set up for shielded communication. She mentioned to him her intuitive worries about Senator Greene and her wish to start the special police force training program.

"You know, Ellen," answered Jack, "Cecile and I were discussing this ourselves and feel exactly as you do about Lyle Greene. He has a rather unsavory reputation around Washington and we both thought he would bear watching, much as John and you did also. The elite police force is a great suggestion. We will most likely need such a force; especially if any problem from Senator Greene turns up."

"Jack," asked Ellen, "do you know of anyone we could get to manage and help train such a force? It would have to be someone we could trust that would be agreeable with our Earth-shepherding project and our anonymity."

"You know, Ellen," answered Jack, "there is a Navy SEALs commander, Paul Traynor; who recently had to leave the service because of the discovery of a far-advanced liver cancer that had spread throughout his body. It was caused by a past infection from a parasite incurred on duty in Africa. He's a relatively young man; still very fit in his forties, and a legend in the SEALs with the reputation of being the best in his profession.

He is living in an apartment close to the Naval Amphibian Base (NAB) in Coronardo, California, where he had been training new Navy SEALs. The scuttlebutt I've heard is that he's just waiting to die. He apparently is not a prospect for a liver transplant because the tumor has already spread to his lungs and bones. Chemotherapy and radiation have apparently done little to slow the progression of the cancer. I don't believe he has any relatives and he's not married.

[2] See "The Synthetic Race," by Jack Randall, PublishAmerica, 114-115, May, 2004

I know about this man because one of Josh's college friends went into the SEALs, and raved to Josh about his commander's fantastic reputation and training abilities and the terrible disease that had made him quit the service he so loved. He had tried to get Josh to join the naval program and Josh looked into it and discussed it with me; including telling me about this legendary commander. It sounds like he might be a candidate to become a Gnor-human, and would thus be the perfect choice to lead your new police force."

"Yes, indeed," said Ellen. "Jack, do you think you could set it up for us to talk to Commander Traynor. We could get Zeltor to fly us out to Coronardo close to his apartment. Let me know if it can be arranged and we will talk to him about saving his life with transplantation and engaging him to train our Special Forces personnel."

"I'll see what I can do and get back to you as soon as possible," answered Jack. In the meantime, Cecile and I will continue to plan on the trip to the space platform next week with John and you unless this changes our plans.

"Great!" responded Ellen, "we hope to hear from you soon.

***

Commander Paul Traynor was billeted in a Navy apartment located just off the NAB in Coronardo, California where a grateful commanding officer had allowed Traynor to stay while he was undergoing treatment for his cancer. Jack Nelson had been able to make arrangements to talk to the commander and arranged to meet Ellen and John in a remote, densely wooded grove fairly close to his apartment. Zeltor used electronic jamming and flew his scout vehicle close enough to the grove to allow Ellen and John to transport into it by the Portal. The three met there and then proceeded through the dense woods to a secluded dirt road where Jack had left his car. Zeltor gave the three instructions to signal him when he was required to transport them up to the ship for departure after Commander Traynor had been interviewed by them.

It took about three quarters of an hour for the three to arrive at the commander's small apartment on the outskirts of the base. Jack had been advised of where it was by the base commander and had no difficulty locating it. As they approached the front door they were able to see Traynor through the front window. He was asleep in front of the television set, wearing a khaki T-shirt and trousers, and a half-full glass of beer was on the table next to him. Jack approached the door and rang the bell. Commander Traynor awoke with a start and went to the door and opened it. You could see that he was experiencing pain as he winced when he pulled open the door, and his face was lined with the deep creases that belied chronic outdoor exposure to the elements.

"Good afternoon, Commander Traynor," began Jack. "We'd like to talk with you about a possible position with the company of the two people with me. I'm Jack Nelson, an undersecretary of the EPA, and this is Ellen James and John Scott, of Waste Management."

"How do, Mr. Nelson, Ms. James, Mr. Scott," the commander nodded towards each in turn. "You say you're offering me a position with your company? I don't believe you will want me when I tell you about my current problem. But please come inside."

He ushered the three into the living room and indicated that they be seated on the large couch beside the TV set opposite his chair. He then immediately sat down in the chair with a small grimace of pain, and the three could readily see that he was quite weak and fatigued.

"You see, people," the commander began, "I am dying of an incurable cancer and probably won't live long enough to even start a new job. Believe me, if it were possible, I'd still be out there training SEALs."

"We know about your cancer, commander," said Ellen. "But that won't be a factor if you agree to our proposal. We have the means to cure your cancer; but you will have to remain with and work for us if you agree to allow us to undertake to do so. What we want you to do for us is not at all different from what you have been doing for most of your military career; that is, to train an elite special police force to work for our company. The other thing I can tell you, commander, is that your sense of duty to protect your country from harm that we have been told is your greatest motivation, will not be much different working for our company when we tell you who we are and what we are trying to do. Are my words at all interesting to you, Commander Traynor?"

"Are you kidding, Ms. James?" replied the commander. "They don't expect me to live but a few more weeks. What do you mean, you can cure my cancer? The doctors here have all said nothing can be done to save me as the tumor is all through my body and not responding to any of the treatments they are giving me."

"We cannot save your body, either, commander," said Ellen. "But we can save your brain; at least long enough to encase it in a synthetic body like John and I possess. You will then be much better and stronger than you have ever been before, and will have an unbelievable longevity by human standards. You can see how valuable this type of individual might be to an unscrupulous businessman or military commander; and thus our company's requirement of an elite police force to keep these individuals honest."

Commander Traynor sat slumped backwards in his chair with a look of amazement and disbelief on his face.

"Ms. James," he half croaked out, "what are you talking about? What do you mean when you say you are synthetic? You mean you are robots? You certainly look and act like live people. Mr. Nelson, are these two new pentagon and EPA developments?"

"They are not US developments, commander," answered Jack, "they are two human beings just like you that have had their brains transplanted into a synthetic body to keep them from a situation that would have unequivocally caused their death. This great boon has been presented to them by an alien race called Gnormen that had come to Earth for help from the human race in their development of an almost immortal synthetic body and brain. Ms. James has been instrumental in helping this race accomplish this goal. The race has now left Earth and gone back to their home planet, leaving Ms. James in charge of a colony of Gnor-humans as they are called, that are now residing on the planet Mars and at a base on the dark side of the Moon. They remain here to shepherd Earth's peoples and try to keep them out of trouble in the future. They are capable of time travel and so will know which paths must be avoided or changed. The first Earth challenge has been the damage they have witnessed in the future caused by toxic and nuclear wastes. They have established a high Earth orbit space station and have set up the company you were told about during the earlier introductions. This company plans to rid Earth of her wastes by shooting them into the sun from the space station. There are nefarious business people about who would obviously reap great benefit if they controlled the Gnor-humans and their technology. That's why Ms. James wants an elite Special Force trained to protect the Gnor-human endeavors in shepherding Earth from future dangers to the planet and its peoples."

"And you obviously," interrupted Ellen, "are the ideal candidate to do that training of the Gnor-humans that we will need. It will mean that you will never be able to return to Earth or the Navy to train SEALs again. But we think your contribution to protecting our Gnor-human endeavors to help Earth with the formation of a well-trained elite Special Force will be just as important for Earth and its peoples' continued prosperity and protection as your SEALs have been for the US Navy and the United States. Many of the Gnor-human colonists rescued were submariners and other sailors that should feel quite at home being trained by you and vice versa. John and I will tell you much more about the history of the Gnormen who came to Earth and actually had a great deal to do with how the Earth's peoples evolved into what we are now. They were very similar to us in their distant past and the wars, pollution, and diseases on their planet, much like our own, caused them to have to develop a synthetic body to survive. They have had time to evolve over the eons into highly ethical and moral people —yes, people, even though they are totally synthetic, including their brain; thanks to help from us Gnor-humans. What do you say, Commander? Are you willing to join us and supply a vital link to the protection of our endeavors at shepherding Earth?"

For the first time the three visitors noted a change in the attitude of the SEALs commander before them. He seemed to lose the expression of fatigue and depression that he had had when they first entered his apartment and began to look excited.

"Do you mean, Ms. James," said the excited navy man, "that you could transfer my living brain into one of your synthetic bodies and I would be able to go on as myself, without the cancer, and with a new stronger and more durable body? Is that the truth?"

"Yes," said Ellen, with a broad smile on her face, "and we have had no problems to date with any of our transplantation operations. Of course, you must know that you would not be able to return to your old life on Earth again. Perhaps in the future we can return to Earth, when it may then be safe to introduce ourselves to Earth's peoples and work directly and openly with them. Many of the current humans running the planet now are definitely not able to be trusted to do the right thing for all the Earth's peoples, but are more likely to try to gain everything for themselves with no thought of other people. With the process of continued human evolution and use of chemicals developed by the Gnormen over the centuries, we hope in the future to eventually develop the high ethics and morals in humans that our Gnormen friends have already developed and put into us. This will obviously take time and we will probably need your elite Special Force very critically during the early years. However, since the Gnor-human body has almost a thousand year longevity, we should have time to accomplish our shepherding endeavors. What say you, Commander, are you with us?"

"Ms James, Mr. Scott, Mr. Nelson," and the commander's eyes were now sparkling with tears and excitation, "please lead on. Only a fool would want to do anything else in my current situation. I will miss my SEALs trainees, of course, but I'll have a whole new cadre of students to train; and from what you've told me and what I've seen in you two, they should be a fantastic force!"

"We think the same, commander," said Ellen. "Especially since you are training them. If you are agreeable then, I see no reason why you cannot come with us to our city on Mars unless there is something you need to do here now."

"I would like very much," replied the commander, "to go and thank the commanding officer of the base who has been so kind to me by bending the rules and letting me stay here. He knew that at some point I was going to go to a hospice situation so I'd like to go and tell him that that time has come. If you could take me over to his office I'll say that you are the hospice people come to take me there. I have already told him that I don't want any fanfare or any visits to occur when this finally happens so I don't think there should be any problems with my departure. I have no relatives to contact either."

"That can be done easily," said Jack. "Let's get you in the car and we'll take you over to his office right now."

The commander gathered all the treasures of his past existence as a SEALs instructor in a small cardboard box, including what would have been a very full chest of medals had he chose to wear them, and left the apartment with his three visitors. At the door's exit he took a long look around the apartment and mused,

"It looks like this place will not represent the end of life for me after all, but actually may become instead the place from where I launch what certainly appears to be a new and very exciting life."

The farewell at the base commander's office was short and poignant with the three "hospice officials" being told by the Vice Admiral commanding officer to take good care of this man who was the finest officer he had ever known. The Vice Admiral's voice cracked a little as he spoke and a tear started in the corner of his right eye. The two men hugged each other, and Commander Traynor thanked the admiral for all his support over the years and the apartment he had recently allowed him to use. The two men then sharply saluted one another and the four left the Admiral's office.

"I think that was tougher on the Admiral than it was on me," said the commander, as Jack sped the car away from the base towards the rendezvous with Zeltor and the scout vehicle. "Unfortunately, I couldn't tell him that my life is not ending, but actually beginning again!"

"We will have another surprise for you when we get to the ship, commander," said John. "You'll meet Zeltor, our pilot, who is a genuine Gnorman alien who stayed behind to help us shepherd Earth when the rest of his fellow Gnormen returned to their planet."

"And I think the ship itself will be quite a revelation to you as well," smiled Jack.

When they reached the thick woodlands where they had disembarked from their ship earlier, Ellen, John and the commander stepped out of the car and Jack took leave of them to drive off to return his rented car. He stated he would see them again shortly as they were all to go out to the space station construction in a few days for further observation and obtaining pictures of the station's construction progress for the EPA Secretary. Ellen contacted Zeltor with her communicator and suggested they transport the three of them up to the ship with the Portal as the commander was too weak to transport there with a gravity belt. This was accomplished rapidly by Zeltor and the commander was extremely impressed by the maneuver.

"It's just like a Star Trek episode!" he enthused. He was amazed by the scout vehicle itself and remarked upon his introduction to Zeltor that he expected to meet an unusual-looking alien life form and not another typical human being.

"How do you do, commander" smiled Zeltor. "Actually, you look like us because of the DNA and other substances we put into your ancestors many, many years ago here on Earth at the time of the dinosaurs. But Ellen and John will tell you all about that history while we fly back to Mars, and you'll meet the two gentlemen who were responsible at that time for developing the human race as you know it today. So sit back and relax and we'll get you there 'in jig time', as you humans say."

The commander did take a comfortable seat and was briefed on the Gnormen and Gnor-human history, the colony on Mars and the dark side of the Moon, the space station for getting rid of toxic and nuclear wastes, and a little about his upcoming operation. They informed him that he would get a complete rundown on that by Dr. Dik Ran and the technologists who would perform the operation when they arrived on Mars. As the scout vehicle approached the Starship that would carry them to Mars, Commander Traynor gazed at the huge silver ship with awe.

"Our world has nothing like this massive ship!" he whispered. "I halfway didn't believe all you've been telling me, but I do now after seeing this fantastic spaceship!"

Once they had docked and established Ellen, John, and the commander in more comfortable quarters, Zeltor proceeded to the bridge and took over the helm of the great silver ship to begin a rapid ascent towards the First City landing port on Mars.

***

They soon arrived on Mars for disembarking at the First City landing port. Commander Traynor was helped into a survival suit and Ellen and John escorted him to the Oxygen Quarters where he was introduced to Dr. Ran. The doctor was informed of the circumstances of Commander Traynor's condition and his willingness to undergo a transplant operation. He was informed of the commander's SEALs background and that he was to become the trainer of the new elite Special Force that would probably be needed to protect the Gnor-human endeavors in shepherding planet Earth. Dr. Ran agreed with Ellen that this was a prudent plan, and he proceeded to discuss the upcoming operation with the commander.

The two seemed to hit it off almost immediately, and as time went on they were to become fast friends. The commander was established in his quarters and Dr. Ran left some medication orders to help with his condition prior to his operation. The procedure was set up as quickly as possible to spare the commander from any more suffering than was necessary from his cancerous condition.

The time quickly passed to the day of the operation and Commander Traynor sailed through it with flying colors. After the time of his rehabilitation had passed he was almost obsessed with his new body's physical and sensory abilities. He often said that if he had had SEALs with these abilities he would have been able to develop an unstoppable force with them.

"And so we hope you will have with our group, Commander," Ellen had replied to him.

"I really look forward to accomplishing this," the commander had eagerly rejoined to Ellen. "When will I be able to start, and when can I meet the people I will train?"

"All in good time," Ellen had returned. "My daughter Molly has a group of young friends that have been working out together for some time now, and they all are quite anxious to start this endeavor. My husband and I are also interested in this training as well as Dr. Ran's son, Ares. In addition, there are several other Gnor-humans who are interested, including a host of former navy men and women that we have rescued from disasters at sea. Oh, there will be no lack of candidates for your Special Force, Commander; and we are all as anxious as you are to get started with the training as we fear there may be trouble brewing with some as yet unknown factions on Earth. You need to have a little more time with your rehabilitation Dr. Ran says, but you should be ready soon enough to start. In the meantime we'll get you acquainted with some of the famous people we have rescued that have opted as you did to join our colony of Gnor-humans. We'd also like to get you more familiar with our Gnor history and our mandate to shepherd and protect our planet Earth."

"That will be great, Ellen," replied the commander, "I'm ready to begin with that group you mentioned just as soon as Dr. Ran says I can start."

In the next few weeks, as the commander's rehabilitation needs drew to a close, the start of the training of the new elite Special Force of Gnor-humans was set up in the site in First City where Ellen's daughter Molly had exercised with her friends in the past. The commander proved to be an excellent trainer as Ellen and Jack Nelson had thought he would be, and the Special Force soon proved to be exactly what the colonists had wanted and needed for protection of their identity and their projects on the Earth. The formation of this Special Force did not come any too soon as the Gnor-humans were about to find out.

***

Meanwhile the space station for waste disposal in high Earth orbit had been completely constructed and was now ready for use. Molly and Josh had returned to Mars and Josh and Jeanne then returned to Earth. Molly and Ares quickly became involved with the new Special Force being organized by Commander Traynor and Jack Nelson informed the EPA Secretary that the space station was now functional and Ellen's company was ready to begin its disposal activity. The Secretary set up a collection of nuclear wastes that had been scheduled for transport to the Yucca Mountain Facility after it was opened to be the first shipment tried with Ellen's company's techniques. Jack convinced the Secretary that the transport of the wastes should be carried out by Ellen's company's specialized technical employees and in their specialized trucks that had been specifically constructed for the job. He stated that the transportation would be monitored and protected by a Special Force that the government had allowed Ellen's company to utilize for this work. The Secretary was happy that this was to be done; thus offering some measure of protection to the EPA if something happened during this undertaking. There was one development that caused some uneasiness when the Secretary asked if Senator Lyle Greene could visit the disposal site in South Dakota as he had asked to do so to advise his congressional committee as to the progress of this new endeavor. Jack had disclosed this request to Ellen and John who told Jack to put him off by saying that because of the secrecy necessary to protect their new transportation technology, they could only show him films of the procedures that masked that valuable technology. There would be enough in the films to enable a thorough disclosure of the waste transport to the space station and later delivery into the sun. Fortunately, the Secretary said he understood completely and so advised Senator Greene that he would have to be satisfied with films of the event. The Senator was not happy with this.

***

"Hello?" spoke Senator Greene into the special red telephone from his desk drawer. "There's something peculiar going on with this waste disposal company. They won't allow anyone to observe their facility or operation. Only Jack Nelson and his wife have been allowed to visit the space station, and otherwise no one has any knowledge of what is up there or how they accomplish their disposal operation. They have made their system operational in a remarkably short time, and by the films I have seen they have some unbelievably advanced technology already in place and working. It may be that you will have to find a way to get Jack Nelson or his wife to talk about this company and what it has. If what they are proposing to do is successful, we can say goodbye to our Congressional lock on the waste disposal assignment at Yucca Mountain and the tremendous wealth you and I would have obtained from that assignment."

"No worries, Lyle," answered the low voice on the red phone line, "we'll pick up Nelson and his wife and find out just what is going on with this company. If something were to happen to those two, since they are the only ones on this project, perhaps you could get the Secretary to allow you to take over the surveillance of it. Therefore, if we are unable to get them to talk, we'll make sure they will be unable to work at the EPA for some time, if ever. Goodbye, Lyle; I'll get right on it."

***

Jack and Cecile had finished their work that Friday at the EPA office and were moving to the parking garage to get their car and drive back home for supper and a great weekend of discussion with their two children about their adventures on their recent trip to Mars and the space station. As they entered the garage a dark-colored van with opaque windows pulled up and obstructed their path to their car. Four men jumped out of the van and forcibly subdued the two of them, dragging them into the van. It then quickly sped away with the two captives.

"What is the meaning of this!" shouted Jack to his assailants, who had blindfolded and handcuffed the two of them. "Who are you, and what do you want of us? Cecile, honey, are you OK?"

"I'm OK, dear," answered Cecile, "but very frightened! What is going on here? Why have you people kidnapped us?"

"All in good time, Mrs. Nelson," a voice answered Cecile. "There is some information our employer wants from you. He will let you know what that is when we deliver you to him very soon."

"What information are you talking about?" said Jack to the voice. He correctly began to suspect that these people probably wanted information about the waste disposal activity and was worried for Cecile and his safety. It was here that he was grateful that Ellen and John had been fearful of this very thing happening and he knew about the trained Special Force that was preparing for just this sort of problem. Ellen had given Jack a special sensing device on his wristwatch that if activated, would alert them that something untoward was going on and that they probably would need help as rapidly as possible. Fortunately, Jack was handcuffed in front and so was able to push the control on his watch. He knew it would take some time for Ellen's Special Force to arrive on Earth, but he had allowed a device to be implanted under his skin that emitted a signal that would lead the Force to his whereabouts. He also knew that in a pinch they could use the time warp mechanism to retrace time if any fatalities had occurred.

"I don't know what information you would want from us," Jack went on. "We are just EPA workers and don't have any vital government secrets that would interest anyone. You've kidnapped the wrong people I'm sure. Don't be upset, Cecile dear, I'll contact the Secretary and other officials as soon as we meet and straighten out this fellow who has erroneously kidnapped us."

Cecile knew at once that Jack had summoned Ellen's Special Force when he spoke thusly, and was relieved that this had been done. She tested the handcuffs with her superior Gnor strength but was unable to break the strong metal bonds.

After this little was said as the van sped along and eventually they reached their destination. The van slowed and stopped and the four men stepped out into what was now darkness, escorting their two captives towards a nearby house. Jack could hear no automobiles going by and there were very few sounds other than a loud chorus of crickets singing. With her enhanced Gnor senses, Cecile could smell and sense that they were in a wooded area. The men led the two into the house which had all the blinds drawn, and sat them in chairs, releasing their blindfolds but keeping them handcuffed.

"This will be your home for the next two days, Mr. and Mrs. Nelson," the leader of the men informed them. "We will be watching you at all times and escape attempts will be met with harsh punishment!"

"Our kids will be missing us shortly and will alert the police to look for us," said Jack. "You'd better let us go right now before you are in very big trouble!"

"We've already told your kids that something had come up and you would be tied up all weekend at the office, and not to expect to see you until Monday. That should give our employer ample time to get the information he wants from you. If you do not give us the information we want, I'm afraid your children may find you missing permanently."

"What do you mean by that remark?" said Jack. "I told you, we are EPA agents, not secret government agents! You have the wrong persons! Now stop this nonsense; you are frightening my wife!"

"You two might as well retire to your room through that door," said the leader of the captors, "since our employer won't be here until tomorrow afternoon to question you. There is a bed and a bathroom in there, but there are no windows or doors; and if you try to escape by any other means we have orders to shoot you, so I wouldn't try anything. If you give us the information we want we will return you home. If you tell us, Mr. Nelson, that you will have to get information from your office, we will keep Mrs. Nelson hostage until you return and one of us will go with you to make sure you return with that information. Now go into your room and remember, don't try to escape!"

"Can you please remove these handcuffs," said Jack: "it will be hard in the bathroom with them on, and we certainly aren't going to try to go anywhere."

"OK, we can do that," said the same man, "but no funny stuff or dire consequences will happen!" With that the two handcuffs were removed and Jack and Cecile went into the room the men had indicated. The door was closed and locked after them by their captors.

"I have already sent a signal off to Ellen's Special Force team," whispered Jack into Cecile's ear. "And you remember, I have that chip locator embedded in my chest wall, so they should be able to track us down. So don't you worry, honey; Ellen's group will be here in time."

"I hope you're right, dear," returned Cecile. "Still, I'm more worried about you than me. I have a Gnor body that will be hard to deal with compared to your frail human body!"

"What do you mean, frail!" said Jack with mock injury on his face. "You haven't complained about me much in bed!" With that he smiled, put his arms around his wife and kissed her on the cheek. "Be assured, dear, our friends will find and rescue us."

"I certainly hope so," returned Cecile. "But before anything happens to you I'll be praying they do get here in time."

"Since there's nothing we can do at this time, let's eat the sandwiches and coffee I see they left us on that little table over there, and try to get some rest on the bed afterwards. We will need to be as rested as we can if we are to get through this. I'm almost positive this will be related to the space station waste disposal company that we have been so carefully protecting. In fact, it probably is evidence that we have been doing an excellent job at the protection. It is a credit to Ellen's thoughtfulness that she anticipated this and set up the Special Force to counteract it. I think we'll soon see how well her Commander Traynor has prepared his group."

"I'm kind of glad they lied to the kids," said Cecile. "At least they will be spared the worry for now."

"Yes," answered Jack, "It is better this way as they would have been very upset if we didn't come home for dinner tonight. Well, for now let's consume our dinner and try to get a little rest afterwards."

***

The following evening the man arrived who was apparently the employer of this group of thugs that had kidnapped the Nelsons and imprisoned them.

"Well, Mr. and Mrs. Nelson," the man began pleasantly enough. "I'm sorry for this inconvenience to you, but, no worries, it will be all straightened out after you answer a few questions I have for you."

"What questions?" exclaimed Jack. "I told your men here that we were simple EPA workers and had no secret government knowledge about anything. What do you want of us?"

"Well sir," the man replied, "Senator Greene and I are extremely interested in this company, Waste Management, which seems to have such remarkable new technology for disposing of toxic and nuclear wastes. I would like to talk to the leaders of this company to see if we might be able to assist in their endeavor to rid the planet of these scourges. Since you seem to have knowledge of and connections with them we were hoping you might supply us with information about the company or an introduction to its leaders."

"Just what information are you interested in, sir?" said Jack. "This company has some very advanced technology and does not want to share it with anyone at this time. They have told me that they would be willing to do this at an appropriate time in the future, but for now they feel it would undermine everything they want to accomplish with it at this time."

"Does this mean that you will not give me any information about them, Jack?" smiled the man.

"I'm afraid that will have to be the case," answered Jack. "What they are able to do with their technology is far too important to be placed in the hands of anyone not above board; as this kidnapping certainly puts your group into!"

"Well, I'm sorry to hear you say this, Jack," smiled the man again. "So I guess we'll just have to try another way to get you to give us the information we want."

With that he barked to the other men, "Tie his wife into a chair and start beating her until he says he's willing to give me the information that I want!"

The men brandished their guns on Jack and two grabbed Cecile and bound her to a chair in the center of the room. One man slapped her very hard across the face, but Cecile did not cry out and struggled harder to break the ropes that bound her.

"Cecile, honey," said Jack, "are you all right?" And addressing the man, "What is the matter with you, you damn fool! Release my wife at once or you will regret dearly what will happen to you!" With that he rushed toward the man with his arms raised to strike him, but was shot in the back by one of the other men in the room. Jack fell to the floor with blood trickling out of his mouth and was unable to rise or speak. Cecile snapped the ropes holding her with a supreme effort and knocked the man closest to her unconscious with one blow. One of the other men fired his gun at her which penetrated her left shoulder just before she reached him and threw him to the floor, breaking his right arm in the process. Just then the door and two windows burst open and Ellen and Commander Traynor's Special Force team broke into the room.

***

Commander Traynor had received the distress call from Jack and he quickly assembled his Special Force for immediate deployment to Earth to locate Jack via his embedded locator chip. He called Ellen and told her about the distress call and she stated that she and John would like to go along with the team. The Special Force assembled quickly at the landing port at First City and Zeltor took them rapidly by Starship to a high orbit area on Earth. He activated a cloaking field around the Starship to avoid detection from below and then flew the Special Force to Earth in a scout vehicle similarly cloaked; arriving in the evening close to the area where the locating device told him Jack and Cecile were held.

"I'll wait for you here," said Zeltor. "Let me know if all goes well below. I'll keep the ship camouflaged with electronic cloaking so there shouldn't be any problems on that score. Dr. Ran will remain up here with me and can be dispensed to the ground rapidly with the Portal if he's needed. Good luck!"

The team rapidly deployed in the cargo hold and donned gravity packs for their descent to Earth from the scout vehicle. Commander Traynor had been accompanied by Ellen, John, Molly, Ares and several of Molly's friends that had formed the elite Special Force trained so well by the commander. On his command they all left the ship and proceeded to Earth in rapid orderly fashion, assembling in a woodland thicket close to the house where the Nelsons were held captive.

They immediately progressed to the front door of the house and to two of the side windows to the room where they could hear people talking excitedly. Two shots rang out and Commander Traynor ordered the Force to enter the house at once! They burst through the door and the two side windows and quickly subdued all of the remaining men in the house that had not already been taken care of by Cecile.

"Are you all right, Cecile?" asked Ellen as she collared the apparent leader of the group.

"Yes, I'm OK," answered Cecile, "except my left arm isn't working right after being shot through the shoulder. But Jack has been shot in the chest and I fear he may have a serious wound. Is Dr. Ran with you?"

"He's in the scout vehicle" answered Ellen, "I'll call and he will be right here by Portal." She quickly summoned Dr. Ran to the scene with her communicator and he appeared almost immediately outside and rushed into the house. Jack was conscious but obviously gravely injured.

"It's time for my operation, doc," Jack smiled wanly to Dr. Ran. We better get on with it pretty quickly."

"Yes, indeed, Jack," responded Dr Ran as he stabilized his patient. "Let's get you back right away. Ellen, I'm leaving with Jack and Cecile right now. The Force should keep these people collared here for now until we can get back. You will have to figure out what we'll do with them."

"Of course, Dik," said Ellen. Get Jack and Cecile back right away for treatment and after we corral these idiots I'll call and let Josh and Jeanne know what's happening. I'm sure they'll want to be there for their dad's operation and be reassured about their mother's injury. Zeltor can pick them up when he picks us up as well."

"Ellen," said Cecile, "this fool mentioned Senator Lyle Greene when he first came into the house, the congressman we were worried about."

"I'm not surprised, Cecile," answered Ellen. We'll check it all out. Now you and Dik get Jack quickly back to the Life Factory for his surgery and get that shoulder of yours looked at!" She called to Ares who was standing nearby, "Ares, could you please go with them and see if you can look at Cecile's shoulder and repair it when you get back to First City?"

"Of course, Professor James," said Ares. He went over to Cecile and examined her injured shoulder. "We should be able to fix this without much trouble, Mrs. Nelson. I'll make the arrangements when we get back to the Life Factory." The three of them immediately transported back to the scout vehicle for fast transit to the Starship and then back to Mars. In the meantime, Commander Traynor had all the remaining men tied up and said he would arrange for their incarceration on kidnapping and weapons charges.

"Jack has set me up as a government Special Forces MP" he said to Ellen, "and I'll say we've been after these people for some time now. I don't think there will be any trouble putting them away for quite a while."

"That's great, Commander," said Ellen. "It's dark now so John and I will use our gravity packs to get to Josh and Jeanne at the Nelson's home to let them know what's going on. It's not too far from here and Zeltor will pick us up with you people after he gets the Nelsons set up on Mars for their treatment. See if you can find out the relationship between this man and Senator Lyle Greene. I suspect they may be linked together in this plot."

"OK, Ellen," answered Traynor. "Will do! I must say this little activity for our new Special Force worked out pretty well, don't you think?"

"It was perfect, commander," smiled Ellen. "John and I are off, but we'll see you all again when Zeltor picks us all up for transport back to Mars." And with that the two of them donned their gravity packs and took off into the night.

They arrived at the Nelson home and found Jeanne and Josh inside watching television.

"Well, it's certainly a surprise to see you two," said Josh when he answered the front door. "My mom and dad are working late at the office this weekend, so if you're after them you'll have to go there to talk with them or maybe catch them on the telephone."

"No Josh," started Ellen. "Please sit down there by Jeanne on the couch." Josh went over and sat beside his sister.

"Your parents are not at the office. They were kidnapped by someone trying to gain information about our company. Fortunately, your father had had us install a locator chip under his skin and an activator on his wrist watch, as we thought something like this might happen. When it did, he activated it to let us know that something had happened to him and that he needed our help. We were able to locate where he was and rushed to the spot with our new Special Force and rescued both your mother and he."

"Are they alright?" exclaimed the two Nelsons together, leaning forward anxiously in their chairs. "Did anybody get hurt?"

"Your father was shot in the chest," answered Ellen, "but Dr. Ran stabilized him and whisked both your mother and he back to Mars where your dad is going to have the brain transfer that your mother has already had."

"Dad's going to be alright isn't he, professor?" said Josh. "He should do as well as Mom did, won't he?"

"Dr. Ran is very confident that he will do so, Josh" answered Ellen, "so don't you two worry."

"How's my mother?" asked Jeanne. "Did anything happen to her?"

"She was shot through the shoulder," said John, "but Ares examined her and said he and the technicians could fix that up quite easily in the Life Factory back on Mars. Zeltor flew Ares, your mother and father, and Dr. Ran back to Mars immediately to start that treatment, and he'll come back and pick us and the Special Force up shortly to return us all to Mars where you can be with your folks."

"Wow!" breathed Josh, sitting back into his chair, "that's a lot to take in so quickly. Still, both Jeanne and I know everything will be handled well, so we're worried, but not massively so. Dad's been talking about having the transfer for some time now, so I guess that time has now come."

"It looks like it," agreed Jeanne, "and I'll probably be the next one."

"Well," said Ellen, "don't worry about that just yet, Jeanne. They'll be plenty of time to think about it later on."

"It is interesting, kids," said John, "that your parents, Ellen, and I were right about Senator Lyle Greene. He apparently was in league with this group of thugs that kidnapped your folks."

"You know, John," mused Ellen, "I bet Senator Greene has not told any of his Congressional Committee about our company and the waste disposal. I think we may find that this man's group and the senator have a company that stood to profit from a waste disposal company of their own that we were endangering. That's probably why they became desperate and kidnapped Jack and Cecile to try to force the information about us from them."

"I think you're right, Ellen," returned John. "But little did it benefit them. The man and his thugs will spend several years in federal prison now, and Commander Traynor should be able to get the man to incriminate Senator Greene for a deal to lessen his sentence."

"Well, we'll see about that later," said Ellen. "Now I'm anxious for Zeltor to pick us up and get us back to Mars. I'm just as anxious as the kids to make sure Jack and Cecile are doing alright; although I'm confident that Dr. Ran and Ares will have the situation well in hand."

It seemed like only a short time later that Zeltor arrived and signaled Ellen and John that he would beam them all aboard with the Portal, and did so. He then picked up Molly and the rest of the Special Force, leaving Commander Traynor and a couple of the Force to assist him in bringing their prisoners to nearby Washington, DC for prosecution there. The commander ironically used the criminals' autos to get to the nearby city. Zeltor then rapidly returned back to Mars with all his passengers so they could check on how Jack and Cecile were doing.

When they arrived at First City, Josh and Jeanne had to don survival suits to transfer to the Life Factory, unlike Gnor-humans Molly and her parents. Arriving there in the Oxygen Quarters they removed their survival suits and joined the others who had quickly made their way to the Life Factory where Cecile was being treated by Ares and his technicians, and her husband was undergoing emergency brain transfer surgery in the OR by Dr. Ran and other surgeons.

A short time later Ares came out to join the others as they were awaiting the outcome of Jack's procedure. Ares went over to Jeanne, who was sitting in a wheelchair, and took hold of her hand.

"Your mother is fine, Jeanne," he smiled down at her. "She's really a tough woman, and her arm is now functioning perfectly again. She'll be out with us in a minute or two. She's really worried about your father, but I told her that my dad hasn't lost a patient yet." And he smiled and squeezed her hand.

Jeanne looked up at Ares and said, "Ellen said you would take good care of my mom, Ares. Josh and I are so thankful you were able to fix her up." And she smiled at him and squeezed his hand back.

"Yes, indeed," added Josh sincerely, "we can't thank you enough, Ares." Then he looked down and winked at his sister who gave him a rapid frown. Molly also smiled and also winked at her mother and father who were happy that their daughter was not upset about Ares interest in Jeanne. Just then Cecile came out from an inner room and approached the group with a smile on her face. She flexed her left arm and shoulder and said to Jeanne and Josh, who had rushed over to her, "There! See that! Good as new! Ares, you and your technicians are absolutely marvelous! Thank you so much!"

"A genuine pleasure, Mrs. Nelson," returned Ares. You're a great patient!"

"Ellen, how is my husband doing?" asked Cecile. "Have you heard anything yet?"

Just then Sarah Ran emerged from the direction of the OR suite and walked over smilingly to the group,

"I just returned from bringing the OR crew some material they had asked for, Cecile," she said. "Jack is doing great and the operation is going along without a hitch. The material I brought was a new type of skin that Dik and the other surgeons have designed that they thought would be appropriate for Jack after what just happened to him. It's similar to what you may know in the U.S. as Kevlar, but is much stronger. The person still won't exactly be bullet proof, but will be able to withstand a lot more firepower than ever before. It still looks and feels like human skin, which is remarkable. I sure would have liked to have had this skin when I was a detective! Dik says he is going to install this type of skin onto all the Special Force people to protect them better in their future work."

"That's great news about Jack, Sarah," said Ellen. "And I'd like for Dik to give that skin to all of us that continue to work on the Earth as well. It would seem to me that it probably should become a staple of the Gnor-human condition from now on. We may encounter more and more problems in our shepherding of Earth that could put us in harm's way from people like Senator Greene and other such individuals."

"Your right as usual, Ellen," John remarked. "But it looks like you've given Dik and Ares a very full work schedule for the immediate future to get all that skin changed."

"Don't worry, John," rejoined Sarah, "my two men will relish every minute of it, although I'll miss seeing them as much as I usually do." And she smiled over at Ares, who returned her smile. Jeanne noticed the obvious love between mother and son and felt the attraction between her and Ares growing stronger. The look Jeanne gave to Ares was not missed by Josh or for that matter by Ellen, Molly, or John either.

Ellen whispered to John, "It looks like we may be right about the kids, at least Ares and Jeanne anyway!"

Just then Dik Ran emerged from the Operating section of the Life Factory and went over to Cecile and gave her a big smile.

"Jack has done very well, Cecile," he said to her. "I would expect him to progress without any complications. His left lung and the edge of the heart were nicked by the bullet and it would certainly have been touch and go if we had been trying to save his human body rather than transferring his brain into a synthetic one. If all remains stable he should be ready to resume work at the EPA within a week or two. Unlike what we did with you and the earlier brain transplants, we now are able to directly transfer the consciousness and memories from the living brain into the synthetic one. This is what Jack wanted us to do."

"Yes, Dr. Ran," returned Cecile. "Jack and I had talked about it before and it is what he wanted to do if the time came. Are you sure, though, that Jack will get the same results as I did transferring the old way?

"Don't worry, Cecile," replied Dr. Ran, "this new technique works better and is safer than the old two step brain transfer we used to do. Jack will do fine, and be ready to continue his life much sooner than you did.

We also installed a new type of skin that is much hardier than the skin you have now. It should give him additional protection if he runs into similar problems in the future."

"Yes," answered Cecile, "Sarah just explained to us about the new skin and everybody here said they would love to have such skin for themselves as well."

"So my wife is drumming up more work for her son and husband is she?" Dr. Ran laughingly remarked. "Actually, we were going to present it to the Council for their opinion as to making it the standard for Gnor-human skin from now on. It will help us on many fronts; not just with bullets, but with radiation and other deleterious exposures."

"Doctor," said Cecile, "can my children and I see my husband now?"

"Of course you can," answered Dik, "but remember; it will be some time yet before he can respond well as his new synthetic brain will cause him to be somewhat dazed for a little while as it takes over all the functioning of his synthetic body. It will be important for you all to see that he still looks like Jack Nelson, and will continue to do so in the future, and also remember and feel like himself as well."

"Of course, Dik" answered Cecile. "That is exactly why I wanted Josh and Jeanne to see their father; to see that this hasn't changed him very much, just like me."

Jack did progress very well, and soon returned to the EPA with Cecile, continuing their work with the US nuclear and toxic waste project. The application of the new protective skin on all the Gnor-humans that were to be involved in Earth shepherding in the future had also progressed speedily and well; in fact, it was apparent that soon all of the Gnor-humans would be in possession of this helpful addition.

***

Several months had gone by and at this time the Waste Management project was proceeding well in the United States. Waste collection routes were becoming well established and the Special Force of Commander Traynor was working effectively to keep everything done by the company confidential. The US president had ultimately agreed to this confidentiality as the outcome for the country had turned out so positively that he realized it would be counterproductive to do otherwise. Several firings of nuclear and toxic wastes into the sun had occurred without any complications whatsoever. The U.S.Congress had rescinded their Yucca Mountain burial plans and Lyle Greene was dismissed from the Senate because of his nefarious scheming to enrich himself at the country's expense. The President had presented Ellen with a Presidential Medal at a highly publicized special ceremony honoring her company and the great forward progress made in making the disposition of U.S. nuclear and toxic wastes safer for the country and the Earth.

France, who by 2004 had over 80 per cent of its electric power coming from nuclear plants, had become extremely interested in Ellen's company. The French President inquired of the U.S. President if that company could be made available to help France get rid of their wastes also. The long and short result of this inquiry found Waste Management now extended into France; and soon it extended into most of Europe. At this juncture, no problems had occurred with the Gnor-human collection vehicles and the firing of the wastes into the sun from the space station. Each country seemed satisfied with the confidential requirements of using the company; otherwise, Commander Traynor's Special Force was able to force such confidentiality on any one that tried to steal the technology.

Eventually, the company found itself doing business worldwide; and surprisingly enough, gradually found less and less trouble with maintaining confidentiality in the different countries. One of the main reasons for this was because Ellen made sure that much of the large sums of money being accumulated by the company in its waste disposal efforts were substantially returned to the local people of the different countries for use in projects necessary to improve their health and welfare. Ellen found herself involved in financing research and treatment for many worldwide disease scourges such as AIDS, tetanus, malaria and tuberculosis. She tried to keep herself as free from notoriety as possible, but it was becoming harder and harder to do so. Her name and countenance was becoming as well known as was Mother Theresa's from an earlier time period had become. Finally she decided to start delegating the cash distribution to many different people and eventually the company itself became known as the Good Samaritan and not any particular individual in the company. This pleased Ellen very much as it gave her the anonymity she needed and a chance to start thinking about the next shepherding project the Gnor-humans should consider.

This came about after she and her original crew made a discovery trip into the future to find if the havoc they had seen before that had been raised by toxic and nuclear wastes was no longer present. There was now almost no evidence of the terrible birth defects and cancer they had found on their previous mission. It seemed that the way nuclear and toxic wastes were now being disposed of had made the difference they had hoped to accomplish. Ellen did not find the Earth's future now so terribly bad with their changing the time line and she reported this to the Council which received the news with great relief and joy. Even Rol, who had been very apprehensive about changing the time line, admitted the results were encouraging. They did find, however, that the effects of global warming were still very much in evidence, and it was obvious to Ellen that this problem would have to be next on their Earth-shepherding agenda.

There still remained one problem that the increasing worldwide waste disposal efforts were engendering; and that was the need of many more Gnor-humans to staff the different collection efforts burgeoning up around the world. It was evident that Ellen and her group would have to rescue more humans to create and train this needed staff of Gnor-humans before they were to start on the new shepherding project for Earth. Gnor-humans were much less susceptible to the effects of radiation than humans, so Ellen had not wanted to recruit the work force necessary from local people. She had called a Council meeting on First City and suggested that she and John start historical research for some new rescue projects to supply this additional workforce that was needed. The Council unanimously agreed with her proposal and commissioned the two Gnor-human leaders to start research on the new rescue missions.

Ellen and John thought their first rescue could be the crew of the Edmund Fitzgerald, a freighter that had been sunk on November10, 1975 in Lake Superior in the US, losing 29 men whose bodies were never recovered.

"Lake Superior was known to the local Chippewa Indians as 'Kitchi-Gummi', remarked Ellen to her husband John as they were discussing the rescue mission.

"What does that mean, mom?" asked Molly, who was present and enjoying the conversation between her parents.

"It means 'great-water'," replied Ellen. "Lake Superior is the largest of the five Great Lakes in the United States and Canada and is close to 1300 feet deep at one point. It has a shoreline of over 2800 miles and many hundreds of ships ply its waters each year, traveling out the St. Lawrence Seaway sometimes as far away as to Europe. Iron ore is one of the many common cargos carried by the ships in the lake, and was what the Edmund Fitzgerald was carrying when she sank. The lake is large enough to influence the weather quite significantly; especially in November when intense low pressure systems pass over the lake when the surface water is warm and the air is exceptionally cold at the same time. This combination can cause very severe storms with high waves and hurricane force winds. The local Indians call these storms the 'Witches of November'. It is not unexpected that the bottom of Kitchi-Gummi is actually littered with over 350 ships that have fallen prey to these storms. We may find that we can rescue more people from some of those other ships if we can locate research identifying what happened to the ships and their crews."

"That's quite interesting, Ellen," said John, "I had no idea how extensive was the shipping through Lake Superior, or that such storms could occur on an inland waterway."

"Yes," returned Ellen, "my eyes were opened as well when I first began researching the sinking of the ship. It should be possible for Zeltor or Lt. Kennedy to take one scout vehicle and retrieve the 29 crew members before the ship goes down. Again, it might be reasonable for someone to go on board the ship to make sure all the crew is rescued, as we did on the Titanic when we rescued Molly."

At the reference to her rescue, Molly looked over at her mother and father with a loving smile on her face.

"You know, mom and dad," she said softly, "I will always remember that night when dad pulled me from the cold rushing water in the sinking Titanic and transported me seemingly by magic to the cargo hold of Zeltor's ship to reunite the three of us. I can still feel the three of us standing together in the cargo hold with our arms around each other and the crush of cold, wet, confused and frightened people all around us."

"Yes," replied her father, "it's something I don't believe any of us will ever forget." He walked over to Molly and hugged her, and she hugged him back. Ellen smiled at the picture of the two of them standing together.

"It's a good thing we don't form tears any more you two," she smiled, "or I'd be losing my mascara right now!"

Molly immediately ran over to her mother and hugged her.

"Oh, mom," she said. "I love you." And she kissed her on the cheek. Ellen hugged her back and then they took their former chairs and continued the discussion of the rescue.

"The Edmund Fitzgerald was a pretty large ship for an inland waterway," began Ellen. "It was built and launched from the Great Lakes Engineering Works shipyard in Ecorse, Michigan in 1958. It was 729 feet long and 75 feet wide and could carry 27,500 tons. At that time she had a state of the art 7500 horsepower engine built by Westinghouse Electric Company, and set many shipping records."

"Whew!" whistled John, "that certainly was a pretty big and powerful ship, Ellen. You wouldn't think it would have had very much trouble, let alone, sink, on an inland lake."

"Well, dear," replied Ellen, "the Titanic wasn't a slouch in power and size either, and it sank!"

"Your right, of course," John replied, "you can't fool with Mother Nature and expect to get away with it."

"The captain of the ship," continued Ellen, "was Earnest MacSorley and he took his ship loaded down with iron ore out of the Superior, Wisconsin dock around 2 PM on November 9, 1975. Because a gale warning had been issued, MacSorley decide to steer closer to the shore to avoid any large waves that might form. He radioed that he had chosen this position to the Anderson, another ship that had launched behind him. The typical November storm intensified and eventually developed winds over 100 miles per hour with enormous waves that battered the two ships mercilessly. The Anderson, although damaged severely by the storm did survive it; but in the middle of the storm the Edmund Fitzgerald suddenly disappeared from the Anderson's radar screen and was never heard from again. The coast guard mounted an investigation of the sinking and surmised that the big ship with its heavy cargo was unstable and listing (as had been reported by MacSorley to the Anderson). This probably made her unable to ride out the massive waves hitting her and she foundered and sank, causing her to break in half when she hit the bottom of the lake. She now lies in 500 feet of water where she was located by the coast guard. A Canadian singer-songwriter, Gordon

Lightfoot, wrote and performed a wonderful ballad about this shipwreck that tells very clearly what often happened when these "November Witches" attacked shipping on Lake Superior. The last lines of his ballad were particularly poignant:

The legend lives on from the Chippewa on down
Of the big lake they call 'Gitche Gumee'.
Superior, they said, never gives up her dead
When the "Gales of November" come early!

Since none of the bodies were ever recovered, these crew members should be excellent candidates for our rescue."

"I certainly agree," said John. "Let's find Zeltor and Lt. Kennedy and find out which ship can help us on this mission."

When the two pilots were contacted they suggested that two ships be used to do the mission because of the relatively violent storm that was going on at the time the rescue would be done and two ships might be needed if something went wrong.

***

Zeltor and Lt. Kennedy had left the Starship in high Earth orbit under an electronic cloaking and had flown their two scout vehicles, similarly cloaked, far enough off the port of Superior, Wisconsin so they wouldn't be identified. They had set their time warp mechanisms to arrive there simultaneously a few hours after the Edmund Fitzgerald and the Anderson had left port on November 9, 1975.

"There's already a pretty good storm going on here, Joe," Zeltor communicated to the pilot of the other scout vehicle. "Stay close to me so communication will be easier. We obviously will have to use our Portals to get this crew out safely."

"Agreed," answered Lt. Kennedy. "Is Professor James going to transport on board to make arrangements for the whole crew to be in one spot so we can remove them all at once?"

"Yes," answered Zeltor, "she and John are here with me and she will transport over and back by Portal to make sure we get everyone off….. Wow! All of a sudden this storm has really picked up. I'm reading 115 mph winds down there with huge waves, and my ship is beginning to be tossed around quite a bit. How're you doing, Lieutenant?"

"I'm getting the same bumps, Zeltor," Joe returned. "We better get these people out and leave here just as soon as we can!"

Zeltor instructed Ellen to prepare and then transported her by Portal to the deck of the ship. She immediately moved to the bridge of the ship and entered, just as Captain MacSorley was issuing the message to the Anderson that he was 'holding his own'.

MacSorley looked up and noticed Ellen standing there.

"Who the devil are you?" he shouted. "And where in hell did you come from?"

"I came from a nearby 'airplane', Ellen lied. "Captain, your ship is about to go under in this "November Witch" with most assuredly the loss of all your lives. We've come to rescue you. I have to make sure we get all of you. Can you assemble all twenty nine of you in one place? It will be easier to rescue you that way."

"Yes, I can do that, Ma'am," MacSorley answered. "But how the devil will you get us off the ship in this storm?"

"Please don't worry about that, Captain," replied Ellen, "just get going now and assemble them!"

The captain was able to get everyone together in the ready room except for the radio engineer who was trying to get the radio working again as it had just failed in the storm.

"We're all here now," MacSorley said to Ellen, "all except the radio engineer who's still trying to get the radio working again."

"Where is that room located," asked Ellen.

"Two decks below," answered the captain.

"OK," said Ellen, "I'll go get him but you all stay here. Don't stray from here at all costs." With that she dashed from the bridge to the radio room two decks below. There she found the radio engineer who was completely mystified by her appearance. The howling storm made it fairly easy for her to convince him of her rescue mission. The two of them left the radio room and went to the outside deck to speed their progress to the ready room above where the others were. Ellen urged the radio man to hurry on ahead and that she would be right behind him. When he disappeared from her sight she used her communicator to give the coordinates of the ready room to Zeltor's scout vehicle. When the engineer had safely entered the ready room she called to Zeltor to immediately transport the twenty nine men over with his Portal to his ship's cargo hold. There John was waiting to explain things to the befuddled captain and his frightened crew.

As Ellen was about to give her transporting coordinates to Zeltor a violent gust of wind blew a flying object across the deck and it struck her with great force across the back of her head and shoulders. She fell forward and her communicator went flying from her hands and was lost into the sea. Just then a huge beam fell on her and pinned her to the deck, and even with her great Gnor strength she was unable to extricate herself from underneath it. An unbelievably huge wave came after that wind gust and smashed into the ship causing her to founder; and she almost immediately went under and began to dive straight to the bottom of the lake. Ellen was afraid that her death was near unless someone on one of the ships could pick up her signs and come to rescue her as she had lost her communicator and couldn't budge the beam that was holding her.

"Strange," she thought to herself, "this situation is exactly like what happened to my John when he was rescued by Dort and Zandor in 1932. I hope someone will be able to do the same for me."

By this time the ship was almost at the lake bottom and as it hit, it broke in half. Ellen lay on the now exposed deck imprisoned by the beam, and the cold and pressure of the deep was beginning to have numbing effects on even her powerful Gnor body.

"I guess this is it," she thought. "I shall miss everyone so much; especially my John and my Molly, and the shepherding of the Earth I love so well."

***

John was worried. They had transported all the crew successfully on board Zeltor's ship, but Ellen had not called to be transferred back herself yet.

"Do you think she believes there is someone else still on board, Zeltor?" he queried of the pilot.

"It's possible," Zeltor answered. "I'll ring her up on the

communicator to tell her we have them all…that's funny; there's no link to the communicator. I'd better scan for her. Oh! Oh! The ship just got hit by a monster wave and she's going down right now! And I think I've located Ellen. She's on an exposed deck and I believe imprisoned by a large beam! I don't think I can transport her over safely until she's loosened from that beam!"

"Can you go after her!" exclaimed John. "If you could get near her, I could go out and free her and you could immediately transport us aboard!"

"I'm afraid I can't do that with these oxygen-breathing humans aboard, John," answered Zeltor. "But I'll transport you over to Joe's ship and let him know about the situation. He can follow the ship down and you can rescue Ellen as you just mentioned. Take a laser sidearm with you; it's what saved your life back in 1932 when Dort had to blast away a similar beam that had you imprisoned on the deck of that burning, sinking ship you were on!"

John did exactly as Zeltor suggested and soon he and Lt. Kennedy submerged and were plunging after the sinking Edmund Fitzgerald.

"Keep your coordinates on me, Joe," he instructed the pilot and transport us back immediately after I have freed Ellen from that beam!"

"Right, John," answered the pilot. "OK, we're there. Good luck! And hurry!"

John had Joe transport him by the Portal to the exposed deck where Ellen was held captive. He quickly made his way to his wife's side and blasted the head of the beam with his laser sidearm, freeing her almost at once. He took his wife in his arms and called to Lt. Kennedy.

"OK, Joe," he called over his communicator, "transport us now!"

With that the two shortly found themselves back in the cargo hold of Joe's ship, John still holding his wife in his arms.

"Oh, Ellen," John said, "I almost lost you!" and he bent forward and kissed his wife firmly on the lips.

Ellen opened her eyes and smiled at her husband.

"Am I in heaven?" she said with a twinkle in her eyes.

"No, but I am," John smiled down at his wife, "now that you're safe." And they kissed again.

As everyone expected, the entire crew of the Edmund Fitzgerald agreed to brain transfer and the ranks of the Gnor-human Martian colonists swelled by twenty nine more people.

Continuing their Lake Superior rescues, soon many more men and a few women were rescued from some of the 350 shipwrecks that had happened in Kitchi-Gummi. Ellen and John's research was able to determine which people didn't survive and were not recovered in these disasters so no serious problems were put forth to the time line. When this fairly large contingent of new Gnor-humans could be trained and installed around the world, it was felt that the toxic and nuclear waste disposal work force would become measurably enlarged and improved. Ellen knew, however, that there was a very good chance that more Gnor-humans would be needed in the future and that rescue missions such as these would have to continue for the time being.

***

Several weeks had gone by organizing and arranging these Great Lakes rescues, the waste disposal project from the high Earth orbit space station was progressing fabulously across the globe, and Ellen thought that the Council might now consider working on another Earth problem that the Gnor-humans could help with; that of global warming and its accompanying serious consequences for the people of the Earth. Ellen had called the Council together at their First City chambers to ask for their advice concerning this new project for Earth.

"I have called the Council together," Ellen began, "to ask if you think it is time now for us to consider working on another great problem on Earth; that of global warming. As already noted by our short travels into the future, the continued burning of fossil fuels is causing all sorts of serious problems there. I will recite for you the following litany of nine of the findings on two of our trips into the future and our concerns about these effects of global warming on the Earth.

We found:

Great losses of potable water into the seas by the melting of mountain snow, glaciers, and ocean ice. This had led to rising seas causing less and less land on which to grow food and the consequent appearance of famines here and there across the Earth.

Larger and larger defects in the ozone layer causing epidemic increases in malignant melanoma and other skin cancers (not strictly fossil fuel related but a similar wrong choice of product use that will need to be corrected).

Increasing air pollution causing an epidemic in asthma in children, and other lung problems for the increasing elderly contingent of the population.

Mercury pollution of the water and fisheries of the world with resultant organ disease and defects in adults, children, and newborns.

Increasingly severe weather with violent storms devastating man's civilization infrastructure on a massive physical and economic scale.

Intense heat waves often killing hundreds of susceptible elderly people and children.

Higher temperatures causing dehydration in the plant world leading to inhibition of photosynthesis and corn, wheat, and rice fertilization; ultimately decreasing the amount of food for the people of the Earth.

Higher temperatures causing increased desertification around the globe. This was enhanced by consequent loss of many aquifers from the necessary increase in pumping them excessively for irrigation to grow food.

Increasing numbers of plant and animal species trying unsuccessfully to travel away from the equatorial heat to survive, with hundreds of species already having become extinct.

This is a depressing litany indeed, but we have seen its start and partial fruition in our travels into the future. I believe we should go back to the beginning of the twenty first century and try to help the Earth get out of the cause of this dilemma.....the burning of fossil fuels for energy; and the overproduction of methane gas from agricultural and other endeavors. Other sources of energy were known and available at that time and I propose we use some of the great wealth we are gaining from our waste disposal project to fund their research and development. After all, it was the desire to amass large amounts of money by the fossil fuel corporate world that has inadvertently led to this problem, so why not reverse the trend and expend large amounts of money to fix it! Man has the technical capacity to switch to other sources of energy; he just needs the will to stop supporting only finite fossil fuels for energy and switch rapidly into using the renewable energy from wind, solar, and other alternative sources of power instead. As we encourage this change in thinking about utilizing renewable energy only, we can endeavor to get Earth to take the next logical step to establish a clean, hydrogen-based fuel cell energy economy. As a final maneuver, we can introduce our fusion generators as an addition to the hydrogen-powered fuel cell energy source if it is needed. It seems reasonable that if the people of the Earth had a plentiful source of free energy for all, that there would be much less reason for the wars, poverty, terrorism, and suffering that was prevalent in the early 21st century. This similar evolution of power sources did indeed lead to a peaceful state on the Gnorman planet, Mekan. Peace remained for many eons, even after they had become synthetic; and only changed with their misadventure with the synthetic lesser beings they created trying to build a totally synthetic brain. My friends, I await your thoughts and suggestions."

Dort, one of the Mayors from the city, Mekan II, was the first one to rise to speak.

"Madam Chair...Ellen," he began, "I agree and strongly believe that this project you mentioned should definitely be started now. If we continue with our shepherding of Earth there may be a good chance that we will be able to stop the deterioration that doomed our planet's race on Mekan to have to become a Synthetic Race. As you all know, Zandor and I feel that we have been instrumental in the development of the human race because of our DNA experiments here on Earth back in the time of the dinosaurs. Of late we have been having some different thoughts and feelings comparing our long life and synthetic condition to that of a shorter finite living status. We do have the advantage of longevity and great physical strength; but there is something to be said about a living finite existence as well. We can both see how that in time, when and if most of Earth's problems are erased, a finite living existence could give just as much happiness as our long-lived synthetic one does; perhaps even more. We believe our thoughts began to see this when the assimilation of the rescued human children made into Gnor-children made us realize that our race's childless existence, though quite reasonably happy, was somewhat lessened by the lack of children and the love and happiness associated with them. There certainly would seem to be arguments to conclude that both ways could work for happiness equally well; after all, we did create the Gnor-children that we now love. It has long been obvious to the Gnorman race that enduring happiness is the only true measure of reward to sentient beings; and both races are sentient beings. And we have found out that enduring happiness does not come from wealth, power and possessions; indeed, these modalities often cause its destruction. There is certainly room in this wide universe for several different kinds of races to produce happiness that is uniquely specific for each one. We both feel that to be able to help preserve the Earth people as a living race would be a very worthy endeavor and we are all for it! Perhaps, under the right circumstances, the Synthetic Race of Gnormen could have remained instead as a living one; with a completely satisfactory measure of happiness obtainable with the much more finite existence than we now have. Zandor and I now believe that an acceptable measure of true happiness certainly can be obtained by either a long lived Gnor or Gnor-human race or a short-lived human race."

"My thoughts exactly, Dort" smiled Ellen. "It is comforting to hear you speak in this way. The race of man, however, unlike the Gnormen, still needs to be taught that wealth, power and possessions do not necessarily produce happiness. But I also feel that if we continue to help Earth solve some of her continuing problems, these solutions will go a long way towards educating people to realize this truth. Some day all people will realize that sharing with, and helping the other person will give them much more of that elusive reward than trying to get and keep everything they can for themselves."

All of the Council members were in agreement with Ellen and Dort's thoughts and were ready to embark on helping to correct the global warming that Ellen and the others had found on their trips into Earth's future.

"The alternative sources of energy," Ellen began again, "such as wind, solar, geothermal and hydroelectric power are all pretty well established on Earth and have industries already producing the technology. We can help the ones out financially that need such help.

However, I believe we should concentrate our assistance with the fledgling companies that are developing hydrogen-powered fuel cells. The Gnormen had utilized this modality in their past before they developed cold fusion generators, so we should be able to jump start Earth into this technology with Dort, Zandor, and Rol's help."

"We will all be very willing and happy to do so," responded Dort. "Incidentally, right now there is a tiny company in the US in the state of New Jersey called Millenium Cell. It has developed a system it calls "Hydrogen on Demand" which is not very dissimilar to what we utilized on Mekan for our hydrogen energy system. The substance used by this company is sodium borohydride which is derived from borax, or sodium borate, a common mineral found all over the Earth. This mineral was prevalent on Mekan as well and is also what we used for our hydrogen fuel cell system using solar energy to combine the mineral with water and obtain the hydrogen safely by electrolysis within the fuel cell itself. When we finally began to run out of the mineral we were able to develop our cold fusion technology to continue our power needs."

"Yes," chimed in Ellen, "You know I remember my mother using a laundry cleaning agent like that when I was a little girl. The can had a picture of a 20-mule team on it and the name on the can was 'Boraxo'. Is it the same stuff?"

"I believe it is," returned Dort. "And the largest deposits of this mineral in the world are mined in the Death Valley desert in California in western United States. It is also found all over the world in mountainous areas in Chile, in the Andes, in Turkey, and in Tibet; so it is available for use everywhere."

"How does it work?" asked Ellen, "Is it as good as the fossil fuel that is being used now?"

"It is better by far than the current fossil fuel energy source," answered Dort, "because it is a clean one and will prevent all the terrible consequences to the planet that we saw from the global warming caused by fossil fuel burning. Its end products are water, electricity and heat; all clean products. There are no deleterious carbon emissions to cause global warming from this energy source like there is from fossil fuel burning. The water that would be produced by fuel cell fixed home energy systems could be available for use since it is obvious that the water supply may be markedly diminishing from many areas in the world in the future.. The heat produced can be used to heat the buildings so equipped with the system. And, of course, the electricity is the clean source of power made available by the process.

As to how it works; the fuel is made by mixing sodium borate (borax) with water to form a solution of sodium borohydride (SBH) and sodium hydroxide. This is the fuel to be used; and it can be stored in light weight plastic containers as it is non-flammable, non-explosive, needs no compression, and is thus very easy to transport safely. The SBH is exposed to a catalyst which produces a small amount of hydrogen gas and the byproduct sodium borate, which can be removed from the tank and reprocessed back to sodium borohydride for use again on site or at another location. The hydrogen gas is then directed to a proton exchange membrane (PEM) where it combines to form water, electricity, and heat. Thus, you have a very neat reusable fuel that doesn't pollute and produces three very useful products; water, heat, and electricity for power. A wonderful property of this half-water fuel is that it has almost the same consistency of gasoline. Thus, the gasoline could be emptied from the gas station tanks around the world and the SBH fuel placed within them. The byproduct sodium borate could be removed from a refueling automobile's tank at the gas station and reprocessed on site or sent off site for it to be done. The automobile tank is then refilled with SBH for continued driving again. Not really very different from what is done now with gasoline; and there would be very little cost converting to this system worldwide. This system is very similar to what we used on Mekan before we went to cold fusion generators for power."

"This is very exciting," said Ellen. "It would seem that we should try to encourage and help finance this technology as it would certainly obviate many of the deleterious changes we have seen happening in the future. And it looks like it might be one of the more plausible technologies to get the Earth into a clean hydrogen fuel cell economy which could definitely stop the destruction we have seen coming in the future from global warming.

"Another thing to consider, Ellen, however," said Dort, "is that this substance has a very high pH of over 13, so it is quite caustic and must be handled carefully. With more rescues of humans, we might be able to supply each gas station that reprocesses its own SBH with one Gnor-human to do the reprocessing on site there. We could have Jack Nelson set up a "Certificate of Excellence in SBH Reprocessing" that the EPA will require everyone by law to have so that each one of the Gnor-humans we assign to each station will have one and be there to do the work much more safely than a human would do. Once a human is properly trained in the safety measures necessary to work with this material, and obtains a Certificate of Excellence, the Gnor-human could leave the site. Of course, the places off site from the gas stations that have been making the SBH for years without any significant human casualties, like U.S. Borax in Boron, California, USA, should continue to do the recycling and reprocessing of the spent fuel. We could supply these companies and any new ones that start up with Gnor-humans that are proficient in running these systems and who could then train humans to work with the necessary safety measures needed so that they could eventually take over and run them themselves. Thus, we could protect humans from being hurt and keep the technology from getting a bad name because of injuries from the caustic liquid. Knowing the tenacity of the fossil fuel corporate world, they might try to use this propaganda to slow down the adaptation of this technology to replace fossil fuel energy sources."

"Dort is correct," spoke up Rol, who had risen to speak from his seat beside Zeltor behind their "Time City" placard on the table. "What we saw in the future from fossil-fuel-induced global warming is well worth attempting to correct and this should go a long way towards accomplishing this!"

With that Rol sat down and various other Council members stood to give their opinions on what Ellen had proposed. All were in agreement that the next project should be that of attempting to correct global warming by eliminating the burning of fossil fuels in order to obtain energy as much as possible. They all concurred with Ellen that they should use their finances to support alternate technologies like wind, solar, geothermal, and hydroelectric power; but that much of their effort and money should be to try to get a hydrogen fuel cell technology such as that presented by the Millenium Cell Company's "Hydrogen on Demand" system to the forefront of Earth's energy economy.

Nuclear power, although now less of a problem than it was before the waste removal situation had been solved, still had a considerably potential chance for possible disastrous complications to occur. It was felt that if it could be gradually phased out for the cleaner, safer hydrogen fuel cell technology, it would be better off for the Earth in the long run. Eventually, when and if Earth people and Gnor-humans could safely become known to one another, the instigation of cold fusion generators for power could be utilized to supplement or even replace the fuel cell technology. This would finally guarantee the availability of free energy for all with eventual equalization of opportunity for all countries, cultures, and peoples and a good start at the elimination of most of Earth's ills so prevalent at this time.

"Thank you all for your input," said Ellen as she rose to dismiss the Council meeting. "We shall start on our financial and other support endeavors to correct the global warming that threatens Earth's peoples. But although we have all been encouraged here by a possibly successful and hopeful outcome for our efforts, we must remember the old Earth proverb, 'There's many a slip between cup and lip'. But that should not deter us from making our best effort to get this job done."

***

Lieutenant Kennedy had called upon Ellen and John the night after the Council meeting had taken place.

"Since we're going to need more Gnor-humans to staff our global warming project," the lieutenant began, "and we know how much you and John like history, Lt. Willy and I wondered if a historical instance that we have been interested in might be worthwhile to set up for a rescue."

"Well, lieutenant," Ellen replied, "we certainly will probably need more colonists; what interesting situation did you have in mind for a rescue?"

"We have both been fascinated by the sinking of the civil war submarine, CSS H. L. Hunley," Kennedy answered. "It is the first submarine in history to sink a ship, and we were hoping that you and John could do the research necessary for us to take part in a rescue of the supposed nine crew members that were lost on February 17, 1864. The sub was recovered in August, 2000, about 136 years after she sank, but only eight skeletons were recovered. What happened to the ninth crew member or if there even was such a crew member has never been solved definitively. It makes the rescue even that much more interesting. Maybe we won't be able to use these sailors, however, unless Dr. Ran and the other surgeon technologists can come up with a way to hide the surgical openings in their skulls when their brains are removed. Since eight of those sailors' skeletons were recovered, the telltale operative openings in their skulls would be hard to explain."

"Yes, that might be a problem, Joe," said John, "but the mystery of the missing sailor is very intriguing, and it would be very interesting to be able to find out the truth, wouldn't it. On the whole, it sounds like a great idea, Ellen, doesn't it. You know, it's fascinating how you two pilots have become so interested in submarine rescues since you did all those for the WW II subs, the Thresher, and the Kursk."

"Yes," answered Kennedy, smiling broadly, "my navy brother Jack would be proud of us. Please let us know what you find and what Dr. Ran says about whether we will be able to mount such a rescue."

"Of course," said Ellen, "it sounds very interesting, especially about that ninth man; we'll get started on it right away. We're planning to visit the Millenium Cell Company soon to start our financial support and garner suggestions from them how we can help to jump start this technology. We'll have some time before getting started on this which should give us a chance to do the research and take part in the rescue if it becomes feasible. We'll let you know as soon as we can make a decision with Dr Ran on whether or not the rescue is possible."

"That's great, Ellen!" said the lieutenant. "I'll go and tell Will the good news. See you later!" With that he started to leave the room just as Molly was entering it.

"Hi, lieutenant!" smiled Molly, what's up?"

"Your mom and dad are going to set up another rescue for us, Molly," he smiled back. "Nice to see you, 'bye!"

"What rescue, Mom, Dad?" asked the young Gnor-woman with excitement creeping into her face. "Can I go on it too?"

"Well, we'll see about that, Molly," her father answered. "Your mother and I will have to do research on it first. It's about the sinking of a U.S. civil war submarine, the Hunley, in which Lieutenant Kennedy says there apparently were no survivors. The strange thing is there were supposed to be nine crew members on board, but 136 years after its sinking the sub was raised and only eight skeletons were recovered in it."

Yes, dear," put in her mother, "it sounds like an interesting case for a rescue, and since the skeletons have now been recovered we will have to check with Dr. Ran to see if something can be done about concealing the surgical openings in their skulls."

"You know, mother," said Molly, "Josh is really interested in history; it's one of his hobbies. He may know something about the sinking, and I know he'd be very interested in going on the rescue."

"Well, we'll see," answered her mother, "in the meantime I'll get started on the research. Since the sub was located in the year 2000, it would be reasonable to look at research done in 2003. More information should be available about it by that time. We can get Zeltor to fly us to Earth around that time and I'll visit the appropriate library to get the information."

"Can I go with you, mom?" asked Molly, smiling broadly. "I'm older now and won't get into any trouble like that first time I went with you to an Earth library when I was a little girl."

"Yes, of course you can come," answered her mother, also smiling. "I guess I can trust you not to get picked up by any strange men this time. And if you do it will probably be their misfortune, what with all the training you've had recently with Commander Traynor's Special Force." All three smiled, remembering the time when Molly had been kidnapped on Earth and they had had to rescue Sarah Ran from death at the hands of the little girl's kidnapper. "As for Josh, we can pick him up on Earth just before we travel back in time to get to the location of the submarine's sinking. Why don't you contact him and set that up, Molly?"

"Great, mom," Molly replied, "I'll do that right away. I know Josh would love to go and it will be fun to have him along."

"What about Ares?" asked her mother, with a knowing look towards her husband. Do you think he might be interested in going also?"

"Well," responded her daughter, "I think Ares is very busy working on some new technology in the Life Factory, and has already arranged to contact Jeanne and bring her up here for a personal tour of the facility. I can ask him, but I think he'll be much more interested in the tour with Jeanne than the rescue mission with us."

Ellen walked over to her daughter and put her arm around her shoulder.

"How are you getting along with Ares these days, dear," she said. "You two used to be pretty good friends in the not too distant past."

"Yes," chimed in her father, "and Ares usually would jump at the chance to go on a mission with you."

"Slow down now, you two matchmakers," smiled Molly. "Ares and I are still very good friends like we always have been. That will never change; but I think Ares has been bitten by the love bug with Jeanne. I certainly don't begrudge him for that at all. I love Jeanne and think she's a wonderful person and I'm happy that Ares feels about her the way he does. So stop worrying about us, you two. We're the good friends we've always been and probably will continue to be forever."

"It's good to hear how you feel, dear," said her mother, giving her a hug. "Your father and I have noted the changing relationships going on between you young people and are happy with it as apparently you are also. And on that subject, how are you and Josh getting along these days?"

Molly looked at her mother and smiled. "It's darn lucky I can't blush, mom," she said, "or else I'd probably be beak red right now. Seriously, though, I guess I really am attracted to Josh a lot. The sad part is, though, Josh apparently feels very inadequate because he does not have all the abilities that we Gnor-humans have, and I think it inhibits him in how he relates to me. It makes no difference to me whatsoever, because I feel deep inside that I am just as human as he is; but unfortunately it does affect his thinking."

"Don't sweat it, Molly," said her father, "Jeanne and Josh have spoken to us about how they are seriously considering brain transformation now that their parents are both Gnor-human. It looks like there is a good chance that you will all be the same very shortly."

"Oh, daddy," said Molly beaming, "that would be wonderful!" And she ran over to him and gave him a hug.

"Well then," said Ellen, "it's all settled. We'll get started tomorrow on the research and check with Dik Ran about the skull problem.

***

Ellen and John had spent some time on the research of the Hunley's sinking and had invited Lieutenants Kennedy and Willy over to their apartment in Harvard Square to discuss what they had found out about the possibility of doing a rescue mission of the vessel. Molly had requested to be in on the discussion since she was going on the mission with them as well. They were informed that Josh would also be present and had been very pleased that they had considered taking him along. The lieutenants informed Ellen that they had discussed submarine history with Josh when they had been introduced to him in the past and were impressed with his knowledge and passion about the historical aspect of the U-boats.

"Well, lieutenants" began Ellen, "there was more than enough information available about the Hunley in the Charleston Library. And guess what? Dr Ran informed us that they had already developed a process that allows them to transfer the consciousness and memories from the living brain into the synthetic brain without having to open the skull anymore. He said they have been doing this for some time now just in case some of the bodies did get recovered at some later time. He said that in many of your WWII submarine rescues the sailors had the benefit of this process in force when their bodies were returned to the ships. It apparently has become a quick process that they now do routinely. So it looks like there is no reason why we can't perform this rescue mission after all. It could get us as many as twenty-two more Gnor-humans for our global warming needs if they are willing to join us."

"That's great!" remarked the two pilots. "What did you find out about the submarine?"

"You know," replied Ellen, "what's particularly interesting is that this submarine actually sank three times; once on August 29, 1863; again on October 15, 1863; and finally for the last time on February 17,1864. The first sinking happened during training and three men escaped and five drowned. We know who did what so we should be able to rescue the ones who drowned after the ones who survived get out. In the second sinking, again during a training run, eight men drowned; including the designer and captain of the ship, H.S. Hunley. They gave his name to the submarine after his untimely death, calling her the CSS (Confederate States Ship) H.S. Hunley. We should be able to save all eight and get the bodies back in the submarine before it is salvaged. In the last and final sinking nine men supposedly were drowned; but when the ship was finally salvaged in August of 2000, almost 136 years later, only eight skeletons were recovered from the ship. If there actually were nine men in the submarine as history has held for 136 years, when we rescue them we will not have to put the ninth sailor back in the submarine since only eight skeletons were recovered. In this time line it would have to mean that one sailor must have escaped, which will leave us the moral dilemma as to what to do about him. If we find out that he escaped from the ship, drowned outside and was pulled out to sea by the tide and never found, then we can rescue him earlier and not put him back into the sub as we said originally. If instead he swam safely to shore we will have to abandon enrolling him for our purposes and be content with rescuing only the other eight. At any rate, it should be a very exciting rescue with a final solution to what has been a 136 year old mystery for many concerning the actual number of sailors that were present in the Hunley. Zeltor and Rol said they would be very happy to fly one of the starships to Earth and wait for us in high Earth orbit to return us to Mars. They have to fly supplies there to the waste removal space station anyway and it would be reasonable to combine the two missions. You two can then fly us to the surface in a scout vehicle under electronic jamming cover to pick up Josh at an appointed rendezvous spot. After we pick him up we can travel on to the different Hunley sinkings using the time warp mechanism we'll have on the scout vehicle. It would be reasonable to submerge a distance away from the area and proceed underwater to each of the sinking sites and thus easily avoid being discovered when we rescue the sailors.

Well, what do you two think of our plan?"

"We love it!" said Lt. Kennedy, smiling broadly at his companion who nodded in agreement. "When do we go?"

"Zeltor said we could be ready for early next week," answered Ellen. "We'll plan to leave on that date. See you then!" With that the meeting broke up and the two pilots left the room to return to their apartment in Hyannisport.

"Oh boy!" almost squealed Molly, "I can hardly wait! This should turn out to be a tremendous rescue mission!"

"It should certainly be different," said her mother. "That's for sure!"

***

They approached the Earth high orbit waste removal space station and Zeltor docked the great silver Starship flawlessly.

"I'll be here waiting for you when you return," he said to Ellen and John. "Good hunting!"

"Be very careful of that possible ninth man in the third sinking," admonished Rol. "It could be devastating to the time line if he had escaped, made it safely to shore and lived; and then we kept him with us, changing everything in the time line that would have happened to him and his relationships with others in the past."

"Don't worry, Rol," said Ellen, "we'll be very careful."

Lts. Kennedy and Willy flew the rescue party to Earth and using electronic jamming, picked up Josh without being discovered. Then they set the time warp mechanism to get them to the site of the first sinking on August 29, 1863, the night before it happened, and submerged the scout vehicle near the area and waited. Molly and Josh set up to monitor the sensors and make tapes of them to be able to convince the sailors that they were about to drown and had been rescued by the team on the scout vehicle.

With the Portal they were able to rescue the five men who were left in the submarine to drown after the first two men escaped from the front hatch and the last one from the rear hatch. All five of the men agreed to brain transfer after they were informed of what was to happen to them and shown the tapes of it happening. Being part of a very innovative technology for their day, they were amazed and excited about the scout vehicle and its technology and listened in awe when it was explained to them by Ellen and John and the two pilots. They were all amazed at Molly's and Josh's sensor tapes that showed them drowning in their future.

The scout vehicle then rapidly returned to the Starship where surgeons and technologists transferred the sailors' consciousness and memories from their living brains into their new synthetic ones and copied their faces to their new synthetic bodies. The old bodies were then returned to the submarine before their recovery could be accomplished by the Confederate navy.

The second rescue on October 15, 1863, was set up in a similar fashion, arriving there beforehand, submerging, and waiting. This time all eight men in the submarine were to be drowned and it took some time for the people above to recover the ship, so they were able to rescue the men easily. A similar flight back to the Starship was made again with brain and face transfers as with the first group. Again the bodies were returned to the ship before it was recovered.

The scout vehicle returned to Charleston Harbor on the evening of February 17, 1864, submerged, and waited again for the submarine CSS HL Hunley to appear on its mission to sink the blockading ship, the USS Housatonic. The scout vehicle's sensors soon picked up the Hunley as she was approaching the Housatonic as both the scout vehicle and the Hunley were on the same side of the Housatonic.

"The submarine is on the surface, not submerged!" exclaimed Lieutenant Kennedy. "I guess they've become a little gun-shy because of the drownings that occurred when they submerged in training."

"Maybe not," said Ellen, "perhaps they can make more rapid speed on the surface. This would enable them to get closer to the Housatonic to attach the torpedo they're carrying on that extended shaft out in front of the main body of the submarine before they are discovered and easily sunk by the warship. They may then submerge and wait or retire from here for there certainly will be a plethora of boats all over this area once the torpedo detonates and sinks the Housatonic as we know it did. They will have to worry about the tide as it is going out rapidly right now and could carry them out to deeper water where the chance of drowning is even greater. Well, we'll soon know what happened and if there are eight or nine men in the Hunley."

"Josh," asked John, "can the sensors tell us yet how many men are in the Hunley right now as she approaches?"

"It's a little muddied at this moment but should clear up in a second," Josh replied. "Jackpot! There are nine men in the submarine!"

"It looks like history was correct," said Molly.

"Yes," remarked Ellen, "and now we have to find out who that ninth man was, or I should say "is" at this juncture, and how he escaped from the submarine while the others all perished. It is best we just observe exactly what happened and then return to the proper spot for rescuing with the time warp mechanism. That would include enough time to be sure about what happens to that escaping man and whether he lives or dies; Rol was very explicit about us doing this and protecting the time line."

"Right," agreed John, "We'll just have to sit and watch the show for awhile before we do the rescue. Molly, will you and Josh make a tape again of the sensors' findings like you did on the other two sinkings? We will need it to show the crew to convince them of their imminent deaths."

"Sure, dad,' answered Molly. "We'll set it up right now."

***

Lieutenant Dixon gathered his eight crewmen around him before they entered the submarine to set sail to attempt the sinking of the USS Housatonic, which was leading the Federal blockade of Charleston harbor, two and one half miles off the Charleston Bar near Sullivan's Island.

"Men," the lieutenant began, "We will start out at night and travel on the surface to approach the Housatonic much more rapidly than what we can do underwater. This should let us get to the ship before we are spotted and fired upon. After we have attached our torpedo to the hull we will detonate it and rapidly back off and then submerge. There will be a great number of boats swarming around here right after the detonation so we will have to stay under water as long as it is possible before we surface and try to escape. We can travel a little distance out towards Sullivan's Island, but we must deploy our grapple to hold us from being pulled out to sea by the tide where we will surely drown. When your candles go out it will mean that there isn't enough air left for us to breathe and then we will have to surface at once. At that time, Chamberlain, you will have to start baling the water from the aft ballast tank while Wicks and I do the same with the forward tank. That should get us up to the surface where we will have air and can propel the ship to safety or escape from the hatches and swim to shore. You men on the propeller cranks must apply yourselves like fury if we are to back away from the Housatonic and not be dragged down with her as she is sinking. Can you do it, men?"

"Yes sir, Lieutenant Dixon!" the men all shouted.

"Good!" replied the lieutenant. "Everybody get on board now and we'll be off to the destiny of being the first submarine in history to sink an enemy ship." And with that the nine-man crew rapidly boarded the submarine and took their positions within the ship.

Ezra Chamberlain approached the rear hatch where he would climb in to take his position at the rear ballast tank. His friend, Jim Wicks, stood next to him as he waited for Lieutenant Dixon to climb in through the forward hatch, after which he would follow him in to man the forward ballast tank.

"Jimmy," said his friend to Wicks, "what do you say we switch dog tags for luck? We may need some to get through this encounter." The two were an interesting pair on this ship as they both had switched sides from the Union to the Confederates.

"OK, Ezra," replied Wicks, "but don't worry, my friend, we'll all make it; and history as well!" And the two then switched their dog tags, placing them around their necks and started down the forward and rear hatches into the ship.

The Hunley was able to make it to the Housatonic and detonate its torpedo. She then submerged and the sailors cranked the propeller shaft with great force and were able to successfully back away from the torpedoed ship as she sank. The Hunley remained submerged and continued out towards Sullivan's Island at about three knots. Lt. Dixon released the grapple as planned so they would not be swept out to sea, and they felt the submarine's rapid flow out with the tide suddenly jerked to a halt as the grapple took hold.

"Now we wait," said Lt. Dixon. "When the candles start to flicker out, Chamberlain on the rear ballast and Wicks and I on the forward one will pump out the water in those tanks like fury to float us to the surface. If it is safe when we look out the hatches, we will try to bring the ship back to a safe port. If there are Union boats all around, we will scuttle the ship and try to swim to shore and escape in the darkness."

A variable time later the candles flickered and started to get dimmer. All of a sudden there was a tremendous rush of water from the rear hatch that rapidly filled the submarine. In the darkness that immediately occurred everyone in the ship drowned in a matter of seconds as the air had been almost totally deleted from the ship even before the water rushed in.

***

"Look!" exclaimed Josh, who was monitoring the sensors, "someone's emerging from the rear hatch on the submarine!"

"Yes," said Ellen, who was looking over his shoulder, "let's see if he makes it to the surface and lives. He doesn't seem too lively on the sensors."

Partway up to the surface the figure suddenly became limp and then started to slowly sink back down to the depths where his body began to be pulled out to sea with the tide.

"Well, Ellen," said John, "he obviously didn't make it and most likely his body will never be recovered."

"Yes," answered Ellen, "so now we can go back with the time warp mechanism and rescue all nine men."

"But won't we have to rescue them after they blow up the Housatonic ?" asked Molly.

"You're right, Molly," answered her mother, "but there should be a big enough window of time for us to do it successfully."

Lt. Kennedy maneuvered the ship back to a position underwater that would be favorable to transfer the sailors by the Portal. Lt. Willy adjusted the time warp mechanism to get them back to the time just after detonation of the torpedo as the submerging Hunley crew was desperately cranking away from the sinking Housatonic. Lt. Willy then transported the entire crew to the cargo hold by the Portal. Ellen, Molly, Josh, and John awaited the crew in the cargo hold to explain to them where they were, who the crew of this ship were, and to show them the sensor tapes of what was about to happen to them. They were told that the other crews of the Hunley that they all knew had drowned previously in training had been rescued in a similar manner. When told that the other crews had opted for brain transfer rather than drowning, all nine men agreed to do so also. Lt. Kennedy surfaced the scout vehicle some distance at sea out of view of any other vessels and flew back to the Starship at the Earth high orbit space station. The nine brain-transfers were accomplished and all faces copied successfully. They became some of the first Gnor-humans to assist in the fuel cell stations that were to dot the countryside when the global warming project was started. Only eight bodies were returned to the sunken Hunley, including Jim Wicks, with Ezra Chamberlain's dog tags still around his neck. Chamberlain's body was commended to the deep with Lt. Kennedy playing the Navy Hymn as he had done in past submarine burial services. A poem written by a southern Yankee and found by Ellen in her historical research on the Hunley was enjoyed by all involved in the project:

On a dark and chilly night in 1864,
Nine men walked their way to death and to the ocean floor.
They laid beneath the harbor and the decades they passed by.
Imagine what went through their heads that night before they died,
Losing all the air they had and rolling with the tide.
So now that we have found them there,
Let's bury them with pride.

***

Ellen and John had started the discussions back on Mars in the Council for their collaboration with the Millenium Cell Company to help start a shift to a fuel cell electric economy to replace the carbon burning one that was harming the Earth by its causation of accelerated global warming. They also encouraged assisting the companies using wind, solar, and other alternative sources of power with the funds they were accumulating from their waste disposal efforts that were now so successful worldwide. The Council established several committees to go out and identify themselves to the companies already engaged in wind, solar, and other alternative sources of power and offer Waste Management's financial aid to their businesses. They also were to encourage and financially help new companies to get started in these modalities as well. One way they could help was to pay for widespread advertising about the new technologies and why it was necessary to get out of dependence on fossil fuels, emphasizing the danger to the Earth and its people if fossil fuel burning persisted.

Ellen herself wanted to concentrate on helping companies like Millennium Cell start the fuel cell technology going, so she made arrangements to visit the company's executives in New Jersey to discuss helping them finance their operation, including paying for appropriate favorable advertising. This would make it possible for them to become better able to have the ability to push the technology more rapidly than they were able to do at present. When they met with the company heads they could see the company was dependent upon many factors happening before they could start to expand. One such critical factor was the development of the appropriate engines for autos, trucks, buses, aircraft, and watercraft to be able to use their fuel. This was happening very slowly because of the inertia of the fossil fuel driven vehicles and consumer preference for them dominating the production scene. There were some fuel cell driven autos and buses out there but very few at present; and there were no aircraft or watercraft engines available as yet. One such company with viable fuel cell vehicles was Ballard Power, Inc. They had been successful in putting out small numbers of such vehicles in a couple of cities around the world. It had been quite impressive when the mayor of Chicago introduced a small fleet of fuel cell buses that were to travel in that city. At this ceremony to present these buses to the city he placed a glass under the tailpipe of a running bus and then drank the contents of what drained from that pipe. Of course it was potable water, one of the byproducts of the fuel cell process—electricity, heat and water! Ellen explained how she thought every gas station in the US could be easily changed to carrying Millenium Cell's safe hydrogen fuel, and how her company could supply experts to help run the systems at each station. The company executives were excited about Ellen's suggestions; especially when she volunteered to help push the auto industry into producing fuel cell automobiles as fast as possible and to help finance whatever was necessary to expand their business. She left them with a suggestion that perhaps a fuel cell unit for each home might be a more reasonable product to start to produce since it would be easy to utilize wind or solar power at each home to supply the electricity necessary to turn out the hydrogen for the fuel cell unit. It would then produce clean heat, water and electricity for each home; commodities that could become quite scarce in the future. It seemed to Ellen that this product might be able to be brought on line business-wise quite a bit sooner than the automobile, which would first require the auto industry to speed up making appropriate fuel cell engines and the gas stations to be retrofitted into fuel cell stations. At any rate she left the company quite excited and happy about Waste Management's offers to help the company grow its business. Ellen also promised to lobby the governments of the world to allow tax breaks and discounts to all alternate energy companies and their related subsidiaries. It did not take much intelligence to realize how wealthier and better off health wise everyone in the world would be when these alternate energy systems with all the subsidiaries in parts and maintenance that would be necessary to support them started being manufactured in greater and greater quantities and being placed in service across the world.

As time passed, this and other companies did start the manufacture of individual fuel cell units about the size of a large refrigerator that easily supplied an individual home with abundant heat, water, and electricity. Homes with this power source began to accumulate rapidly, at first in the developed areas of the world, and clean power gradually began to replace the older fossil fuel polluting sources of energy.

***

The need for more Gnor-humans to help in the global warming fuel cell operations around the world soon made it clear that Ellen and the Council would have to continue the rescue of humans as they had been doing since the Gnormen arrived on the planet. Ellen had been asked by some of the naval aviators that had been rescued earlier if it might be possible to consider rescuing the large number of people that had disappeared in the many planes and ships lost in and about the Bermuda Triangle. Ellen agreed that this would be an exciting and rich source of the needed Gnor-humans in the global warming project and decided to bring the Council together to consider this undertaking.

At the meeting everyone agreed with the continued rescues being necessary and enthusiastically endorsed the Bermuda Triangle project. Ellen had done some preliminary research on the ships and planes that had been lost in the triangle and came up with the common denominator that instrument failure was most likely the source of most of them. However, the other peculiar unexplainable disappearances, almost right before the eyes of reputable observers, she found no real explanation for. During the meeting Rol rose from his Council seat as co-mayor of Time City to speak.

"Before we vote on taking on this Bermuda Triangle project Madam Chair," he began, "I would like to speak to you in private for a brief time if that would be all right with the Council?"

"Is anyone opposed to my doing so?" asked Ellen. "Since no one has objected, I will recess the meeting for ten minutes. Thank you. We will restart then in ten minutes." With that she motioned Rol to accompany her into an adjoining room and they sat down to talk.

"What's the matter, Rol?" Ellen began. "Do you oppose the Bermuda Triangle project?"

"Yes, I do, Ellen," he replied. "But first it is important to confess something to you that I have kept secret up to now from all the others. That's why I wanted to speak to you alone."

"You have been somewhat mysterious, Rol," replied Ellen. "What is this secret you are keeping from us all? Does it have anything to do with your frequent short absences that Zeltor has told me about?"

"Yes it does, Ellen," Rol answered. "And like always, you never fail to amaze me with your uncanny ability to grasp the correct situation right away.

Actually, I am not a Gnorman as everyone thinks I am. No, I'm a time traveler; assigned to watch over the Gnormen when they became capable of time travel. There are many potential traps in time for the unwary time traveler, and for the Gnorman's safety someone needed to council them about what they could and couldn't do safely for themselves and their future civilization. The Prime Mover was the only one who knew my true identity and he was the one who kept the Gnormen on the straight and narrow as regards time travel. That's why he gave you so much grief about time line changes."

"Wow!" breathed Ellen. "This is a bombshell, Rol. I do see now why the Prime Mover acted the way he did about time travel. I am curious though; if you're not a Gnorman, what are you?"

"Actually," replied Rol, "I was an alien from another galaxy that really doesn't matter anymore as I was changed secretly into a Gnorman in the Life Factory on Mekan by the Prime Mover. When he returned to Mekan he commissioned me to stay here with Zeltor, presumably to help him with navigation and you with training of Gnor-humans in the same discipline. He has already acquired another time traveler to aid him back on Mekan with any further Gnorman time travel problems there."

"So all those little "jaunts" Zeltor told me about when you weren't around," remarked Ellen, "were actually time explorations to make sure we were traveling in the right line?"

"Correct again, Ellen," replied the navigator. "And in my future travels in Earth's history I have noted some things that you and the Council should know about for the safety and improvement of the people; and that includes Gnor-humans and Gnormen per se. The global warming project is great and should be tremendously helpful to future people on Earth; but the Bermuda Triangle is not a place for you to go at this time."

"What do you mean, Rol?" asked Ellen. "It would seem there are a host of people that could be rescued just before they had entered the Triangle and became lost. And since their bodies were never recovered, it would make the rescues much simpler than we have usually encountered."

"That is certainly true, Ellen," explained Rol, "but this planet has several spots where the magnetic field sometimes changes inexplicably. This can apparently cause anything from time shifts into an alternate dimension, universe, or time to simple disruption of electronic functions and other wave phenomena. These conditions have caused ships to crash, become displaced in time or geographically and even totally disappear forever, perhaps into an alternate dimension, universe, or time. The Bermuda Triangle is just such an area; and there are several other areas on this planet that I have identified and will keep you abreast of their whereabouts. I don't know exactly what is responsible for these phenomena here yet, but on other planets with magnetic fields similar situations can be found. Some of them have been attributable to shifts in the molten fluid flow in the planet's interior caused by internal planetary structure that changes the direction of flow of this liquid and hence the magnetic field at that site. Other possibilities are large stretches of loss of an iron magnetic crust on a planet's surface so there is no magnetic field created since only one side of a flow is present. Earth's magnetic field, which actually protects it from its Star's solar radiation wind effect and sustains life on this planet, is created by an iron magnetic crust with a molten metal center. As the Earth rotates the liquid center rotates opposite to the stationary iron magnetic surface crust due to inertia, essentially creating the magnetic field dynamo. Other planets in this solar system that have similar opposing flowing layers in their structures also have strong magnetic fields for the same reasons. They include Jupiter, Mercury, Uranus, Saturn and Neptune. Mars has a weaker, but present, magnetic field; lesser, because of its size and rotational speed. Venus has no magnetic field because it revolves too slowly to create any opposing field flows; taking 247 days to complete a rotation that takes the Earth only 24 hours. The problem for us is that Gnor-humans or Gnormen depend on motion through a steady state magnetic field to garner enough electricity to function properly. If such individuals come in contact with a changing or absent magnetic field situation it could wreak havoc with them and also with the electronic control of the ship that they are traveling on. The ship could crash, or the people could disappear into an alternate dimension, universe, or time. Until we know more it is far too dangerous to approach the Bermuda Triangle and other similar areas and I would suggest that we scrap the project for now.

Incidentally, speaking about my past future Earth travels, I did encounter a devastating avian flu pandemic. It apparently started in China with a usually harmless-to-humans virus that occured in poultry used for food that mutated into a highly infectious airborne virus that became susceptible human to human. At the time I first encountered it, millions were being killed by it all around the globe and no treatment was very effective. A few years later a vaccine was developed in China where it had started that was successful in ridding the planet of this terrible scourge. Unfortunately, millions of people were lost before the vaccine was developed. I would suggest we abandon the Bermuda Triangle project at this time and instead travel into the future and bring back the vaccine to head off the millions that will die from it in the future."

"Well, Rol," agreed Ellen, "I certainly do agree with your suggestions and will urge the Council not to undertake the project of the Bermuda Triangle at this time. I will say that the data you have shown me about the area makes it too hazardous to attempt rescues there at this time, and that perhaps in the future when more is known we can return there. I will mention the pandemic plague and say that we noted it on one of our time travels and suggest we take on that project now instead. If it is OK with you I will keep your true identity to myself only at this time."

"It certainly is OK, Ellen," replied Rol, "It is the same situation I had with the Prime Mover for years and it worked out fine."

"Good," said Ellen, "then let's get back into the session and I'll speak to the Council about changing our projects."

Back again in session the Council seemed to understand the problem and accepted Ellen and Rol's suggestion to abandon the Bermuda Triangle project for now and concentrate on getting the appropriate vaccine from the future in time to save the millions of people that would become victims of the avian flu pandemic of the early 21st century. Ellen asked Dr. Ran if he would be willing to explain to the Council what the problem was concerning this particular flu since most cases are harmless though uncomfortable to most people.

"Yes, Ellen," began Dr. Ran, "The common human flu virus is easily tolerated by most people, but occasionally a strain comes along that can be deadly to humans. What most people don't realize is that all flu viruses usually come from birds which harbor about 16 varieties. The birds usually tolerate these viruses fairly well, so they are widely spread quite easily. About three of these viruses have jumped over and become adapted to humans and account for the winter strains people get every year. A new vaccine has to be manufactured each year because the three human strains have the ability to evolve a slightly different form each year and the vaccine must be made to match those changes. Humans handle these strains well because their immune systems have become adapted to them. But sometimes one of these other bird varieties can jump directly over to humans or to another mammal and then to humans and create a deadly virus effect as the human immune system cannot handle this new virus very well. From what I've been told, apparently seventy to ninety per cent of the people infected with the virus in this pandemic died. In fact, this virus was unusually deadly to birds as well, not the usual scenario with the avian creatures. Again, the manufacturers of the vaccine were only able to make 100 million doses per year and there are over six billion people in the world. Hence the millions that died in the outbreak. If we are able to bring back the specific vaccine and the methods developed to make it before the pandemic starts, we should be able to control the virus before it becomes widespread by having a proper stockpile to immunize the entire world before the virus appears on the scene with its deadly infection. This should save millions of lives. Without saying, it should be one of our top priorities in our shepherding of the Earth!"

Ellen thought that she, Dr. Ran, Rol, and John could have Zeltor fly them into the future to the place where the vaccine was first prepared and had been successful in stopping the avian flu pandemic. They would also take along Dort and Zandor; as they were fluent in the many Chinese dialects they learned at the time they had returned to Earth and studied its many languages to be able to interact with the people they had helped to create. Rol said that it had been a Chinese physician that had prepared the first successful vaccine in his laboratory in Shanghai, China; and that he would be able to get us to that lab quite easily.

"We are obviously going to change the time line dramatically," Ellen had confided to Rol in secret when they had discussed the project. "How do you feel about that, Rol?"

"I guess I'm getting 'humanized', Ellen," he replied. "I'm willing to chance the new universe we will be creating to save those millions of people. I don't think even the Prime Mover would let all these people die when he could save them; even if doing nothing would mean direction toward the smaller population and minimal timeline interference he cherishes. As you humans say, 'let's do it!'"

***

Zeltor ferried the group to Shanghai, China with Rol setting the time warp mechanism to the proper coordinates to get them to the right time and place. After masking the ship electronically so it wouldn't be discovered, they landed in a densely wooded area on a mountain and proceeded on foot to the city where they then took local transportation out to the suburbs to where the laboratory of Dr. Hu was located. It was midday and they had no difficulty in meeting with the doctor after they introduced themselves as physicians from America who were intensely interested in his new vaccine for the deadly pandemic that had already killed millions of people in the short time it had appeared on the world scene. Dr. Hu was gracious in meeting with the group of Gnormen, and stated that he had sent information to the NIH in America with his findings and had been waiting for an envoy from America to come and view them. He asked if they were that group he had been waiting for. Dort looked knowingly at Ellen and Zandor and stated to Dr. Hu in perfect Chinese dialect for that area that they were indeed part of that group. He stated that they were looking forward to seeing his results and taking back to America the technique for producing his saving vaccine for the American people. Dr. Hu was a true physician and was genuinely delighted to show the visitors in great detail exactly what needed to be done to produce the saving vaccine. Dort and Zandor took everything down and recorded it on the same internal apparatus that they had used when they first came to Earth in 2003. Dr. Hu was extremely hospitable to the group and gave them all the information that they needed. He wanted to invite them to a banquet before they left for America, but they declined the dinner saying that they wished to get back home and begin working on the needed supply of vaccine as soon as possible. Dr. Hu said he understood and wished them well on their journey back home. This turned out to be exceedingly fortunate as no one in the Gnor group would have been able to eat the great quantity of food usually found at a Chinese banquet. Dort thanked the doctor for his life-saving work and the group left his lab with the necessary information. They took transportation back to the outskirts of the city and then hurried on foot the rest of the way to their ship in the mountain thicket.

"It's lucky we didn't get stuck with having to eat at a banquet," said Dort. "It wouldn't have looked well if not one of us ate anything. I think that Dr. Ran, and his surgeons will have to think about constructing a GI tract for Gnormen and Gnor-humans if we are to continue with disguising ourselves from mankind."

"Yes," responded Zandor with a broad smile, "good idea, and won't doctor Hu be surprised when the real NIH group appears shortly. I doubt that they'll ever know who we were or what country we wanted the vaccine for."

"Well, anyway," said Ellen, "We have the necessary information to produce the vaccine. Now we will have to convince the pharmaceutical companies to make large amounts of vaccine that can be stockpiled for future use; and we'll have to go back three years in time before the major outbreak of the pandemic to do this convincing."

"I'm afraid that the only way we will be able to convince the pharmaceutical companies to do such an unheard of undertaking," said Dr. Ran, " is to convince them that this particular flu pandemic is definitely coming and will be world wide. There have been sporadic cases of such flus for many years, and Dr. Hu's work should make it easier and cheaper for them to manufacture the vaccine for stockpiling."

"They still won't do it, Dik," offered John. "We had better count on using our Waste Management earnings to pay them to do it. If we make it worth their while, they'll make the vaccine and stockpile it. Otherwise, the ugly face of the corporate bottom line will rear its head and kill the project."

"I'm afraid I have to agree with John, Dik," broke in Ellen. "But thank goodness we have enough money to light up the eyes of the pharmaceutical CEO's. And since it won't cost them anything thanks to our generosity, and could lead to enormous profits if all their stockpiled vaccine becomes necessary to be utilized, we shouldn't have too much trouble to convince them to do it. It will be like a guaranteed blockbuster drug for them; since we will pay them to make the vaccine the same amount they would have made with selling such a drug. And since we're giving them the method to make the vaccine, there will be no research and development costs for them either. Many of the pharmaceutical companies had decided in 2001 to make mostly so-called copy-cat drugs and only do research and development on a small number of drugs each year; thus there would be room to make the vaccines at that time. It ought to be a shoe-in for us to convince them to do it; especially since we should also be able to convince the governments of the world to help sway them by giving them legislative protection from lawsuits in the vaccine manufacture. The only problem I see is starting back in time far enough to make the amount of vaccine necessary to cover the entire globe and get the people to be immunized."

"Yes," replied Dr. Ran, "I have noted in Earth's medical history that compliance from the world's peoples has always been problematical with immunizations."

"That is true," continued Ellen, "but we should get enough of this effort done to save millions of lives that would have been lost otherwise. Dik, how many years back do you think we should start the pharmaceutical companies working on this vaccine?"

"I would estimate at least three years from the time of the beginning of the rapidly spreading pandemic," answered Dr. Ran, "and they will have to guarantee how much they can make. Also we will have to figure out how much vaccine we will need and thus how many companies we will need to make it."

"Another thing we should remember to do," volunteered Rol, "is not tell the pharmaceutical companies the year Dr. Hu's work was done. Time travel will not be understood by them and would probably kill any chance we might have in getting the pharmaceutical companies to make the vaccine."

"Of course, you're right, Rol," said Ellen as the group had reached the scout vehicle and were entering the ship. "Well, we have our work cut out for us so Zeltor, let's get back to Mars and start our strategy."

"Yes, Ma'am," replied Zeltor with a broad smile, and as soon as all were safely aboard he placed the scout vehicle into hyperdrive and headed back toward the Starship.

***

On Mars the group that had gone to China and procured the vaccine technology reported their information to the Council members who rapidly agreed to starting the project immediately in late 2003 and begin the campaign to enlist pharmaceutical companies to manufacture the vaccine for stockpiling. Ellen and Dort were enlisted to make the pitch to the pharmaceutical companies. Ellen., because of her influence with both the world governments and the pharmaceutical companies from her recognized good work worldwide in waste management; and Dort, because of his fluent knowledge of all the world's languages and his love of the peoples of the Earth whose creation he felt partially responsible for. The two of them started out early in 2003 and began their quest with the NIH of the US government. There were already sporadic cases of avian flu in Asia and Dr. Hu's work was very convincing to the NIH scientists. They recognized, as did the international WHO scientists, that this was a disaster waiting to happen; and they were in complete agreement with the stockpiling of Dr. Hu's vaccine, especially since Waste Management was to pay for most of it. The Congress of the US, also swayed by someone besides themselves funding it, was almost unanimously in favor of Ellen's and Dort's proposal; and congressional leaders agreed to formulate legislation to protect pharmaceutical companies from aggressive trial lawyers. When word was passed worldwide that the US had been in favor of Ellen's and Dort's proposal, they were able to easily convince the rest of the world's governments to also pass legislation to protect the vaccine-making companies as well; mainly because most of these companies were either in the US or greatly influenced by the US companies.

In the meantime, an accurate figure had been postulated concerning how many doses would be necessary and how many and which companies would be needed to produce this amount in time to head off the pandemic about to develop. Ellen and Dort were also successful in selling the project to the needed pharmaceutical companies; since it guaranteed excellent, and possibly tremendous, profits to the bottom line of every company. It was interesting to Ellen and Dort that several of the biggest pharmaceutical company presidents said they had often thought that the governments of the world should pay at least a partial amount with taxpayer money for such a project as this and not leave the economic and legal risk up to the pharmaceutical companies alone.

Everything progressed nicely and tremendous stockpiles of vaccine were produced and stored; waiting to be utilized throughout the world when the avian flu pandemic began to develop in earnest across the globe. It was evident that millions of lives were to be saved by the Gnor-humans' efforts, and new forays into the future by the group that had seen the devastation in the past were greatly gratified to see how many lives were to be saved compared to what had transpired in the old time line. Even Rol, who had been "humanized" as he had remarked to Ellen before, was extremely gratified to see just how many people would be saved by their project.

"You know, Ellen," he remarked, "I believe you were correct in this time line change. I have often thought that perhaps the problem with the Prime Mover's and other Gnormen's fears about changing the time line may stem from a secret believe that there is a plan for this particular universe, perhaps set up by some Omnipotent Being that doesn't want Its scenario to be changed by one of Its lowly creations. Thus the fierceness and often unfathomableness demonstrated by a universe's powers may have made the Gnormen deathly afraid of attempting to change anything at all. But, like you, I'm beginning to understand that the important thing is not to worry about "Omnipotent Beings" and to keep learning the universe's secrets so that you won't be afraid to change things that appear to be safely changeable. At any rate, it is a wonderful feeling to know that we have been instrumental in saving millions of human lives with our project, isn't it?"

"It is, indeed," replied Ellen. "Well Rol, I guess we should continue with our rescues as the global warming endeavor continues to need more Gnor-humans around the globe to help the transition into a fuel cell energy economy. Lts. Kennedy and Willy have found us several more shipwreck victims we can consider rescuing; and some of them apparently have had over a thousand casualties. John and I will start research on them shortly. You know, it would be a lot simpler if we could identify our Gnor-human race to the peoples of Earth and perhaps convince some very desirable individuals with serious illnesses to consider joining us."

"Yes," answered Rol, "but that would really change the time line very significantly, and it would be hard to predict whether its outcome would be for good or evil. I think we should stick with remaining incognito and rescuing the people already dead at this juncture; and consider something different for the future. Certainly with converting a single sick individual, it might be possible to go forward in time and see what that person's survival has done to the time line. However, at this juncture I would be worried about engaging the process with a multitude of people at the same time."

"I see your point, Rol," said Ellen, "but Cecile and Commander Traynor are examples of what I would call good outcomes from changing sick people to Gnor-human status."

"I knew you would mention those two, Ellen," smiled Rol, "and in those cases, I agree wholeheartedly. But remember, we would be revealing the Gnor-human body to the human race and it could lead to great problems if every human is not ready to properly handle Gnor-humanity with its powers and longevity. I feel we should wait for now until the situation becomes better defined. There actually have been a few problems over the years with Gnor physiology; including the effect of the brain chemicals utilized to create and stabilize the Gnor ethical and moral demeanor; and the new synthetic brain has not really had much time to be sure of its longevity and functioning either. Sometimes the desired effect is not forthcoming; you remember what happened with the lesser creatures developed on Mekan. It would not be wise to ultimately change the human race to a Gnor-human one with time travel ability if that race starts to develop problems that could make them a greater risk to the current universe than the shorter-living human race might be."

"I bow to your wise council, Rol," replied Ellen. "For now we'll stick to the selective rescuing of the already deceased."

***

Back in First City, Ellen and John met with Lieutenants Kennedy and Willy to discuss the rescue of a shipwreck that the lieutenants had in mind to add to the needed Gnor-people for the fuel cell global technology transition.

"You know, Ellen," began Lt. Kennedy, "there was another British ship that was a luxury liner like the Titanic, and was later converted to wartime use as a troopship. Her name was the Lancastria; and she was built in Glasgow, Scotland, making her maiden voyage from Glasgow to Montreal on June 13, 1922 under the name of the Tyrrhenia. This 16,000 ton Cunard-built liner was refitted two years after this voyage with a fancy new interior and given the new name,

Lancastria; and she spent many years cruising all the world's oceans. After her last pleasure cruise in 1939 in the Bahamas, she returned to New York and had her structure radically changed; painting her portholes black and mounting guns on her decks to prepare her for duty as a troopship for the British navy.

The Lancastria took part in the evacuation of the British Expeditionary Force from St. Nazaire, France, along with RAF fliers and some civilians on June 17, 1940 during WWII. It was estimated that over 7,000 people were loaded onto the former cruise ship to be taken to England. Unfortunately, the German Luftwaffe located the sitting-duck ship and sank her to a depth of 85 feet in two hours time. Estimates were that 4,500 to 5,000 people died in that attack.

Not many people have heard of this worse loss of life from any sunken British vessel because Prime Minister Winston Churchill felt that the country would not be able to stand the devastation to their morale that such news would bring. Newspapers were forbidden to print the story and survivors were not allowed to speak of the sinking under the King's Regulations. All of the people killed were listed as 'missing in action'.

We feel that these lists could enable us to research exactly who was killed, and since none were buried, that would not be a problem either. Photographs may be able to be obtained and studied, which would allow identification of the people that should be rescued. There are between 4,500 and 5,000 people that we could potentially add to our Gnor-human colonists. We could use the scout vehicles as submarines and transport the people to them via the Portal. So what do you think of our plan? Is it feasible?"

"It sounds great to me!" answered Ellen, and looking at her husband, "What do you think, John?"

"I certainly agree," her husband replied. "That is a significant number of people to be rescued, however. We will have to make careful plans as to how we will accomplish this rescue."

"I think we will have to use six scout vehicles to rescue this number," said Ellen. "I would suggest that the pilots of the ships be Zeltor, you two, Ms. Earhart, Captain St. Exupery, and Glenn Miller's pilot, Lt. Morgan. John and I, Dort, Zandor, my daughter Molly, Dik's son Ares and Commander Traynor will have to transport over to the Lancastria from each ship at the correct time to rescue as many people as we can; as John and I did on the Titanic. It will be more efficient if each person only has one ship to be thinking about, so John and I and five others should go. We should get the proper Gnor-humans in the holds of the scout vehicles to calm the people down when they are transported to our ships by the Portal. And with our time warp mechanism we can retrieve any of us that get into harm's way during the bombing if we can't get away in time.

You know, Lt. Kennedy, shipwrecks may be the most reasonable sites to find larger numbers of people to rescue as they are all in one place. There is no question that the sea certainly has taken its toll on the human race. Keep looking for these as we are becoming somewhat expert at taking part in these sea rescues. It is good that you two are interested in these shipwrecks; they certainly are productive for increasing the number of our Gnor-human colonists. John and I will start our research immediately and let everyone know when we can all get together to plan the project, and thanks as usual for your good work."

***

Ellen and John in their research were able to identify most of the people who were killed at the sinking of the Lancastria, and found most of the photographs of them as well. The plan was brought before the Council, and all the Members agreed unanimously to go ahead with the rescue. Appropriate Gnor-humans were assigned to the cargo holds of the six scout vehicles to calm the people being rescued; and to discuss with them the possibility of their joining the Gnor-human race. All was well-prepared and the project started out smoothly with utilization of the time warp mechanism on each ship enabling them all to get to the St. Nazaire harbor on the morning of June 17, 1940.

Zeltor was to be the lead ship and as they approached the French harbor at St. Nazaire he directed all six scout vehicles to immediately submerge and approach the sitting Lancastria underwater. As more and more people were taken aboard the converted cruise ship the large number of people now present soon made it feasible to transport the six Gnor-humans surreptitiously on board the vessel via the Portal. Because there was so much confusion present they were soon able to melt into the great crowd of passengers being taken on board. All six Gnor-humans quickly went about the business of identifying people that were to die (be "missing in action") and transporting them immediately to the holds of the six scout vehicles residing close by under water. The Gnor-humans assigned to the holds of the scout vehicles had a difficult time trying to explain what was going on to the thoroughly confused people transported on board, but they all did their jobs very well and soon had the situation in the six holds under good control.

Soon they had amassed about six hundred people in the ships. When the count of one hundred was reached in each ship, it sped away from the scene underwater until it reached a spot where it could immediately surface and take off. The ship then would rendezvous with one of the two great Starships in electronically-cloaked high Earth orbit to deposit the rescued people from the Lancastria. Appropriate Gnor-humans were also available on the Starships to discuss with the survivors who they were and what they were proposing to them for their becoming part of the Gnor-human race instead of dying in the Lancastria debacle occurring below. The depositing scout vehicles would then speed back to the Lancastria bombing scene and submerge for more pickups from the six Gnor-humans on board the Lancastria who continued to transport as many people to the underwater ships as they could identify. Anyone who opted for not being rescued and joining the Gnor-human race would be returned to the Lancastria at this time before making any new pick ups.

The project soon had rescued over three thousand people when German Dornier Do17 bombers arrived and began lambasting the hapless liner for about two hours. Many of the people who had been killed in the original encounter in history had already been rescued by the Gnor-humans on board; but some of the ones they had not been able to identify were now massacred by this murderous assault by the German planes. As the bombing became more furious and accurate, five of the Gnor-humans on board were forced to stop transporting victims and evacuate the Lancastria themselves to avoid being destroyed by the bombing. Ellen and John were the last two left on board as they had gone down into the engine room to try to transport everyone down there over to Zeltor's submerged scout vehicle. They knew that all in this area would be killed by an accurate bomb that would be dropped directly down the smokestack into the engine room. Unfortunately for the Gnor-human couple, that bomb drop occurred before they could accomplish the engine room transport to get the crew and themselves out of harm's way. All down there were blown apart by the blast which caused the great liner to roll onto her port side and plunge 85 feet to the sea floor.

Zeltor quickly manned the time warp mechanism when he realized what had happened to Ellen and John and retraced the time to ten minutes before the direct hit had occurred. He then transported himself by Portal directly into the engine room in a spot undetected by the crew there and quickly located Ellen and John, informing them what was about to happen to them. As most of the engine room crew members were all together in one spot, Ellen set the coordinates of her Portal for them and the three Gnor people to be transported to the cargo hold of Zeltor's ship. She then activated it just five seconds before the bomb dropped down the smoke stack into the engine room, sinking the ship and killing the few crewmen remaining that they had been unable to find to transport.

"Whew!" exclaimed Zeltor when they had arrived in the hold of his ship. "That was really close! You know, of course, that if we had remained there for just five seconds more, we all would have been blown to smithereens again by the bomb that sunk the ship; and no one was in my ship to know it!"

"It was that close?" remarked Ellen anxiously, as the three of them made their way through the confused, milling crowd in the hold to the bridge of the scout vehicle. "Did the other four get back all right? Is Molly O.K.?"

"Was anybody else hurt?" chimed in John.

"Yes, yes," said the Gnorman, now with a smile on his face, "everybody had the sense to get back before they were blown apart or otherwise killed or injured. I can't say the same for the leaders of this project though; you were both disintegrated by that bomb, along with the crew that you subsequently rescued. I had to return the time to ten minutes before the occurrence and transport over to warn you."

Ellen moved over to the Gnorman smiling broadly and threw her arms around him giving him a big hug and a kiss on his cheek.

"Thanks for saving us, old friend," she said with great feeling.

"That's one we owe you, Zeltor," said John, shaking his hand warmly. "About how many people have we been able to save so far?"

"It'll probably come close to 4,000 at this point," answered Zeltor. "I would say that we should probably not try for any more as it would obviously need several passes and we may end up losing somebody as the subsequent attempts get closer and closer together. Not only that, but the other five said they didn't think they would be able to identify any other people able to be saved."

"I would agree with that decision," said Ellen. John and I also were already having trouble to identify anyone else just before we went down to the engine room. Let's get back to the Starship and to Mars to see how many will join us as new Gnor-humans. It looks like once again another shipwreck will greatly increase the number of our Gnor-human colonists, thanks to Lieutenants Kennedy and Willy and their interest in these wrecks. Pardon us, Zeltor, but John and I must get back and try to calm those confused people down there." And the two of them sped back down the stairs from the bridge to the cargo hold.

Back on Mars, the seven Gnor-humans who had transported over to the Lancastria to rescue the victims of the disaster, assembled for discussion about their adventure on board the huge liner and why this shipwreck was so little known in history with such a great loss of life. They were all happy with what they had accomplished; and after Ellen and John had related the story of their being blown up in the engine room and then being saved by Zeltor with the time warp mechanism, they were all quite thankful to be alive and talking about it with one another.

Later, on Mars, when all the discussions were over with the rescued people, it turned out that every one of the survivors agreed to become a Gnor-human. And so after all the operations were successfully completed by Dr. Ran and his surgeons, the Gnor-human colonists' number enlarged by almost four thousand more people.

***

The nuclear and toxic waste disposal project, now set up worldwide, was progressing very well at this time, which was fortunate; as the slowing of global warming by the fuel cell project was running into a few snags. The amount of the electric power from solar and/or wind technology at each individual gas station around the Earth was often not enough to allow the electrolysis that was necessary to manufacture the liquid hydrogen product for use in the tanks of the automobiles and other vehicles. In addition, the reconstituting of the spent fuel removed from the automobiles' tanks on site when they fueled up with fresh hydrogen fuel also suffered from this lack of electric power. The drop in power would occur when the sunlight or the amount of wind was not adequate enough to supply the electricity needed to accomplish this. Obviously the governments of the world did not want to go back to a fossil fuel electric grid again, thus continuing the air pollution and global warming problems this had caused in the past; and there were no large enough solar or wind facilities anywhere on Earth at present to supply a national grid adequately. Instead, until a national grid could be powered by these alternate sites constructed on Earth or on the Moon (with the energy transported by microwave technology back to Earth to be changed to electricity), more and more of them began to turn to the use of nuclear power for the energy needed. Since they now had an excellent method for getting rid of nuclear waste through the Gnor-humans' Waste Management space station, the change to nuclear power actually turned out to be a fine interim solution. There still was the problem of the rare possible contamination at the power plant site; but when the alternate energy national grid was completed these plants could be dismantled and disposed of as were all the rest of the nuclear wastes. All this added pressure on Waste Management, however, caused Jack Nelson to humorously complain that it was giving him so much more work that he couldn't see his wife and children as much as he'd like to.

"Some day," Ellen had remarked, "if we are ever able to safely identify our Gnor-human race to the rest of humanity, we will be able to share our fusion generator technology with them. This will result in the instant availability of the free energy that will subsidize materialism for all, and the dissolution of any legitimate reason for war or greed. Power will still be able to be obtained, as it seems that individual humans will always seek this as part of their happiness. But it will be obtained in the proper manner by the ones who will deserve to have it. Methods and incentives to help one another will gradually cause competition to give way to cooperation; especially since with enough energy for appropriate space and Earth-ocean colonization, the thinning out of the population could cause competition to become obsolete with few people doing the same job. This is what has happened on Mekan with the Gnormen."

***

After Molly's return from the Lancastria rescue, she had decided to join Josh again at the space station where he had almost become a fixture as some of his ideas about space station technology had turned out to be extremely helpful in the building of the station. He was very happy to see Molly when they met on the station. He began again to think about becoming a Gnor-human when he saw how easy it was for her to get around the station without the need for oxygen and the much heavier environment suit that he had to wear. Molly was aware of his chagrin at not being able to do what the other Gnor-humans on the station could do; but until he decided to undergo the transforming operation she did all she could to make it easier for him to function there on the station. She began to realize now how much Josh meant to her and was obviously falling deeply in love with him. Josh also had realized that he felt the same about her as well, which made him lean more and more towards considering the operation. It was impossible for them to be intimate in the space station environment and obvious that they would have to wait until they were on Mars in the Oxygen Quarters or back on Earth before their true feelings would be able to be fully realized. Molly day-dreamed about this often on the space station and looked forward to the time when they could express all their feelings for each other on Mars or Earth. She secretly hoped that Josh would undergo the Gnor-human operation soon so that she could be with him completely anywhere.

One day, right after Molly and Josh had observed a nuclear waste-firing into the sun from the aft section of the space station where it was done, a section of debris which had broken off from one of the

Russian satellites which occasionally passed by the station came into a trajectory right toward the section of the station where the two were moving their way along the guide rail back to the operations area. Without warning the debris hit the back of Molly's helmet and knocked her off the guide rail into space. As she drifted away from the station in a dazed state, Josh secured his safety rope to the guide rail and lunged after her. He was able to reach her and she threw her arms around him to secure herself to him. He then called the inside of operations on the station with his communicator to ask for help, moved Molly in front of him for security, and began to pull them back to where his safety rope was secured to the guide rail. On the way back another piece of debris struck the back of his environment suit slashing it open and cutting him deeply across the back as well as exposing him to the cold and vacuum of space. In less than a few minutes Josh was close to death inside the remains of his suit, as the people from the operations area were arriving on the scene to help. Josh managed to get them to the guide rail before he lost consciousness; and the two were quickly grasped and brought into the operations area inside the space station where Molly frantically tried to revive Josh to no avail. She called her mother on Earth who advised her daughter to place Josh immediately into the nutrient fluid tank that was present on the station to be available in an emergency to save the brain of any human that such a catastrophe happened to while there. Molly did so at once and the two of them were transported in a scout vehicle to a Starship which had been bringing supplies to the space station. The Starship then flew them rapidly back to the First City spaceport on Mars and Josh was taken immediately to the Life Factory in the Oxygen Quarters. In the meantime Ellen had notified Jack and Cecile, and she, John, and the two Nelsons were quickly picked up on Earth by Zeltor who ferried them as fast as possible to First City. Dr. Ran and his surgeons were ready for Josh when he arrived with Molly from the space station and took him immediately into surgery where they were prepared to transfer his brain into a synthetic one in the Life Factory. The four parents arrived from Earth and proceeded to the OR waiting room in the Life Factory where they met Molly, who was very distraught over what had happened.

"Oh, Mom!" began Molly, "Josh saved me on the station when a piece of errant debris from one of the Russian satellites knocked me off into space. He dived after me and caught me and brought me back to the platform. But on the way back another piece of debris slashed his suit open and k…killed him. Oh, he has to be all right! I love him so much!"

Ellen put her arms around her daughter to comfort her.

"Don't you worry, Molly dear," soothed her mother, "you know Dik Ran will pull him through this with flying colors. And your father and I know how you feel about Josh. We both also like him very much as well."

"Yes, Molly," said Cecile, walking over to the two of them, "as much as I am a worrying mother, I have great personal confidence that Dr. Ran will pull Josh through this intact. Don't you worry, dear."

"Sure thing, honey," chimed in Jack, "as worried as I am, I also know how talented Dr. Ran is. I'm sure Josh will be fine. And both Cecile and I are also quite happy about you and Josh. Incidentally, he has talked to me about having the operation he is now undergoing and was actually considering doing it."

At that point Sarah Ran emerged from a door leading to the operating suite to inform them about the progress in surgery.

"Dik wanted me to let you know that everything is going very well and it appears that there has been no damage done to Josh's brain at all. At this point he appears confident that Josh will do very well!"

Molly rushed over and threw her arms around Sarah's neck and gave her a big hug.

"Oh, thank you, Sarah!" she exclaimed; and then, a little sheepishly, "I know you and Dr. Ran had always thought of Ares and me getting together; but somehow I have fallen for Josh. Ares knows all about it and says he is OK with it."

"Yes, he is," responded Sarah. "We have discussed it. He seems to have become quite enamored of Jeanne in the meantime. He has told us that he expects that the four of you will remain good friends for some time."

"Yes," answered Molly, "that's how I feel exactly." And she hugged Sarah again; obviously very relieved about Josh and immensely happy about the seemingly successful outcome expected with his operation.

A while later on Dr. Ran emerged from the operating suite and related the good news that Josh was doing very well and he expected no brain damage to have occurred.

"Remember," he said, "even if we find any future problems, we can always go back in time and prevent this. But being a true Gnorman, I'd rather do it this way instead of chancing any problems with the time warp mechanism. The Prime Mover and I have had some discussions about this in the past and since Josh has already discussed with me about doing this, I'm happier doing it this way and not having to change the time line, even a little."

"Oh, thank you so much, Dr. Ran!" said Molly as she rushed over and hugged him. When can I see Josh?"

"You can see him shortly, Molly," answered Dr. Ran, "but remember, his living brain's consciousness and memories have just been transferred to his synthetic brain so he will act dazed for some time before everything settles out and he becomes his normal self again. Don't let his foggy mental condition at this time scare you."

"Oh, yes, I realize that, Dr. Ran," said Molly, "I just want to see him and hold his hand for a minute."

"Sure, Molly," said the doctor, winking at Ellen, "we can arrange that."

Just then Ares walked in to the area and walked over and put his arm around Molly's shoulder.

"Don't you worry, Molly," he smiled at her. "We'll take good care of your boyfriend. Don't forget, he's one of my best buddies as well. We'll pull him through OK."

"Thanks, Ares," answered Molly with a grateful smile on her face, "I know you will, and I thank you for your understanding."

"That's what friends are for, Molly," responded Ares with a broad smile on his face. "Incidentally, where's Jeanne? I thought she'd be with you people. I know how fond of Josh she is. Didn't she come up with you?"

"She didn't feel too well today," answered Cecile, "so we didn't bring her up. We'll do so probably tomorrow. She really wanted to come up today, but we thought it might be a little too much for her."

"Is she OK?" asked Ares, with a concerned look on his face. "I know she has a metabolic problem that bothers her."

"Yes," answered Jack, "it seems that her condition has been worsening lately. I keep a connection with her activated at all times just in case something does happen. It's similar to the one that Commander Traynor had on me that was so helpful when Cecile and I were kidnapped that time."

"Well," said Ellen, "I guess John and I will head back to Earth with Zeltor, now that it appears Josh is doing well. We are looking into some problems with water on Earth, which might be the next project we may need to take on. Zeltor can bring Jeanne on his trip back if you wish."

"That would be great!" said Jack. "Then we'll probably all be going back ourselves a few days later; when it looks like Josh is progressing as planned." Cecile had wanted me to go back with you and check on Jeanne and come back with her, but I think I'd rather stay and be sure about Josh and let Zeltor bring Jeanne back."

"Dad," said Ares to Dr. Ran, "would it be OK if I went back also? I would like to help Jeanne get prepared for the trip here and make it more comfortable for her. You probably won't need me right now."

"OK, son," answered his father with a wink at his wife, "I'm sure you won't be worth much until you're sure Jeanne's condition is stable. Go ahead."

"Thanks, dad," said Ares. And the two men and Ellen went out to prepare for the trip back to Earth.

On the way to Earth in the Starship an emergency message was transmitted to the ship saying that Jeanne's distress signal had been activated and could they check on her as soon as they arrived there. Zeltor replied that they would go there at once in the scout vehicle and keep the Starship electronically cloaked in high Earth orbit in case they had to take Jeanne back immediately.

When they arrived on Earth, Ellen, John, and Ares proceeded directly to the Nelson's home and found Jeanne in a compromised state with increasing lightheadedness and great weakness in her muscles. Apparently her metabolic problem had suddenly become much worse. She was unable to get out of bed by herself so Ares picked her up and carried her out of her bedroom into the living room. Ellen called Zeltor on her communicator who transported them all aboard the scout vehicle with the Portal. Ellen called Dr. Ran and told him to prepare possibly for the last Nelson to have a brain transplant because Jeanne's metabolic problem had rapidly deteriorated and she was having considerable trouble at this time.

Then Zeltor dashed the scout vehicle back to the Starship which rapidly flew back to First City on Mars. All the way back to Mars Ares remained next to Jeanne, supporting her head and comforting her with reassurances that his father would be able to restore her to perfect health as a Gnor-human.

"I believe this as well, Ares," she said, looking up at him with her eyes sparkling, "I have been looking forward to this procedure so that then I can be to you what I want to be."

Ares looked down fondly at the pale young woman and bent his lips down close to her ear.

"I would want that very much myself, my darling Jeanne," he whispered to her. "I will look forward to it after your operation is completed."

At that moment Ellen approached the couple and spoke reassuringly to Jeanne about her upcoming operation.

"Don't be too worried about this procedure, Jeanne, dear," she said. "We've all been through it and have all done extremely well. Ares father and his surgeons are all fantastic technicians. You will be very pleased with your new Gnor-human body, and will feel and really be the same as you were before but much better and stronger than you have ever been; you will love it!"

"I'm sure I will, Ellen," answered Jeanne, "and thank you so much for your kind interest in me."

"You're very welcome, dear," said Ellen. "By the way, your brother's operation went through without a hitch and he is already on his way to complete recovery. I called your mom and dad to inform them about what's happening with you and about your choice of undergoing the operation; and they said they were glad you decided this way and were anxious to see you. Your dad had his usual humorous remark in the face of something he is really concerned about; and said to me that it looked like Dr. Ran was issuing "Green Stamps" for Nelson brain transferences, doing two Nelsons in less than twenty-four hours."

"Yes," said Jeanne, smiling, "that sounds like Dad. He always jokes when he's worried, God love him!"

When the Starship docked at the First City spaceport, Zeltor transported Ares, carrying Jeanne, directly into the Life Factory Oxygen Quarters by the Portal where Ares deposited her onto a waiting OR stretcher. This saved Jeanne from having to don an environment suit to transfer from the Starship spaceport to the Oxygen Quarters; something that would have been very difficult for her to do in her current condition. Cecile greeted her there, hugged and kissed her and told her not to worry; and that she will love her body afterwards.

"Yes, and so will Ares," whispered her father, who had just entered with Ellen and John, bending low to her ear and winking at his daughter.

"Oh, Daddy," blushed Jeanne; but then seriously, "yes, I really do love him Daddy, and he loves me."

"Yes, I know dear," said her father, "your mother and I are very happy for you both. Now go in there and have your operation! We will see you later with your spanking new perfect body." And with that he bent down and kissed his daughter on the forehead.

Jeanne's operation also went smoothly and it appeared that her metabolic disorder had nothing to do with her brain but was just a muscle-wasting type of illness. Therefore, a completely normal brain's consciousness and memories were transferred during the operation to her new synthetic brain. Several weeks later both Josh and Jeanne Nelson successfully became full-fledged Gnor-humans; and just like their parents, assumed normal human activities back on Earth. Both, however, were anxious to become full-fledged Gnor-human "Shepherds of Earth."

The four friends; Molly, Ares, and the Nelsons; became even closer after the two Nelsons successfully completed their brain transference and became Gnor-humans like the other two. They joined Commander Traynor's Special Force and all four greatly enjoyed working out together, honing their physical and mental skills to a sharp readiness. Commander Traynor was very impressed with the four's constantly improving abilities and discussed with Ellen and John about developing a top tier elite group from his Special Force of Gnor-humans that would work independently in very difficult assignments reserved for their special expertise.

"It would be made up of the young Nelsons, Molly, Ares, me, and three others I have personally trained," the commander explained to Ellen. "You, John, and the older Nelsons could consult on and take part in certain assignments that you wanted to be a part of or that we needed you on."

"I think that's a splendid idea," said Ellen. "Don't you think so, John?"

"I do, indeed," replied her husband. "I for one would definitely want to be at least on the thinking part of this team. I'm sure there have been many times in the past, and will probably be just as many in the future, that will need a specially-trained, mobile, talented group different from your regular Special Force unit. Specific situations detrimental to mankind might be handled best by just such a specially-trained team."

"Yes," said Ellen, "set up your elite team, Paul; John and I would be proud to be a member of this team, able to help out in any way we can. I will speak to Jack and Cecile, and I'm sure they will also want very much to be a part of this team as John and I do."

"Great!" said Commander Traynor, "I'll make all the arrangements and let you know when we should meet for instructions and practice sessions. I'll arrange the mandatory sessions to take place both on Mars and Earth so that the training will be convenient for everyone. The mandatory sessions should be enough for any Gnor-human to become well-schooled in what will need to be learned. Later, individual practice sessions will be arranged at convenient times and places for everyone. Eventually the team will be ready for any of these specific situations that might come up where expertise above that of our standard Special Force is needed. I'll get a time schedule out to everyone involved very shortly. I have already discussed this with the young people I mentioned before and they are all excited about creating this elite team as I'm sure you both knew they would be."

"Yes," answered Ellen, "It's certainly like them. John and I will look forward to the training sessions; but Paul, please let us know with enough time so that we can plan our other commitments. Also, have you considered giving this group a special name? How about the Gnor-human Intelligence Team (G-HIT)?"

"That's pretty catchy, Ellen," answered the commander. "G-HIT, I like it! If everyone agrees, then that's what the team's name will be!"

***

Everyone involved was excited about creating the new elite Special Force team, G-HIT, and tackled their training sessions with great enthusiasm. Commander Traynor was especially pleased with the performance of the seven young people he had asked to become a member of this team. He confided to Ellen, John, and the senior Nelsons during one of their training sessions together on Earth that he was very proud of the way they had progressed and was certain G-HIT would be able to perform the duties required of it very well and very soon.

"That's good to hear, Paul" remarked Ellen. "I'm sure we'll need the team in the future, and you never know exactly when that might be. It's very reassuring to hear that you think it will soon be ready. How do you think our older contingent is doing? Do we pass muster yet?" All four were smiling broadly at Ellen's question to the commander.

The commander smiled back but then answered in a more serious mode.

"I'll tell you the truth, Ellen," he remarked, "You four are very little different in your responses to the training; although you don't have quite as much enthusiasm as your younger teammates. None the less, I would not be worried about any of your abilities being enough to help any of our missions to be successful. It is especially remarkable to me how well you and John perform, Ellen; knowing as I do how old you both are. It is a great tribute to your Gnor-body!"

"It is a wonderful thing, indeed, Paul," answered Ellen. "That is why it is such a great privilege to be able to help in shepherding our human brethren through their trials and tribulations since they don't have such a body to help them as we do."

"Incidentally, parents," began the commander, "I'm not sure if you know so I felt that I should inform you; Ares and Jeanne have become very fond of each other. A similar situation exists between Josh and Molly. I suspect that each couple will be coming to you shortly to ask if they could consider living together in their own apartment. I overheard Josh and Molly talking about it after a training session. I hope I haven't upset you but I thought you should know; they are all obviously very much in love."

"No, Paul," answered Ellen, "You haven't upset us, and the four of us have suspected this would happen at any time. We've been waiting for them to tell us and will gladly give them our blessing to do so. We all know that the liaisons between them will do nothing to dim the great friendship they all have for each other. John and I were recently discussing how it is too bad that there is no marriage ceremony between Gnor-humans. The brain chemicals given to us in the Life Factory may help our fidelity to one another, but since we don't seem to have lost our human emotions, it is too bad that such a ceremony couldn't be restarted again. Maybe we can do so with our four young people; we'll see what develops when they talk to us about their love for each other as I'm sure they will."

***

Amelia Earhart had sought an appointment to converse with Ellen in Ellen's capacity as Chair of the Council, about mayoral matters in her city, Electra. The conversation drifted away from the mundane political situations being discussed and progressed to a dialogue about women flyers. Amelia remarked about how sad it was when she encountered in her reading of space flight history that all seven of the astronauts aboard the space shuttle, Columbia, which included two women, had been killed in a tragic reentry of their ship coming back from its successful mission in space.

"Yes it was tragic, indeed," said Ellen. "Rocket transportation out of Earth's gravity has always been hazardous; one in every two thousand launches has often ended in disaster. If it becomes possible for us to identify ourselves to humanity, we will introduce them to our magnetic climbing drive and fusion generators for the safe power needed to leave their gravitational prison to travel to places beyond Earth. As you know, we already are using such powered craft in our waste disposal operation; which is why it is so successful; but unfortunately we still must keep such drives under wraps until it becomes safe to reveal them to humanity."

"Yes," remarked Amelia, "I can certainly understand that. But Ellen, have you considered the possibility of rescuing those seven astronauts? I noted in my reading that there was a loss of contact with the reentering shuttle for a period of time just before it disintegrated. During that brief period it might be possible to extract the crew by the

Portal into a nearby cloaked scout vehicle. This would give us some excellent potential pilots, and pilots are becoming more and more needed as we expand our shepherding of Earth's peoples."

"I didn't know about that brief period of time before the ship disintegrated, Amelia," said Ellen thoughtfully. "I believe you may be right and we could rescue those seven! They certainly could help our burgeoning pilot work load, that's for sure. John and I will do some further research on the crew and then call a meeting of the Council and see if they would sanction our attempting to rescue that unfortunate group of individuals. I agree that it's a good possibility for us to be able to do so."

The research by Ellen and John revealed that the Space Shuttle Columbia was the first ship in NASA's orbital fleet. The ship was constructed in Palmdale, California starting in 1975. It was delivered to the Kennedy Space Center for trials in 1979. During this early testing at the space port two workers were killed and four others injured. Thus, the beginning and ending of this ship's service was not very auspicious. Between these two tragic periods, however, the Columbia managed twenty-eight successful missions into space. The ship was named after the Boston sailing ship, Columbia, which was the first sloop to sail around the world. Several "firsts" were enjoyed by Columbia. The first mission occurred in 1983 with six astronauts; one being the first non-American. In 1986 Columbia launched the first Hispanic astronaut, as well as the first Congressman, Bill Nelson into space. In 1998 Lt. Col. Eileen Collins was slated to become the first woman commander of a future Columbia space mission, which she never was able to fulfill because of the disaster on February 1, 2003.

The Columbia, on all of her missions, took part in 28 flights, over 300 days in space, finished 4,808 orbits around the Earth, and traveled over 125,204,911 miles in her exemplary service to NASA. Just as the sailing ship she was named after might have been dubbed the 'Gem of the Ocean', perhaps she could have been said to be the 'Gem of the Skies'.

Rick Husband, a colonel in the USAF, was commander of the Columbia's mission; which included sixteen days in space where eighty research experiments were carried out working twenty-four hours a day on two alternating shifts. William Mc Cool, a commander in the USN, was the pilot; Michael Anderson, a Lt. Col. in the USAF was a specialist; David Brown, a captain in the USN, was one of the physicians; and Laurel Clark, a captain in the USN, was the other physician on the mission. Ilan Ramon, a specialist, was the first Israeli astronaut; and Kalpana Chawla, another specialist, the first female Indian astronaut on such a mission.

On February 1, 2003, Columbia entered the atmosphere and NASA lost radio contact about 9 a.m. The craft was expected to land at Kennedy Space Center in Florida around 9:16 a.m. but disintegrated in flames over Texas, 39 miles above the Earth traveling at a speed of 12,500 mph. All seven astronauts were lost.

It was this short period of radio silence that the Gnor-humans were to try to extricate the living astronauts from their doomed ship to the cloaked nearby scout vehicle piloted by Zeltor.

When Ellen called the Council meeting together, it quickly became obvious that all were enthusiastic and agreeable to rescuing the seven unfortunate space travelers. With this positive commitment by the Council, Ellen suggested that Zeltor be the pilot on the mission, and that she, Amelia, and Lt. Kennedy be available in the cargo hold to greet the astronauts and explain what had happened to them and that we were offering them the possibility of joining our Gnor-human race. It was expected that there might be a good chance that both Amelia and Lt. Kennedy would be readily identified by the astronauts because of their known requisite educational background in aviation history. This might make it easier for them to understand what was happening when they were brought aboard by the Portal. All the Council members agreed to the personnel suggested by Ellen for the rescue mission and preparations were started for the endeavor to take place on February 1, 2003, around 9 am. At this time Ellen's research had revealed that there had been a brief loss of radio contact with Earth control hopefully giving them time enough to make the Portal transfer of the astronauts from the Columbia just before she disintegrated during reentry. Zeltor was granted his request to take Rol as his navigator to run the time warp mechanism and the Portal; and planned when they arrived from Mars in the Starship to leave the big ship electronically cloaked there in high Earth orbit. Then, in a similarly-cloaked scout vehicle, he would head to the site over Texas in the United States where the Columbia had been destroyed. Ellen, Amelia, and Lt. Kennedy would be ready to greet the astronauts when they were transported from the doomed space shuttle to the cargo hold of the scout vehicle where they would be awaiting them.

Ellen had remained on the bridge with Rol and Zeltor as they approached the 9 am radio-loss time and the site over Texas where the shuttle's destruction was to occur.

"There's the Columbia!" exclaimed Ellen, as the doomed ship came onto the telescreen. "I'm off to await our friends. Good luck, gentlemen!"

"Thanks, Ellen," said Zeltor, as she dashed from the bridge on her way to the cargo hold. "Rol, when I'm close enough, and have them all in the sensor, activate the Portal at just after 9 am. That way we'll be able to transport them at the exact time when Earth control will lose contact with them."

"Right," answered Rol as they approached the space shuttle. "I'm all set!"

"OK!" shouted Zeltor, "They're all in the sensor now"

"It's a few minutes after 9am," said Rol. I'm activating the Portal now!"

Just then the Columbia began to burst into flame and parts of it flew apart and disintegrated in the intense heat of the reentry.

"I hope we got them all!" said Zeltor as the two watched the shuttle's destruction on the telescreen. He addressed the intercom to the cargo hold, "Ellen, did they all come over?"

"Yes, Zeltor," Ellen replied, "everyone is accounted for; great job, you two!"

The seven astronauts were completely baffled by what had happened to them and were intensely curious as to what kind of a ship they were in.

"Who are you people?" asked Colonel Rick Husband, the commander of the mission. "Is this some sort of new recovery ship? And how did you get us all over here? It seemed to be like a Star Trek 'beaming' transportation."

"It was very similar to that maneuver, Colonel Husband," answered Amelia. "Your shuttle was about to disintegrate and we had to take you aboard before you all burned up. Apparently a piece of the insulating foam peeled off during your launch sixteen days ago and struck the edge of the wing. This made a hole that filled up with hot gases that will destroy your ship and all of you upon reentry."

"If you all will look at the telescreen over there on the wall," interjected Ellen, "our pilot on the bridge of our ship will show you what will now happen to your ship. Zeltor," she spoke into her communicator, "could you please activate our telescreen here in the cargo hold? Thanks." With this the cargo hold's telescreen sprang to life showing the flaming destruction of the Columbia. The catastrophic demise of their ship had a sobering effect on all seven of the astronauts; which was soon changed to jubilation from the fact that they had survived the holocaust.

Captain Laurel Clark was the first to speak after the destructive viewing,

"Who actually are you people, and where did this marvelous ship come from? I know you'll probably think me daft," Captain Clark began addressing Amelia, "but you bear a very striking resemblance to Amelia Earhart!" The others all murmured agreement with Captain Clark's observation.

"That's because I am Amelia Earhart," the aviatrix answered. "I was saved by these people the same way you were today; as were my two companions, Professor Ellen James and Lt. Joseph P. Kennedy, Jr. I'm sure you'll all probably recognize Lt. Kennedy now as well from your studies as astronauts." All seven murmured their assent.

"You see," broke in Ellen, "We are alive today because of being saved by an alien race that had come to Earth for our help to save their race from disappearance. The history is complex, but the human race actually came from their race and thus look very much like them. The three of us will explain everything to you in great detail. You all were actually burned up, but we have the ability to traverse time and were able to extricate you before this happened. You can never go back to your old life, but you can join our Gnor-human race and continue with us to shepherd Earth from its coming problems until the time it will be safe for us to reveal who we are to all Earth people. Although we look like normal human beings, we are now totally synthetic but still have all our feelings and memories from when we were living human beings. We can live for hundreds of years now and age ourselves at the proper time every hundred years. Come with us now to the bridge of the ship where you will meet the two alien Gnormen who are piloting us. After we have discussed with you in detail who and what we are, you will have to make the decision as to whether or not you will have the operation necessary to make you into Gnor-human beings. If you agree to this you will have great strength, longevity, and our commitment to shepherd our Earth brethren in the right way to avoid coming problems that will threaten to destroy them. As you will see," Ellen smiled, "we are very friendly aliens! If you decide not to join us, we will put you back into your shuttle again and let what happened occur. As it has always been with everyone in the past, it is your decision completely; we will do whatever you decide you want to do. Come up to the bridge now and meet our 'aliens'."

The seven accompanied Ellen and her two companions to the bridge and were introduced to Zeltor and Rol.

"Why they look just like us!" said K.C., the astronaut from India.

This brought smiles from both Gnormen.

"Actually," smiled Zeltor, "You are the ones that look like us. Ellen will describe to you how two Gnormen came to your planet in the time of your dinosaur age and planted our DNA into arboreal tree shrew mammals which evolved into creatures very similar to us—you! In fact, you will meet those two Gnormen if you agree to undergo the operative transfer of your brain's essence into a Gnor synthetic body; that incidentally, will still look and feel exactly like you!" This will occur on our colony on Mars, where we will take you now. On the way there Ellen and her companions will discuss with you everything about Gnormen and Gnor-humans. I know some of you have had hopes to eventually fly to Mars; well, now you're all going there in style in that Starship just ahead." And with this Zeltor turned on the telescreen and revealed the huge majestic Starship they were approaching.

"How did you keep this big ship we're in, and this immense Starship up ahead, from being picked up by Earth surveillance?" asked Lt. Colonel Michael Anderson.

"We have both ships electronically cloaked so they won't be seen by any Earth apparatus yet available, Colonel Anderson," answered Rol. "You remember in some television programs such as Star Trek, that Klingons and some other races had such devices. Eventually, this technology usually becomes available. All it takes is continued progress in the inventiveness of intelligent beings like you and us."

"Thank you for that vote of confidence, sir," said Colonel Husband, "but it will certainly be some time before we can reach your position in science."

"It is our fondest hope, Colonel Husband," remarked Ellen, "that eventually we will be able to let the people of Earth know who we are and how we can help them as much as possible. For although we are now Gnor-humans, we still retain all our human traits; but they are modified somewhat by certain chemicals in our brain that enable us to corral the baser qualities of greed, lust, and excessive violence that unfortunately are strongly present in some human beings. Because of what the Gnor-human body represents and can do, it is not safe yet to reveal ourselves to the peoples of Earth. We already have had a few skirmishes with people that have wanted to control what we can do and utilize it for their own personal gain. Sad to say, mankind may never be able to handle the gifts we can bring to them as humans. Greed, lust, and excessive violence will have to be either controlled, as it is in us, or espoused from human nature before it will be safe to give our technology to the people of Earth. Until that time we have decided to remain hidden from view by the people that we will be trying to shepherd away from trouble. Please gather around the table here and we will try to give you more detail of who and what we are all about and answer any questions you may have about us and what we have planned for you if you will accept it."

Ellen and her companions then went into great detail about the history of Gnormen and Gnor-humanity and answered a myriad of questions from all seven of the astronauts.

"Many of our present Gnor-human colonists on Mars and the Dark side of the Moon have told me that when they consented to become Gnor-humans, they thought secretly that they might be able to do certain things later on that they knew might be detrimental to the benevolent plan of shepherding Earth. What they found out was that those chemicals that we mentioned before that are inserted into the synthetic brains of Gnor-humans at operation modified them into losing the driving forces of greed, violence, and insatiable lust they might have had before. They lost nothing of reasonable ambition, the drive for perfection, logic, emotions of all types, their libido, and love. The one overriding tendency that seems to develop in all Gnor-humans in time is the desire to think of the other person before themselves; which most likely is an offshoot of getting rid of greed, violence, and lust. It has become obvious to these Gnor-humans that the mollification of those strong detrimental drives leads to strengthening of all the other drives; that then help the individual in any kind of a society to be happy and live life to the fullest."

The seven astronauts boarded the great Starship after Zeltor skillfully landed the scout vehicle inside one of its several docking stations in the part of the ship that contained oxygen. Discussions continued, and by the time they had reached the spaceport in First City on Mars and transferred there to the Oxygen Quarters in First City's Life Factory, all seven had decided that they would agree to become Gnor-humans. The pilots were excited about the possibility of their being able to learn to fly the scout vehicles; and all were dedicated to the idea of being able to shepherd Earth from future problems. All underwent living brain consciousness and memory transfers into a synthetic Gnor body and brain with excellent results. They all understood that they could not go back to their old life, and that brain chemicals instilled at operation would help them to live up to this edict.

One day Colonel Husband asked if he might speak to Ellen and John at their apartment in Harvard Square City and proposed that the two of them consider thoughtfully something that he felt might be able to be done by Gnor-humans on Earth.

"I would suggest," the Colonel began, "that perhaps certain Gnor-human individuals could have their faces completely changed in the Life Factory and return to their home cities to be near their loved ones. They would never identify themselves, but perhaps could just be around to help their family cope with the problems of life that might have become more difficult without their lost spouses. In a way it would, on a much smaller scale, be similar to the shepherding of Earth Gnor-humans were doing on a grander scale with endeavors like their waste removal system. Waste removal, after all, is being done without Gnor-humans identifying themselves to humanity as such. With all the gas stations now being manned by individual Gnor-humans initially, before they train their human counterparts, it might be easy for certain people to be near their loved ones and watch over them while performing their jobs at the stations or elsewhere.

Other friendships or relationships could be established in stores, organizations, etc. that would not identify them as their lost loved ones, but would allow them to keep tabs on their family and in many be able to assist them in day to day problem solving. Indeed, how many people can you remember who were friendly to you and gave you advice and help along your path through life that were not your immediate family?"

"Colonel." returned Ellen, "your suggestion is very interesting and has considerable merit. I do believe this is something that could calm a fear John and I have had for some time now. Since we don't lose our affection, emotions, or our love for our family when we become Gnor-humans, in spite of the mollifying chemicals present in our synthetic brains; John and I have worried that these deep feelings might lead some Gnor-humans to identify themselves to their loved ones with consequent possible devastation to the Universe's time line. If Gnor-humans could do what you have suggested, it would go a long way toward ameliorating that fear. I'm sure that Gnor-humans could cope much more easily with their feelings for their family if they were allowed to do this."

"Yes, indeed," added John, "but I feel we may need to add specific psychological training to what is already taught at the Life Factories after their brain-transferring operation. This will be needed to help them understand why, and prepare them for how they will have to act to keep our presence on Earth completely secret."

"You are quite correct about that, my husband," said Ellen, and then addressing the Colonel, "but this is exciting, Colonel, and I will discuss this with the Council at once and invite you to be there to present your very interesting proposal to them. Dr. Ran has already realized that the closeness of the many Gnor-humans around the globe now occurring in the hydrogen fuel endeavor has necessitated that they develop some sort of vestigial GI tract to allow Gnor-humans to mimic the act of eating to preserve the deception that they are human. This has definitely been a problem for the Nelsons while working at the EPA. Dr. Ran and his surgeons have developed a system that works very well; with a swallowing, propulsion, storage, and evacuation apparatus that mimics the human condition very well. They have even included an anal opening in the same spot as found in humans and are already retrofitting each individual Gnor-human on the planet with this system. I'm sure they will install the same system into you as well if you decide to take part in this endeavor."

"Thank you, Ellen," replied Colonel Husband, "I shall look forward to being there to present the idea to the Council members; and I definitely would like to do this myself."

***

Ellen and John brought this before the Council and had Colonel Husband discuss his proposal with the members. There was some very lively discussion that ensued and it was finally decided that the proposal would be started with very specific individuals and monitored very carefully to be sure that no problems occurred. Since doing this with all past Gnor-human transferences would be hazardous to the time line because the prior families would have already progressed into fixed time line changes; it was decided that only the current new Gnor-human colonists could take part in this endeavor as they would be creating a new future time line as yet unformulated and not changing an old, already established one.

Four of the Columbia astronauts sought permission and were selected to pioneer this project with their families; Colonel Rick Husband, Captain Laurel Clark, Commander Willie Mc Cool, and Lt. Colonel Michael Anderson. All four had their faces changed and GI tracts installed so they would not be recognized by their family and be able to fit into human society. They secured various jobs that would enable them to make contact and develop a friendship that could be used to help their families with any problems that came up in their lives.

***

Evelyn Husband was anxiously sitting in her church's choir-practice room awaiting the entrance of the choir director, as one of her two children had recently showed great interest in joining the church choir. Her husband, Rick, had always enjoyed singing in church, and lately her children had fostered a desire to do the same thing; so she was here to help make the arrangements for them to possibly join the choir. A tall good-looking man, who was not the choir director, entered the room and asked her name and if he could help her.

"My name is Evelyn Husband," she said. "You're not the choir director are you, sir? I wanted to see if my children might be able to join the choir; something my late husband enjoyed very much."

"No ma'am," answered the man, "I'm not the director; my name's Ralph Smith, and I'm helping him out while he is away on vacation. I'm sure we could set up your children to join and sing in the choir. What do you think may have caused this new interest in singing?"

"Well, you see, Mr. Smith," began Evelyn, "it was a favorite pastime of my late husband, and I think it may be a way for the children to keep their dad's memory fresh in their minds." A small tear had formed in the corner of Evelyn's right eye and was beginning to run down her cheek.

"Of course, Evelyn," said Ralph, "it's perfectly understandable that they would do so. Please don't fret yourself for a moment. I will take personal control of overseeing your children's entrance into the choir, and I'll see to it that they get the proper instructions in choir singing."

Ralph Smith took hold of Evelyn's hand to reassure her that everything could be done without any trouble at all and that she needn't be upset about it. Evelyn dabbed at her face with her handkerchief. Then she smiled and thanked Mr. Smith for his kindness.

"I guess I miss the take charge ability my husband always displayed about these things, Mr. Smith, she said to him.

"Now don't you worry, Evelyn," he said, "I'll take personal charge of being around to make sure everything goes well for the children here." Then he smiled at her, shook her hand, and gave her a brochure with the rehearsal times and some other data about the choir. As he walked her to the door exit he mentioned emphatically that he would look forward to seeing her and her family in church from now on."

As Evelyn exited the room, Ralph glanced at himself in the small mirror there on the side wall of the room.

"Well, Rick Husband." he thought, "I guess you've got some work ahead...some work you've been dying to do." And the thought was not intended as a bad pun.

***

Jonathan Clark was upset. His secretary had become ill and suddenly had to leave his employ. He was trying to hire someone to take her place, and several women had applied for the position. The one he chose finally was an older woman, close to his own age he imagined. She was quite talented in her interview, coming with an impressive resume and seemed very personable with an almost perpetual smile. Her name was Monica Green, and she quickly became indispensable in the running of his office; as well as in advice for his activities with his son.

"You know, Monica," Jonathan was saying one day in the office, "your advice about things for me to do with my son is so apropos that I'm sure your own family must run like clockwork. You know you've never mentioned your home life; just that you have a son. Do you do the same great things with him that you set up for my son and me to do?"

"Oh, no, Mr. Clark," answered Monica. "I never see my son much any more; not since I left my husband. But I did do the things I'm always suggesting that you do with your son."

"It's hard to believe that you would have left your husband," Jonathan remarked. "You've always told me what a great person he was, and you're so personable here in the office...what on Earth would have caused you to leave?"

"Well, believe me," Monica answered, "it was not something I wanted to happen, but circumstances occurred that made it happen, much against my will. But I am now making the best of it and pretty much accepting the situation; besides, I enjoy my work here and take great pleasure in my suggestions for you and your son to take part in."

"Yes, Jonathan replied, "and we appreciate those suggestions very much. You know, I don't mean anything personal by it, but your suggestions remind me of very similar ones that my late wife, Laurel used to make for us."

"Nothing personal taken, Mr. Clark," Monica replied, "I'm just glad I've been able to help."

After Jonathan left her office, Monica mused to herself, "You're welcome, my husband, your Laurel enjoys doing it more than you'll ever know!"

***

Sandy Anderson was concerned about her two daughters, especially since she didn't have her husband to help her with them as they went through the troubling time of growing up. She also was worried about them eventually wanting to drive her late husband's Porsche, and she thought about this each time she took the car to be serviced at the garage where her husband had always taken it. There was always a turnover of mechanics at this particular garage, and Sandy was never sure that the finicky Porsche was being correctly serviced. Recently however, a new fellow named George Casey had come to work there who instilled a great deal of confidence in Sandy, and she came to rely more and more on his advice about the car. She became very friendly with him and wished she could have obtained his advice about when he thought her daughters could be considered to drive the car, but she never went as far as to ask him this personal question. One day, during a check up session at the garage, out of the blue George asked her if she were going to allow her daughters to drive the car eventually. This floored her for a moment, as she never remembered telling him that she had two daughters.

"George, how did you know that I had two daughters?" she asked the mechanic. "I don't remember ever telling you that."

George looked at her a little sheepishly.

"You told me about them one time when you were talking about your late husband's love of this car, Sandy," he answered her.

"That's funny," she replied, "I don't seem to remember that, George. But no matter; I'm glad you brought it up as I am worried sick about it. It is a very fast car and the young people today sometimes don't appreciate what can happen if you're not careful when driving such a powerful machine."

"You're certainly right about that, Sandy," replied George. "Say, I'd be glad to talk to them and even give them some driving lessons if you'd like me to. You know, just like they get in driver's education in school, only I'll instruct them in how powerful this car is and how they must drive it properly and take good care of it. You know how much I love this great car of yours, and I easily have the time to do it. What do you say?"

"George," replied Sandy, "that would be wonderful!" "Are you sure it would be no trouble for you? I'd be glad to pay you for doing it. It certainly would ease up my concerns about the girl's driving this car."

"I'd be glad to do it," said the mechanic, "and don't bother about paying me. Just driving more in this great car will be payment enough. Bring the girls around the next time you come in for a checkup and I'll get to know them and start educating them about this car. Don't worry about me; I'm not a pervert or a child molester as anyone here at the garage will attest. And you will come with us any time we do any driving. OK?"

"Yes, great!" said Sandy. "I'll bring the girls with me next time I come in. Thanks George, you're a lifesaver!" With that Sandy entered the Porsche and drove away. As she disappeared down the street George thought to himself,

"No, Sandy Anderson, your Michael says that you are the lifesaver!"

***

Lani Mc Cool was ferrying her two boys to the school where they took their weekly guitar lessons.

"How do you like your new instructor, kids?" she asked them as they drove up to the door of the school. "What did you say his name was?"

"It's Mr. Don Perry, Mom," they both chimed in, "and he's really great! I hope he doesn't leave; he's much better than the last fellow we had. During the break he played chess with us; just like Dad used to do. We really like him, Mom."

"That's good," said Lani, "feeling a little twinge when the boys mentioned their father's chess playing; I'll come in today and meet him if that's OK with you two?"

"Sure, Mom," the boys replied, "you'll like him; he's really neat!"

Lani entered the building with her two boys who ushered her into the room where they played their guitars. Don Perry was seated at a desk in the front of the room and rose to greet the two boys and their mother.

"Mr. Perry," said one of the boys, "this is our mother. Mom, this is Mr. Perry."

Perry came over, smiled, and shook Lani's hand. She noted that it was quite cool to the touch.

"I'm very happy to meet you Mrs. McCool," he said. Your boys are doing very well with their guitar lessons; they're quite talented! They told me your husband played the guitar also. That certainly may be where they get their talent from."

"Thank you, Mr. Perry," answered Lani, "my late husband enjoyed playing the guitar very much and we enjoyed listening to him play. That's why I'm glad the boys have taken up interest in the instrument."

"Well," remarked the instructor, "the guitar can certainly be at the least a very satisfying pastime; and if you become good enough at it, it can become a great profession."

"The boys seem to like the way you're teaching them very much, Mr. Perry," said Lani. "They were just telling me in the car how much they enjoyed your teaching and that they hoped you wouldn't be leaving soon."

"Well, Mrs. McCool," replied the instructor, "there's no danger of that; I'm here to stay for some time now. By the way, please call me Don; Mr. Perry sounds so formal."

"OK," smiled Lani, "but you must call me Lani as well. Incidentally, the boys told me that you played chess with them. We used to do that with their father who loved the game very much." And she stared out the nearby window in the room with a sad look on her face as she remembered this.

"I'm sorry to have brought up any sad thoughts to you, Lani," said Don.

"Don't be," answered Lani, "my thoughts are always happy ones where my late husband is concerned." She turned to leave.

"I was very glad to meet you, Don," she said. "I'll pick up the boys at 4 o'clock when they've finished their lesson. I look forward to their recital in the fall. Thank you for helping the boys to learn to play the guitar; their father certainly derived much pleasure from doing it as well."

As Lani closed the door softly behind her, Don smiled inwardly to himself:

"And your Willie still continues to get immense pleasure from doing it."

And thus began the first human and Gnor-human interactions of former family members on planet Earth. After the rapid refitting of different faces and new GI tracts into the recently-formed Gnor-humans already scheduled to or working on Earth's fuel-cell project, it became possible to work out the logistics of locating them close to their former loved ones in a position where they would be able to help them with their problems. This situation was monitored extremely closely for many months by the Council, but nothing untoward happened to change the minds of those who had arranged it. It was an unmitigated success; and Colonel Husband ("Ralph Smith") was congratulated for his original proposal by Ellen and the Council.

***

Ellen and John were sitting quietly reading on either end of a couch in the living room of their Harvard Square apartment when their daughter Molly entered the room with an overly serious look on her face.

"Mom, Dad," she began, "could I talk to you two for a minute about something that has happened to me?"

Ellen looked across the couch at her husband with a knowing glance.

"Why of course you can, dear," said her mother, patting the space on the couch between them. "Come and sit down here between us and tell us what the matter is. You look very serious about something."

Well, Mom," began Molly, I wanted you and Dad to know that I am very much in love with Josh Nelson, and he feels the same about me."

"That's wonderful, Molly," said her mother, "Josh is a terrific young man. But we already knew that about you two; we've talked about this with you in the past. Now why are you looking so serious about this?"

"Yes," chimed in her father, "I feel the same about Josh, so what's troubling you, honey?"

"Well, Mom," Molly said putting her arm around her mother's shoulder, "Josh and I feel so strongly about our love that we both want to live together in our own apartment...and not live with our folks any more." Molly looked down at the floor after she spoke.

Ellen gently put her hand under her daughter's chin and elevated it so she was looking right into her daughter's eyes. She smiled at her daughter in a warm, motherly way and kissed her on the cheek.

"Oh, Molly," she said softly, "please don't you fret at all. Your father and I think what you just said is a wonderful idea and we will help you to set it up."

With her mother's words and her smile, Molly threw her arms around her, and then looked from one parent to the other with her eyes sparkling.

"Oh, I knew you'd understand," she said. You are the best parents ever! I'm so lucky to have you, and Josh thinks the world of you both as well."

"Of course we'd both be delighted to go along with this, Molly," joined in her father, "we feel the same about your young man; and your mother and I have been discussing the possibility of re-introducing the old human custom of marriage once again; starting with you young people. What do you think about that idea?"

"Oh, Daddy," Molly burst out, almost bouncing with excitement on the center of the couch they were on, "I think that would be a wonderful idea! I'm certain Josh would go along with it, too! I'll talk with Josh and see how he feels about doing it."

"We could have a big party on Earth," said her mother, "once Dr. Ran has installed all the GI tracts into the Gnor-human wedding attendants. In that way, all of Josh's human friends could come and enjoy the wedding as well. I'll bet we could install another face on Glenn Miller and bring his band down to play at the wedding also; I know he'd love to do it!"

"I'm going to find Josh right now," enthused Molly, "if he agrees, let's make the arrangements right away! Oh, I love you two!" Molly shot two intensely loving glances at her parents and rushed out the door of the apartment to find Josh and tell him the news.

Of course Josh was ecstatic about how Molly's parents were so in favor of the two of them getting together and agreed wholeheartedly with Ellen and John's plan for a wedding on Earth. Both of the Nelson parents, when Josh informed them about his intentions with Molly were delighted as well, and everyone looked forward to the wedding with great excitement.

Molly had asked Jeanne to be her Maid of Honor, and Josh had asked Ares to be his Best Man. Both were delighted to fulfill those two positions, and Ares had secretly asked Josh if he might be enticed to be his best man if ever his sister Jeanne might consider doing something similar with him. Josh was very happy to hear this and informed his friend that he knew his sister cared a great deal for Ares and that he should get on the stick and ask her.

Buoyed up with this knowledge, Ares approached Jeanne one night after one of their G-HIT workouts in First City and invited her to walk with him to the overlook near the spaceport.

"Mars's two satellites are low on the horizon tonight," he said to her, "and Zeltor says they are very beautiful to behold in this position that doesn't happen very often. He said you can see them very clearly at the spaceport overlook. Would you like to go with me now to see them?"

"Oh, yes, Ares," said Jeanne, looking up smilingly at him with her striking brown eyes and pale, beautifully-chiseled face, "I'd love to go; it sounds like it will be very pretty to see it."

"Yes, it should be worth seeing," Ares rejoined, "although I'm sure it won't be as pretty as you are, Jeanne." He looked at her with a fond expression on his face.

"You're such a flatterer, Ares," she answered, "but looked up sideways at him, smiled, and squeezed the hand he had extended to her as they started out to the overlook.

When they arrived at the overlook they were greeted by the beautiful spectacle of the two satellites low in the western sky almost gleaming like two reddish yellow coals in the fading light of the Martian day.

"Oh, my!" said Jeanne, "that is gorgeous! As foreboding as this planet is, it can certainly be very beautiful at times."

Ares slipped his arm around Jeanne's shoulder and drew her closer to him.

"Jeanne," he began, "is it presumptuous to ask how you feel about me? I'm afraid I have fallen head over heels in love with you; and with what's happening between your brother Josh and Molly, I must confess that I am wishing the same thing might happen to the two of us some day. Is there any hope for this ever to happen, Jeanne, dear?"

"Oh, Ares," murmured Jeanne, "you don't know how long I've wanted to hear this. When I was only human, and sick, I felt that we would never be able to be as close as I wanted to be with you. And now with my new Gnor body I have longed for the day when you might say what you just did. Oh, Ares, I love you very much!"

Jeanne threw her arms around him; and Ares kissed her upturned face as they embraced for what seemed to the entranced couple to be an eternity. Finally they drew slightly apart, both smiling, and with adoring looks at one another. Ares was the first to speak.

"Jeanne, darling," he began. "would you consider living together with me in our own apartment away from our folks?"

Oh, Ares," she answered, "in a minute I would. And I would like to marry you as Molly and Josh are going to do with Glenn Miller's band and all our friends there! Oh, Ares you have made me so happy! I can't wait to tell my parents, Josh and Molly what we'd like to do. We can have a double wedding! Molly can be my Maid of Honor and Josh can be your Best Man!"

Ares had a broad smile on his face as he gave Jeanne a big hug.

"Well, it'll be complex, but I think quite doable," he smiled. "Oh, you've made me so happy, darling! Let's get going right away on the arrangements."

When everyone was apprised of what had transpired between Jeanne and Ares there was a second outpouring of great joy among the parents and friends and the wedding plans were then started in earnest.

To make it even more complicated, Ellen and John expressed a desire to be the third couple to take part in the wedding as they had never been able to be married in the past and desired to do so now. John had Dik Ran as his Best Man, and Ellen had Sarah Ran as her Maid of Honor. And so the spectacular triple wedding finally took place on Earth with the wedding guests made up of humans and Gnor-humans together. GI tracts had been installed in all the Gnor-humans so nothing untoward was noticed when food and drink were indulged in. Glenn Miller obligingly had his face changed and brought his band to Earth with him to provide a marvelous big band musical extravaganza for dancing and entertainment. The Nelsons had invited several members of the EPA including the Secretary, and all thoroughly enjoyed themselves. Jeanne and Ares acquired an apartment in First City close to Dr. Ran and his wife Sarah, and Molly and Josh obtained one in Harvard Square city close to Ellen and John's apartment. When asked, the Nelson parents successfully made up a scenario about where their two children were now living that would not disclose their true whereabouts.

***

Dr. Ran and his surgeons had just about successfully completed their installation of GI tracts in the Gnor-humans that were interacting on Earth with their human counterparts. More and more liaisons were beginning to be fostered between recently created Gnor-humans and humans. No complications of inadvertent Gnor-human identification seemed to be occurring and the Gnor-humans were very grateful to have been allowed to help their former loved ones with many of their problems. Husbands or wives were able to assist former spouses; their children, and their parents. In each case friendships were first established and then assistance was able to be delivered without the discovery of the presence of Gnor-humans being on Earth. At no time did anyone identify himself or herself to their former family; a necessity if the program were to continue.

One such Gnor-human, a former sailor rescued from a shipwreck named Joe Palm, was located in the city of New Orleans and had been there helping his former wife and family to recover from a disastrous hurricane called Katrina that had destroyed the levees holding back Lake Pontchartrain just north of the city. His wife was an executive secretary in the office of Mayor Ray Nagin, and in the past Joe and his wife had often discussed the catastrophe that would most likely happen if the levees failed that held back the waters from the lake. The levees did fail; and New Orleans, being built in a bowl many feet below sea level, plunged under water with the loss of over one thousand lives by drowning and economic losses in the billions. When Joe had returned to First City for the installation of his new GI tract by Dr. Ran, he had suggested to the doctor during his post op recovery that perhaps it might be an important project to consider some way of taming the weather, and especially these severe hurricanes that occurred from time to time. Even after the correction of global warming there still would be the occasional severe storm that might devastate widespread areas with great loss of lives and property.

Dr. Ran took Joe Palm's suggestion to Ellen and she was sufficiently impressed by the project's possibility that she called a Council Meeting to discuss it.

Research by Ellen and John had disclosed that in 1999 a Russian scientist named Vladimer Syromyaenikov had attempted to put a 100-foot-wide mirror into space to reflect sunlight to the cold, dark winter landscape of the Russian North. Unfortunately, the mirror never deployed and had to be jettisoned where it burned up upon reentering the Earth's atmosphere. Six years earlier a smaller mirror had been successfully placed into orbit by the Russians that projected a path of sunlight just before dawn across Europe. That path was 21/2 miles wide and was seen as a bright, slowly-moving light; like a full moon emerging from behind a cloud. The project, however, was abandoned when U.S. President Ronald Reagan's spending competition forced the Soviet Union into a rapid decline and stopped any further capital being available for developing the space mirror program.

"Some scientists have entertained the thought," began Ellen before the Council members, "that this concept might be useful in dealing with harmful weather patterns. Concerning hurricanes, typhoons, or cyclones, however, it probably will prove difficult for the mirror's heat to be very effective in controlling them.. The reason why a hurricane, typhoon, or cyclone forms is not exactly known, but there is speculation that it may start with the moist air from ocean surface water over 76 degrees Fahrenheit rising up into the cooler air where it condenses and releases a considerable amount of energy that fuels the swirling winds of the storm. Most storms grow to about ten miles in height and as much as 500 miles in width. As more and more energy-containing moist air continues to rise, the ferocity of the storm increases. On the edge of the storm's calm eye the swirling winds form huge powerful thunderheads that drop devastating amounts of rain often causing flooding. It might be possible to dissipate some of the moisture within these thunderheads with the mirrors; and drying them out might also decrease the amount of lightning forming within them and hence the destruction caused by this lightning. But the mirror would not affect the storm's winds, however; and they probably might continue to build with the aid of the heated air from it. It is recognized, however, that when most of these storms travel over a cooler region (land), they soon dissipate. This is thought to be because the cooler surface no longer contributes energy from warm, moist air rising as well as the fact that the structures the storm encounters on land absorb most of its energy.

Indeed, it is true that the hurricane season seems to start up during the four summer months when the ocean's surface water is heated up to the 76 degrees necessary for the storms to develop. Hurricane control and the taming of other severe weather conditions would definitely be a worthwhile endeavor for Gnor technology in its shepherding of Earth if it is possible to do so. The cost to human life and property is enormous from many different weather conditions.

It definitely may be possible to use the Russian concept of space mirrors for possibly taming many adverse weather conditions other than these great storms. The lens of the mirror would be directed to send the heat of the sun's energy where it could be used to dissipate certain susceptible weather conditions; similar to what most people have done in their youth with a magnifying glass, concentrating sunlight onto paper to cause high heat and combustion of the paper.

From our research, John and I believe space mirror technology could be used successfully in the following conditions that would probably keep the mirror operators quite busy. The mirrors could be used to unblock cities frozen in sudden snow and ice storms, dissipate rain clouds that are causing severe flooding, dissipate dangerous areas of fogging, prevent avalanches near mountain villages, and warm up areas where severe cold snaps have created living and economic havoc. They might be able to be used in agriculture to dissipate clouds, when too much rain or lack of sunshine from too lengthy cloud cover might cause loss of needed crops. And in the hurricanes, typhoons, and cyclones, they could at least be used to dissipate some of the moisture in the thunderhead rain clouds that swirl on the edge of the storm's eye and cause so much destruction by flooding when they dump their moisture.

We do have the means to place these mirrors into space, as we did with the orbiting space station for the management of wastes. We could actually station Gnor-humans on the mirrors to direct their energy accurately and maintain the proper service to them. It would probably entail making living quarters and an operating bridge in a section in the center of the mirror array. The mirror could be fitted with its own drive apparatus or connection couplings that would allow a scout vehicle to move it.

As to Dr. Ran's patient's suggestion concerning the possibility of dissipating hurricanes, I'm afraid that might be quite difficult, if not impossible, to do with a space mirror.

John and I do feel that there is a way, however, that might work quite well. Since it is suspected that the energy from the moist air rising from the warm surface ocean water is the main culprit in the formation of the storm, we should be able to abort its development by cooling that surface ocean water at the site where the storms start. In the case of hurricanes in the northern latitudes that is a spot just off the African coast near the Azores islands, and there are other spots on Earth at other latitudes that are known as well. There are three possible ways we have conjectured that might be able to accomplish this cooling of the susceptible ocean water.

One:- we could carve off icebergs with fusion torpedoes, tow them with the scout vehicles to the areas, and allow them to cool the water to pre summer temperatures when we know the storms will not develop.

Two:- we could generate chemicals like liquid nitrogen or dry ice and use the scout vehicles to infuse these chemicals into the appropriate surface ocean water to again decrease the temperature of that water. Or more reasonably, and we think that this may be the most likely to be cost-effective to accomplish this:-

Three:- we could plow up the deep cooler water by utilizing the scout vehicles as submarines and plow up that cool water from the deep water to the surface. Because our scout vehicles can move underwater more that ten times faster than Earth submarines, the plowing should be able to be accomplished rapidly over the needed fairly wide areas without much difficulty. And the surface water can be monitored continually during those four warm summer months to prevent that water from rising to the temperature necessary to create the severe storms. We may have to increase the number of our scout vehicles but that should be able to be accomplished without too much trouble. And, of course, it will mean more pilot training and rescues for more pilots—something that we are doing anyway.

You have all heard my discussion and proposition; what do the Members think about doing this as our next project in the shepherding of Earth?"

A long discussion followed with many members asking questions about the technology that would be involved. In the final deliberation it was decided to accept this as the next Earth-shepherding project and several top notch Gnor-human engineers were chosen to begin the deliberations that would enable them to come up with the technology necessary to make the mobile space mirrors a reality. It took several months but eventually practical technology was developed that allowed these engineers to build six such mirror arrays; three having their own magnetic drive apparatuses, and the other three to be moved by scout vehicle connection couplings. It was felt that they would need to be mobile to travel to the most advantageous spots from which to deliver their sunlight energy to the particular adverse weather condition that needed to be corrected. It was decided that all six of these mirror arrays would be constructed by their company Waste Management, as the company was already well known to have such a capability by most of the world's governments and they would certainly go along with the protection such machines would afford to the world and its peoples.

The six mirrors were finally completed and manned by six of the Gnor-human engineers that had been principle designers of the arrays. On the first use of one of the mobile mirror arrays it was discovered that certain scenarios had to be treated in a gradual manner rather than all at once. When a city paralyzed by a sudden snow storm was freed up by successfully melting the snow that had caused the problem, massive flooding ensued. This then had to be secondarily treated to get the water to run off thru the usual areas where that occurred, now not available in the cold weather. Melting the drainage areas solved the problem; but from then on a more gradual melting was done to prevent this from happening again. A successful world-wide "hot line" was developed from all the different countries to be able to report where the mirrors were needed to modify the offending weather condition. As time went on several more mirror arrays had to be developed to keep pace with the calls for their use in doing what the meteorologists had originally called BWM (benign weather modification). The coupling technique was abandoned and only self-propelled mirror array vehicles were newly constructed.

In the meantime the ocean plowing had turned out to be highly successful. Only an occasional severe storm developed every few years or so and they were usually not as destructive as the old ones had been during the global warming period. And the excessive moisture in the thunderheads that developed on the edges of the eyes of these occasional storms was usually able to be greatly dissipated by the mirror arrays, so flooding was eliminated as well. At long last, the damaging wind storms and adverse weather conditions previously so prevalent in much of the Earth's history were able to be significantly tamed by Ellen's Gnor-human company, Waste Management.

Thus, once again the Gnor-human Shepherds of Earth were able to help out the peoples of the world in another significant problem that had plagued the human race for as long as that race had memory.

***

The next project that Ellen was convinced was important was to rescue more deceased humans for the needed pilots for the space mirrors. There was already a large backlog of submariners rescued from WWII that were working in other positions. She felt that these people could be transferred to the fleet of scout vehicle submarines needed in the ocean water-plowing endeavor to tame the damaging wind storms around the globe. As the planes lost in and around the Bermuda Triangle were such a rich source of pilots, Ellen decided to summon and converse with Rol once again to try to convince him that perhaps they might be able to rescue some of these pilots safely by modifying how and where they attempted the rescues. When Rol arrived in her Council office she began by asking him once again if it might be possible to rescue at least some of the Bermuda Triangle pilots for use after their training in the submarine scout vehicles that were becoming increasingly needed around the globe for storm dissipation.

"Couldn't we intercept these planes," began Ellen, "just after they had left their takeoff positions before they entered the Bermuda Triangle area where they disappeared? We could research where the take-off site was, cloak our ship, follow them a short distance, transport them to our ship, and then let their ship go on to crash into the sea. We could convince them that they were going to be lost shortly by transporting them ahead in time to prove that they had indeed been lost and never recovered. That would keep us away from the site in the Bermuda Triangle where all the weird happenings occurred and obtain us the pilots we need."

Rol looked thoughtfully at Ellen and finally said, "That might just work, Ellen; provided we could be sure to intercept them at sea, away from sight of other planes or ships and not close to where the unexplainable happenings occurred. I am still worried about what might happen to our ships if we get too close to where these unusual things take place. I agree that allowing the pilot-less ship to crash into the sea is reasonable since it will be lost in that way most likely anyway."

"My research," Ellen replied, "has disclosed that there were 38 military planes lost and never recovered in the Bermuda Triangle area from 1942 to 1965, and 50 civil aircraft lost there similarly from 1978 to 2002. That's a lot of pilots for us to train for our storm-dissipating project, Rol. What do you think? Should we try it?"

"Yes, Ellen," Rol rejoined, "Let's do it. I think if we could rescue the plane's personnel in a safe location, where no one else will witness it, we will be able to get the pilots we need safely. It will be critical, however, that we do not go into the Triangle to attempt the rescues, but get them done before such an entrance becomes necessary."

"It's all settled then," answered Ellen. "I suggest we just use Zeltor and you and one ship to rescue all 88 planes. John and I will start doing the research necessary to find out exactly where each of the planes took off from so we can intercept and follow them to a safe spot where it will be possible to undetectably rescue them."

After several weeks of research had been done by John and Ellen, the rescue project for pilots from ships lost in the Bermuda Triangle was launched. Most of the personnel in the eighty eight planes Ellen had mentioned to Rol were able to be rescued and the rescues were not observed by any other ships or planes in the area. Zeltor's scout vehicle had a few unusual electronic malfunctions occur on a couple of rescues but no permanent damage to the ship or anyone on board occurred, and several needed pilots were obtained for training to fly the additional scout vehicles being constructed for the many projects coming up that they would be needed for.

***

All the various projects shepherding the Earth's peoples were in full swing and straining the resources of Ellen's company, Waste Management, but in discussions at the Council Meetings she was extremely proud and happy with the results coming in from all these endeavors. One day at a private meeting arranged with Ellen and John in their apartment in Harvard Square, Rol started a discussion that caused the two of them to reflect with great seriousness about two very important problems that the people of Earth all faced if not corrected.

"I have traveled far enough into Earth's future," Rol began, "that it has become obvious to me that one of the greatest threats to the Earth's peoples has yet to come."

"What do you mean, Rol?" asked Ellen.

"The Earth's future," answered Rol, "with the current manner the people are utilizing water will end up in a relatively short time with not enough of the precious commodity being available to sustain life in many areas of the world. What is happening is that water is being pumped out of the aquifers world wide to irrigate the crops that are necessary to feed the world's burgeoning population. In parts of the world deserts have become as prevalent as forests. Once the fossil or deep aquifers are depleted, the food supply will disappear and famines will ensue everywhere crops are dependent on these aquifers for their irrigation. These deep aquifers have no known way to be replenished as yet, so when they are gone, so is the food supply that they sustain with their water. Desalinization of the sea water is not practical at this time in history so if there isn't an attempt to manage water correctly, there will soon not be enough to irrigate the crops with and the food supply will dwindle dramatically with widespread famine developing everywhere. In addition, the midwestern United States supplies a very significant percentage of grain to the rest of the world, and it depends on the deep Ogallala aquifer for its irrigation water. Once this fossil aquifer dries up, a significant part of the world will be without food."

"Doesn't the world come up with management techniques to manage the water in the future, Rol?" John asked.

"Well," Rol replied, "you remember what happened when radiation crept into the Ogallala from the Yucca Mountain depot. It wasn't a water shortage that was the problem then, just the contaminated water causing contaminated crops. But it did show how important that aquifer was to the rest of the country and the world and what happened when it was contaminated. It doesn't take much to extrapolate what dire problems would occur if the water were gone from it. And to answer your question, John, as far as I have gone into the future very little had been done about managing the water supply properly. Instead wars have broken out concerning possession of it. In places like India, China, Saudi Arabia and the rest of the Middle East, Pakistan, Mexico and most of Africa, over-pumping of aquifers for crop irrigation has often led to their drying up and producing famines wherever this has occurred."

"Well, Rol," Ellen remarked with some emotion, "it certainly looks like our next project should be water education for the world's governments and peoples. I have had some discussion about the potential water problem with the Prime Mover when he was with us, and he said that what needed to be done was to change the economy to allow it to happen. This means that forests would not be allowed to be decimated for financial gain from lumber; that enough trees must be left standing so that water would not run off into the sea but would be caught up and evaporated into the air allowing more rain for the crops further inland. A specific drip method for irrigation of crops needs to be created to utilize only the amount of water that is necessary to sustain crops, and wasteful over-pumping of aquifers as is done here on Earth now must be stopped. The economy of Earth must be brought into perspective with values rearranged to allow proper assignment of increased value to everything on the planet that is essential for the well-being of everyone and decreased value to unessential things that might be money-makers in the current economy. He felt that one of the greatest needs on Earth at this time was the sharing, not hoarding, of wealth; to decrease the widening gap between different parts of society and thus to supply resources to help accomplish all the necessary things to stabilize and enrich all of society, not just a few individuals. I believe we will have an uphill struggle with this project, Rol; but I also feel it is worth all of our effort to accomplish it. Technologically, if we could create a method of drilling down into the fossil deep aquifers and some way of desalinating the oceans to have enough water to refill these aquifers, we could go a long way towards solving some of this water shortage problem. But the technology will have to be developed to do this; we don't have it as yet. We could tow large icebergs to port cities and melt them for water use, but even that would be hardly cost-effective or practical. No, proper management of water by the Earth's peoples is certainly the way to start."

"Don't sell yourself short, Ellen" rejoined Rol, "the inroads you have made with all the world's governments with your nuclear and toxic waste-removal, fuel cell energy economy, global warming suppression, flu pandemic solution, and weather modification may give you a lot more clout for this water management education than you may realize."

"I would so like to believe that, Rol, replied Ellen wistfully; "but the perpetration of more and more senseless terrorist activity I have seen forming throughout the world here in the twenty-first century discourages me. Is it the inequities created by the excessive wealth being accumulated by a few corporate businesses and individuals that refuse to share with the rest of society that continues to fuel the development of more and more terrorism being promulgated around the globe? Or is it that the race of man has such inherent culturally inbred dislike and distrust of one another that they will never be able to get along; and will continually resort to more and more increasingly violent acts of terrorism toward the other faction they hate? I greatly fear that the future lack of water will fuel terrorism even more; similarly as scarcity of oil did before the fuel cell economy was started. The greatest shepherding that we could do would be to set up a system for the peoples of the Earth that would allow every individual to be honestly educated up to his or her own achievable standard and to teach all that the honest sharing of all of Earth's resources equally with one another is the only chance to create harmony in all the world and certainly help to alleviate the terror that is so unsettling and detrimental to all.

"I would surmise," replied Rol, "that Gnor-humans may eventually be obliged to cope with terrorism on the Earth if the dwindling water supply and other developing problems cause it to escalate further and reduce the Earth to constant killing of one another by rival factions that are incapable of seeing the other's point of view."

"It would appear," remarked John, "that the terrorism in the early twenty-first century was at least superficially based on religious differences that we may find very difficult to overcome. And there are the insecurely stored Russian nuclear weapons from the old Cold War that could be obtained by these killer factions and used in an exceedingly harmful way for large segments of the Earth's population."

"Yes," rejoined Ellen, "there is a good chance that we may find ourselves having to stop terrorist acts while at the same time trying to induce the other faction that is being attacked to stop using so much of the Earth's resources selfishly and honestly share more of them with the rest of the world to encourage a more peaceful and fair existence for all.

Indeed, John and Rol, I suspect our continuing shepherding of Earth will find us very often in the near future having to utilize our elite G-HIT squad to effectively help with her *delivery from terror*!"

Printed in the United Kingdom
by Lightning Source UK Ltd.
136514UK00002B/53/A

9 781424 121908